A Fine Mischief

Also by Cecelia Frey

Fiction
  Breakaway (Macmillan)
  The Nefertiti Look (Thistledown)
  The Love Song of Romeo Paquette (Thistledown)
  Salamander Moon (Snowapple)
  The Prisoner of Cage Farm (U of C Press)

Non-fiction
  Phyllis Webb: An Annotated Bibliography in
    *The Annotated Bibliography of Canada's Major
    Authors* Series (ECW Press)

Drama
  The Dinosaur Connection (CBC, Vanishing Point)

Poetry
  the least you can do is sing (Longspoon)
  Songs Like White Apples Tasted (Bayeux Arts)
  And Still I hear Her Singing (Touchwood)
  Reckless Women (Ronsdale)

A Fine Mischief

Cecelia Frey

Lord, what fools these mortals be!
– Puck, *A Midsummer Night's Dream*

Cecelia Frey
November 28/04

Touchwood Press
Calgary, Alberta

Library and Archives Canada Cataloguing in Publication Data

Frey, Cecelia
    A fine mischief / Cecelia Frey.

ISBN 0-9687861-5-4

    I. Title.
PS8561.R48F55 2004   C813'.54   C2004-904151-7

Canada Council   Conseil des Arts
for the Arts   du Canada

We acknowledge the support of the Canada Council for the Arts which last year invested $20.3 million in writing and publishing throughout Canada.

Published by Touchwood Press
6228 Touchwood Drive NW
Calgary, AB, T2K 3L9
E-mail: jlfrey@telusplanet.net

Guest Editor: Barbara Scott
Book Design & Production: John Frey
Cover Art: BISS Graphics

Printed and bound in Canada by
Priority Printing Limited of Edmonton

Quotes from Shakespeare's *A Midsummer Night's Dream* are from the Airmont Shakespeare Classic Series.
Lines from Edmond Rostand's *Cyrano de Bergerac* are from the Anthony Burgess translation, Applause Books.

for Fred and Ann

ACKNOWLEDGEMENTS

I would like to thank the writers of the Sage Hill novel colloquium who, during the summer of 2002, eased me into an understanding of this novel. Robert Kroetsch, especially, encouraged an expansion of vision. Thanks also go to Cheryl Sikomas and Willie Fitzpatrick who read further drafts and to Barbara Scott whose insightful suggestions helped complete the project.

CONTENTS

NOTE

A reader who looks at a map of the Okanagon region of British Columbia will, indeed, find a Blind Bay on Shuswap Lake. However, the name is where fact and fiction part company, and a search for further similarities between the two will lead only to the reader's own fancies. The setting as described herein, as well as the people and events, alas, are constructs of the author's imagination, an attempt of the pen that *gives to airy nothing/A local habitation and a name.*

PART ONE

THE PLAYERS GATHER

i

Robb Goodfellow adjusted his field glasses. He was standing before a large window, one of a series of windows that wrapped around two walls of his cabin and were designed to give an unencumbered view of the lake and the natural environment. It was five o'clock of a glorious June morning at Blind Bay on the Shuswap.

Nothing was coming through. Hazy images blurred his vision. Vague unidentifiable shapes loomed into view. Blobs of pale green filled the lens. He realized that he was too close to his subject. He was in the trees for Christ's sake. Where was the lake? He fit the circles of glass more firmly into his eye sockets and raised his head.

In profile, the binoculars appeared to be an extension of Robb's ocular organs, a monstrous deformity protruding from his upper face. Full front, he might have been a magnified creature of the undergrowth, one which, because it lived in the dark, had adapted to its environment by acquiring two enormous glossy orbs.

Robb moved his head sideways toward a space between the trees where the lake unfurled crimson and gold satin in the dawn light. Low hills in the distance arrived out of a hovering spotty mist. Above the hills, the sky was striated with layers of shades of red and gold, intense at the horizon, fading as they mounted the dome. He lowered his head, at the same time lowering his cumbersome projection down from the sky, down from the hills. His body tensed.

Out in the lake, smooth concentric circles rippled the water. At their centre, two hands appeared. A swimmer emerged from a surface dive and struck into a front crawl. The low sun cast a golden glow on her shoulders. Water fell from her fingers in an arc of shimmering golden droplets. With each stroke, her arms lifted high in a clean curve through the air. Her hands sliced the water precisely. Even though her pace seemed leisurely, she quickly covered the distance.

Near the shore, she rose up out of the lake, naked as a goddess newly born. Lifting one glorious arm, she pulled a pair of goggles back across her head. She strode, strong limbed, through the shallow water. Her toes gripped the wet hard sand at the water's edge. They burrowed into the warm dry sand as she made her way across the narrow beach. They crushed the wild grass of the path.

Oh, to be that sand! To be that grass! To be massaged by those toes, to have them burrow into him, to be walked on by those exquisite feet, to feel the weight of the flesh of that incredible body!

Robb's binoculars turned as his eyes followed this goddess up from the beach. Strong back, strong buttocks, high breasts, she moved through bending willow and delicate birch. She looked up toward tall branches where robins traded melodies intercepted by a red-winged blackbird's piercing motif, threaded with a sparrow's staccato note and high-pitched trill. Just the way she raised her head, a slow sinuous movement, caused an intake of Robb's breath. Her neck was classic, a shapely pillar holding her superb head high. Her face was Renaissance – oval, full-fleshed, sensuous, with straight nose, straight brows above almond-shaped eyes, a round soft chin and full lips. Robb lingered a moment on those lips, letting himself wallow in the dimple on one side. Again, she raised that perfect arm, this time to remove the band that was holding back her long fair hair, which then settled in wet tendrils against her cheeks and the back of her neck. She ascended the back steps of a two-storey clapboard house and crossed the porch, picking up a towel from the railing and patting herself with it as she moved. She opened the screen.

The door slammed in Robb's face.

To hold the dream a moment longer, Robb turned his glasses back to the spot where his Aphrodite had emerged in all her golden glory. As the sunrise lifted and thinned, the lake water reflected the multicoloured sky. Near the shore, long fingers and broad patches of various greens blended with the blue of the water. It was going to be one of those rare June days in which any normal man would be happy. But Robb was not normal. He was a writer, which was not the worst of it. He was a writer connected to the theatre, which meant that not only did he have to satisfy his own muse but those of other people as well. It further complicated matters that those people were immature egomaniacs who lived in a transitory illusory world. This misery, however, was an ongoing problem in Robb's life and one that he accepted. What was more immediately troubling his mind this morning was that his muse did not see him. She did not honour him with having a place in her life.

Robb put down the glasses and turned from the window. He moved lightly and silently, almost flitted, a thin, wiry being, neat and trim, already showered and shaved. Robb was a man whose appearance stated 'brown' – brown hair, brown complexion, brown denims and shirt. He always wore brown. It simplified life. He did not have to make decisions about something so minor as clothing. It saved time. Time was a valuable commodity. That was one of the reasons he stayed mostly at the lake, as opposed to his apartment in Vancouver. Here, he could live the quiet brown life that befitted a hidden watcher. He could meld into the cedar siding walls of his cottage or the woods outside the walls. Here nothing much happened. Life was composed of reflections on the screen of his mind, which he then transposed to the square screen of his monitor.

In the kitchen, Robb plugged in *Mr. Coffee*. He placed half a cup of beans into the grinder. He forgot his finger on the button. The coffee turned to powder and he had to dig it out of the grinder cup into the paper filter with a small brush. He placed the filter into the basket of the coffeemaker and poured the four-cup limit of water into the back. He stared at the machine as the water burped and gurgled its way through the grounds and flowed brown into the glass carafe.

Sylvia Wilde with undulating hip movement mounted the stairs. In the bedroom, she dropped the towel to the floor and slid into bed beside her sleeping husband, curving the front of her cool fresh body around his warm back, putting her cold feet on his warm legs. Her husband turned toward her...

No, no, no. That was not the way it should happen. He must change the story. Sylvia could not continue to waste herself on an inferior person. Even before he had actually met the husband a few weeks ago when his neighbours had invited him over for a barbecue, Robb knew without a doubt what sort of person he was. Michael Wilde was an actor. The word in Robb's head took on a tone of utter derision. He had long been dealing with the Michael Wildes of the world. He scarcely needed the evidence of his phony smile, his supercilious manner, his habit of catching his image in any and all reflecting surfaces. Robb knew that, while Michael Wilde exuded charm and wit in public, in private he threw tantrums and insisted on having his own way.

Not that Robb didn't like actors. Actors were fine as long as you didn't expect anything of them other than acting. In a way, he loved actors. He had to love them in order to write plays for them. His way of accomplishing this was to objectify them. They were not real people. They were masks, and masks were fine in their rightful place, which was on the stage. Off-stage, if they were not being silly and atwitter with a great deal of nonsense, they were mean and nasty. They were so unabashed in their self-involvement, so completely without thought of other people's needs or desires. Their wishes and demands had to be fulfilled, their wills to be done. As far as he could see, their only function was to be entertaining, on and off the stage. They were simply entertaining objects. As long as Robb kept that perspective he was fine. Never think of them as thinking, feeling subjects.

That was one of his rules. Another was, never become personally involved, which Robb managed easily by having as little as possible to do with them, restricting his own professional social appearances to mandatory first-night parties or publicity sessions.

Coffee in hand and a thoughtful look on his face, Robb returned to the window. He directed his gaze toward the neighbouring property. Through a thin grove of trees, he saw an afternoon three months previous. He saw it so clearly, it might have been happening this very minute. There she was. More properly, there *they* were, but in his mind Sylvia was in focus in the foreground while Michael was a fuzzy background blur. They were standing on the grass down from the back porch steps of the farmhouse, talking with Ernie Simmons, the realtor. Sylvia was wearing a summer dress constructed of some wispy flowery material. On her head was a large straw hat with a flower. Across the space came her laughter, a musical trill bubbling like a brook in spring across silvery stones. Robb ran for the field glasses. Please, please, please, he kept muttering under his breath as he opened and slammed a kitchen drawer, rummaged in a box of fishing tackle, finally found them on a bookshelf. He lifted the glasses to his eyes, panting a bit from his exertion. He held his breath, afraid to adjust the focus. What if she was ugly? What if she looked mean or otherwise unpleasant? But he need not have been afraid. The first time ever he saw her face, and he would never forget that moment, her laughing eyes, her generous laughing mouth, he was smitten.

The next day, he got the low-down from Ernie. An actor who wanted a quiet retreat to rest his nerves between plays, to escape the insane rat race populated by stage managers, directors, other actors, and playwrights who wrote lines that no identifiable human being ever uttered. Hmmm, yes, thought Robb, recalling a Michael Wilde who was making a name for himself in romantic comedy. Theatre critics said that he had a flair for the genre, a 'light whimsical carefree approach which he always manages to keep out of the mire of the sentimental or maudlin.' 'What's more he looks the part,' gushed one female reviewer. 'Tall, dark, slightly rugged features, broad-shouldered although slim, he has a charming casual manner reminiscent of a young Cary Grant.' And how about the lady? Robb had inquired. Lady? The wife, what about her? Ernie had looked at the sheet spread on the desk before his hairy arms. "Cellist," he had said, "but that can't hardly be an occupation."

As a rule, Robb allowed himself only one cup of coffee before sitting down at his word processor with a second. But this particular morning, not only did he pour himself a second, he returned to the window. Setting his cup down on a ledge, he picked up the binoculars. He swung them in the direction of the lake. As a doomed man searches for deliverance, he searched for some remnant of Sylvia's being, some aura that she might have left behind. His eyes, greenish brown, the colour of field grass in autumn, travelled the path that she had taken from lake to house. He saw again her long limbs moving with animal grace through the trees. She was *so* pastoral. So right for this place. His place. Goodfellows had always lived in these woods. That was why it was his responsibility to keep an eye on things. His great-grandparents had settled at Blind Bay, on a small tract of land. His grandparents and parents had farmed the same piece before it was subdivided and sold off for lake cottage lots. And it was Sylvia who had encouraged her husband to buy the old farmhouse. As she related it, Michael would have preferred a yacht. Map and classifieds in hand, Sylvia had come to make her home in the place of his ancestors. This place and Robb Goodfellow were her destiny. But she had betrayed that destiny. She had married the wrong man.

Normally, that is if Robb's life had been going forward clickety-clack, the universe unfolding as it should according to Robb, this problem would not have upset him excessively. He loved his angst, after all he was a writer. Grist for the mill and all that nonsense. He could have worked it into a script. He had enough casual relationships with women to get him through the essentials. In any case, his experience in that area was that, inevitably and invariably, familiarity bred contempt. How many times had he started out in a relationship, full of hope and optimism, only to have it end in disillusionment? The woman chattered like a magpie, mostly about herself. Or she had an underlying mean streak. Or she had silicone-implanted breasts.

Anyway, he had no desire to share his life with anyone, male or female. He was not a marrying man. And when it came to muses, he had found it best to admire them from afar. He preferred to dream about perfection instead of getting to know reality. For weeks after he had first viewed Sylvia, he had let himself be mildly titillated by the sight of her tending her garden or drying her long golden hair in the sunshine. Even after the day she introduced herself to him in the town's only supermarket, even after he took to occasionally crossing the patch of grass between the two houses and tapping on the screen door, even after spending a few spring evenings in her company drinking herbal tea, he was quite content to envision her as pure, inviolate, asexual.

But then things changed. One day, a few weeks previous, drawn to his window by the sound of heavenly strains of music, he had looked out and seen Sylvia perched on a wooden kitchen chair practising her cello. Bosom thrust forward, back arched, buttocks spread and planted, cello clasped between her thighs, her nimble fingers were stroking the strings. At that instant, a physical passion sprang sharply, painfully, into life.

Robb had put in a bad month. He had not been able to write. Never before had this happened. All through the long days and longer nights his flow of words was frozen. He felt the material inside him but it was dammed up by the ice jam in his throat which had travelled down his arms into his hands. His fingers could not get past the obstruction to produce anything worthwhile. It was only through sheer force of will that he got them to tap out a dribble of words. He made a trip to Vancouver. He went out on the town with his producer friend and admitted that his well was dry. His friend pointed out that Robb had written a new play every year for the last six years, that perhaps he was suffering from exhaustion. "Go to Mexico. Bake on the beach. Get drunk. Get laid," was his advice.

Instead of going to Mexico, Robb returned to the lake and

thought it through. Every dawn he watched Sylvia come out of the lake. Every morning he sat down at his word processor and batted out the most terrible drivel. Every afternoon he deleted the file. Some days he would come to with a start and realize that he had been doing nothing but thinking of that cello for the past hour. While he had been contriving fantasies, the light on the screen had long gone out. He would throw down his pen, throw up his hands, get up so quickly his head reeled. He would make more coffee, light another cigarette, ball up paper and fling it at the cat.

He spent hours at his window. He viewed Sylvia as she knelt, delectable in sun hat and gardening gloves, pulling up weeds. He heard her singing as she washed and polished the windows of her house. He heard her "chick-chick-chick" as she fed her few chickens. He saw her bend toward the goat, her golden curls falling around its bearded little face, its knobby horns. He found himself wishing he were that goat. He thought of what male and female goats did together.

He made attempts to return to chastity, to swap his carnal thoughts for nobler ones, but it was no use. Once thoughts have been thought, he thought, they cannot be unthought. The mind cannot be returned to its unblemished state. No, mused Robb, the writer, ever looking for an underlying profundity to life as well as to words, once innocence is lost, it cannot be regained.

This could not go on. Robb knew that. He had to get some work done. He had a deadline, a final one, his producer had told him in that voice he got sometimes, a pleading whine which Robb found more difficult to ignore than an outright stern demand. The new play had to be delivered by the end of August and he didn't even have an idea for it yet. More accurately, he had had several ideas resulting in hundreds of words, all of which had seemed brilliant at the time, all of which had shrivelled like salt-sprinkled snails leaving traces of silvery slime on the page. He knew that the well was not dry. Quite the reverse. He felt all juicy inside. But he could not tap into that juice as long as he could not touch that woman.

He would have to seduce Sylvia Wilde. It was the only solution. He had wrung every bit of magic possible out of their present celibate relationship. The obstruction in his throat which seeped down into his hands was a frozen lump of frustrated desire. He must satisfy this desire and release his feelings. No longer would he watch from the shadows. No longer would he wait in the wings. No longer would he play a minor role in Sylvia's life. He would be the main character, maybe, even, the hero.

But how to do it? He knew from the time he had spent with her that Sylvia was one of those faithful women who would not dally with men other than her husband, even when she should, even when the husband was doing his own dallying. She was one of a rare breed of women that did not see a husband's flaws. Well, then, Robb would just have to remove her rose-coloured glasses and reveal to her Michael's true nature. He would have to cause mischief between wife and husband. It would be easy, the husband being such a defective specimen. All Robb had to do was divulge a few choice tidbits of information, place a few bugs in certain ears, strip a few veils from eyes, then let nature take its course.

By the time Robb drained the dregs of his second cup of coffee on that first day of a summer weekend at the lake, he knew that he would have to break one of his rules. He would have to become involved with an actor. For the purpose of seduction he would have to enter the lives of his neighbours. If he was to save Sylvia Wilde from making the catastrophic mistake of devoting the rest of her life to a vanity-driven excuse for a human being, he must intervene. And save her he must. It was crucial. As his muse, she was essential to his survival.

But even if he pointed out to Sylvia her dolt of a husband's shortcomings, would she turn to him? Might she not choose another? Or choose no one at all? But, no, he would be on the scene to direct her. He could be persuasive when he had a mind to. He could lay it on with the best of them. Of course, in this case, he would be sincere. After all, she was his muse. You don't play fast and loose with your muse – not unless you want a snout full of bad karma. But, he assured himself, he was not being selfish. He was thinking of Sylvia as much as of himself. She deserved a man who would let her take centre stage for once, a man who would *see* her, who would bring her to life.

Robb looked across his shoulder to where his word processor sat in silent reproach. He took deliberate steps toward the beast, sat himself in his special chair designed for hours of comfort in which he had spent eons of agony. He pressed the power button. The screen lighted. As the magic of a June dawn over a northern wooded lake spread upward from the horizon and fanned out into sunny daylight, Robb's fingers found their rhythm on the keyboard. Letters appeared on the screen as if by magic. He had made a decision. Already he felt the lump of ice shrink, just a bit, but enough so that some words could trickle around its circumference.

And if my plan doesn't work... Robb looked up. There was a eureka glow to his countenance. If plan A doesn't work, I can always murder the husband.

ii

Sylvia set the table carefully, folding white linen napkins into the good crystal, foolish perhaps for the terrace, but all meals in the country were occasions. In their small apartment in the city, she and Michael scarcely ever ate together during a play's run. By the time he got out of bed, she was off to rehearsal or lessons or shopping or lunch with girlfriends. By the time he got home in the middle of the night after going out with the rest of the cast for a drink, she was sound asleep, even if she'd had an evening performance. Unlike Michael, she was always exhausted after performing. At the lake, slow meals allowed them to catch up with each other, a factor that Sylvia had considered when she had proposed the project.

And today was a special occasion. As Sylvia merrily mixed up muffin batter, blueberry, Michael's favourite, as she scooped butter into balls and placed them into an iced silver dish, she trilled in a sweet buoyant soprano, *Un Bel di Vedremo*. The poignant aria of Butterfly floated out the window, wafted through the trees, and found its way into Robb Goodfellow's consciousness, inspiring him to type even faster. But what was this? The singing abruptly stopped. Whether it was due to the melancholy subject of the music or the alignment of the stars, Sylvia had just had an unsettling thought, a thought that must have been lying dormant in her subconscious. Otherwise, why would she have thought it? *Something is bothering Michael.*

Sylvia stood stock still in the middle of her kitchen clutter. Michael had been acting strangely lately. Now that she thought about it, lately he avoided her eyes and spoke in his light false voice. It must be this place, she concluded. What else would it be? He hadn't wanted to buy it. He had wanted to buy a yacht. Momentarily, her sunny outlook was overcast, but then the cloud lifted. They would discuss it. They were a happily married couple. Everything could be solved by open communication.

"What's up," said Michael, observing the array, seating himself as though everyone was watching him. "It's not our anniversary is it?"

"Silly." Sylvia's tones were liquid honey. "Summer solstice always puts me into a celebratory mood." She adjusted her body into the webbing of the lawn chair, a little low for the table.

The Wildes were breakfasting on a semicircular flagstone area at the bottom of the back porch steps, which allowed their neighbour an excellent view. Sylvia had set out a large round white table with a colourful umbrella. Overhead, the fanning branches of an elm filtered the sunlight, dappling the canvas with dancing shadows. Behind them was the house, old yet solid, providing, by its very presence, something that seemed, if not eternal, at least enduring. That was why Sylvia liked it and why Michael disliked it, although he insisted that it was growing on him. Before them, through a screen of lacy willow and birch, blossoming dogwood and saskatoon, lay the lake and, beyond it, the hills. The colours had changed since early morning when Sylvia had gone for her swim. Now, it was bathed in bright light, effecting clarity in the tones of green and blue, shades of yellow and splashes of reds and oranges. The berries were coming nicely. Sylvia had planned a berry picking fete for the morrow, a project which she had not yet revealed to her husband.

"The solstice was a week ago." With exaggerated movements, Michael plucked a muffin from out a linen-lined basket and deposited it on his plate. He reached for the butter dish.

"I know, but we're celebrating this weekend. 'Sumer is icumen in, lhude sing cuccu'... ." She poured the coffee in a thin arc from an elegant pot.

"'Groweth sed and bloweth med and springeth the wude nu'," Michael interrupted, rummaging in the butter balls with miniature silver tongs.

"Yes." Sylvia felt the way she used to feel in school, when she knew the answer but someone with a louder voice or more aggressive manner said it first. "I can see why the ancients had rituals around such events," she rallied. "Places, too. There's magic in the air here. I've felt it since the moment we moved in. Even before. I felt it when we were talking to the realtor that day. Didn't you?"

"No, can't say as I did." Michael broke open his steaming muffin and plunked into the crevice the chosen butter ball.

"And this weekend. When our dearest friends are coming to help us celebrate our new place. Don't you have the feeling that all kinds of strange things might happen?"

"No."

"Well I do! I had the feeling when I went for a swim this morning. This is going to be a special weekend. My horoscope says that my ruling planet, Venus, the planet of love and creativity, rises in the east at the very moment of the full moon rising. I'm looking forward to it."

"Well I plan to unwind. Relax. That will be special enough for me. And, apparently, for once the weather's supposed to cooperate."

"I hope it won't be *too* hot," said Sylvia with a furrowed glance at the cloudless blue sky. "The heat can affect people." She lowered her eyes and caught the last bite of her husband's muffin as it travelled an arc up to his lips, hidden by a full moustache. For his last role, he had grown the moustache as well as a mane of hair. He was usually pretty good at reinventing himself back into reality after a play, but this time he seemed to be having trouble. Following a crumb as it moved up and down in the thick black hairs, she wondered how long he would keep up this Zorba-the-Greek thing. The play had been struck two months ago. Since then, he had done a TV commercial for tinned spaghetti, the producer had wanted the Italian look, but that was a month ago. Actually, apart from him constantly losing food in the foliage, which was not like his usual fastidious nature, she didn't mind. She liked men of an expansive, fun-loving nature. Sometimes, Michael was rather niggling. If some of Zorba rubbed off on him, so much the better.

Michael was not into the Zorba-the-Greek thing. He was into the Latin Lover thing. He had discovered, after growing all that hair over Christmas for the January play, that he had to fairly beat off the female sex. Women seemed to go primitive over hairy men. He could not help but encourage them. When the play was over he didn't want to return to his old self, which was no slouch either when it came to attracting women. But he found it exhilarating, for a while at least, to play the swarthy elemental Latin as opposed to the immaculately barbered, suave English drawing room comedy type, a role he had done so often and so well that he was in danger of being typecast.

"Your horoscope says it's an excellent time to get in touch with your inner self," Sylvia said.

"It's always an excellent time for all of us to get in touch with our inner selves. That's the thing about horoscopes. They spout generalities and truisms that apply to everybody."

She did not tell him the other half of his horoscope. 'You may have to wear an asbestos suit to withstand the heat as the sun, Mars, Saturn and Neptune form a heavy T-square.' Instead, she said, "Not only is it going to be a full moon tomorrow night, it's going to be a blue moon. The second full moon in the month. I've read that even during an ordinary full moon, police departments brace themselves. As do lunatic asylums."

"Since we're not criminals and, I hope, not lunatics, it shouldn't affect us too much."

"We should all be lunatics," cried Sylvia gaily with an upward flinging of her arms. "We should all be affected by the moon."

"I doubt Dob will be. Or Pam."

Sylvia lowered her arms. Her voice, too, returned to terra

firma. "You're probably right. He's too befogged. She's too efficient. But how about Jack?"

"I think Jack *could* be affected. In a physical way. Jack's so basic."

"I wonder about his friend. Who's he bringing?"

"I don't know."

"Have we met her?"

"I tell you, I don't know. All I know is, he phoned yesterday and asked if he might bring a friend and, of course, I said by all means."

"Of course. I wonder if they'll need separate rooms."

"If they were actors you wouldn't need to wonder."

"I could put Jack in your study."

"May as well put them in the same room. They'll end up together anyway."

"Still, one shouldn't presume. We don't want to insult her."

"Most of Jack's friends would be difficult to insult."

"Better to be subtle about it. I'll prepare a bed for him in your study. And I'll put her in the small room. I'll put Pamela and Dobbin in that lovely room at the back with a view of the lake. Oh I do want everything to be nice for our friends' first visit to our little country home." On that note of anxiety, Sylvia finally got around to taking a muffin.

"I wouldn't get too worked up about housekeeping details." Michael rested his elbows on the table. He struck a pose, looking toward the lake. "The main ingredients of a successful occasion are art, love and wine."

"That reminds me," said Sylvia. "Dobbin is bringing his latest wine experiment. Remember to be polite about it."

"Don't worry. I wouldn't hurt Dob's feelings."

Sylvia looked at her husband. "No," she said. "You wouldn't." The truth of her statement surprised her. Michael was sensitive, even kind, where Dobbin was concerned. And she could not help but notice that her husband was not always so careful with people's feelings – that poor man next door, for instance. And he was a terrible host. He didn't think it necessary to put any effort into his friends' comfort. Let them look after themselves, was his motto, they'll feel more at home. While his old university friends might put up with him, since they knew him and loved him anyway, other people felt unwelcome. Then she had to step in and smooth ruffled feathers. She didn't mind doing this. She knew that Michael was an artist. If he had to try to be socially pleasant it might be at the expense of his true nature which he must not suppress if he was to be an emotionally honest creative person.

"You're very fond of Dobbin," she continued. "I don't believe I've ever heard you say a word against him."

"Of course I am. Of course you haven't. Why would I say anything against Dob?" Michael's tone was one of bafflement at another's stupidity.

"What I mean, he's important to you." What Sylvia really meant was that not many people were important to her husband. She often doubted that she was. She often thought that he might have found someone else to marry who would have done equally as well. He might not have married at all. He didn't need people.

"Of course he's important." This time the tone was, 'what exactly is the point of these obvious statements.'

"How about Jack?"

"Jack's important too."

"What would you do without your squash games? And tennis in the summer. But with Dobbin it's ideas. The way you two bat them back and forth! For hours on end."

"We've known each other for a long time."

"Pamela, too."

"Yes."

Sylvia's feelings were not really hurt by the exclusion of her name from the list. She had known when she married Michael about the closeness of this troupe from university days. And in truth, she was humbly thankful that they had included her in the close-knit group. But this morning, a morning of strange thoughts entering her mind, a new one arrived. If Michael had to choose between his friends and her, what would be his choice? Shocked by the question, she stared open-eyed across the table at her husband. "We must clean the barbecue," she said, in an attempt to bring to earth her errant notions.

Sylvia was aware of the discrepancy between this remark and reality. She knew that *she* must clean the barbecue. But she was in the habit of saying *we*, a reflection of her thinking of her and Michael as a couple. She considered the relationship itself to be a living, breathing entity. That was why she must bring up the subject she had thought of earlier in the kitchen. It was for the benefit of the relationship to discuss any feelings Michael might still have about the buying of this property. They would clear it all up and everything would be lovely again.

"I might have to send you into town for oven cleaner," she went on, looking up toward the subject of her concern, a dark tarp-shrouded hulk overlooking them from around the corner of the house where the porch continued onto a back deck. The remark was intended to alert Michael against doing a disappearing act, leaving her to cope with all the cooking, cleaning and arranging necessary to entertain his friends. Not that she minded the extra work. After all, they were now her friends too. But she knew from conversations with other women in the orchestra during rehearsal breaks that nowadays married couples, happily married couples, shared chores and entertaining duties.

"A good scrape with the wire brush is all that's necessary." Michael reached for another muffin. "Other than that, the heat cleans them well enough."

"Dobbin won't be able to eat a bite unless those grills are stripped of all former bits and chunks," countered Sylvia, trying to keep her voice free of any note of contention.

"I suppose you're right." Michael broke open his muffin, releasing for the second time fragrant steam. "I remember at university he always brought his own utensils to the cafeteria."

"He's a Virgo."

"That explains it," said in a voice not so much sarcastic as disdainful.

"I hope he'll be all right with the berry picking I've planned for tomorrow."

"Berry picking?"

"It'll be a fun activity."

"Since when could berry picking be construed as a fun activity? As for Dob, he won't do it," stated Michael. "He hates being hot and itchy and dusty."

Sylvia let herself feel a bit discouraged. Why *would* Michael insist on shooting down her plans. "He doesn't have to go," she said. "You don't have to go, either, if that's the way you feel about it."

"My dear girl," Michael looked at her, a small amused smile, his loving smile, around his lips. "I'm only explaining Dob to you. I've known him for more than fifteen years. You've known him for five. I don't want you to be disappointed by his reaction to your agenda."

"Oh, I know." Already, Sylvia regretted her rude words. "And I mean it. You don't have to go. No one has to go who doesn't want to. I'm not going to force people to do anything. Maybe Jack and his friend will want to go. Jack's usually a good sport. You're right about Dobbin, he'll want to work. And you can stay back with Pamela. I'm sure the two of you will find something to do."

A clatter from the other side of the table caused Sylvia to raise her head sharply. Michael was half standing, his coffee cup overturned. Luckily, it was empty. "What's that supposed to mean?"

"What? Nothing. What were we talking about?" Sylvia's expression was one of simple confusion.

Michael quickly recovered himself and sank back into his chair and former position. "We're talking about the berry picking. Pam is sure to want to go. She's always up for things. She'll be leading the charge."

"That's settled then. Whoever wants to go, shall go. Whoever doesn't want to go, shan't go."

"Seems like a good plan." Michael poured himself more coffee.

Sylvia looked at her husband's face. The way it flickered with the flickering elm leaves, reminded her of early reel-to-reel films. Shadow and light, she thought, the basis of theatre, what you see and what you imagine you see. The table, too. What could be more real, more tangible than cups, plates, cutlery, our wedding goblets containing orange juice? And yet in the flickering light and shadow, it all took on an illusory appearance. Perhaps this serene lull would be a good time to bring up the subject she was determined to discuss. "You do like it here, don't you?" she asked. "You have gotten to like it?"

Michael looked at his wife. He must be careful. This might be a loaded question. But her eyes were clear and guileless. She was wearing a white top of diaphanous material and a bright wrap-around skirt. Without makeup and with her hair pulled back into a curly wreath, she looked like a scrubbed and polished child. This innocent quality was what had first appealed to him. It still did. Innocence in the theatre was a rare commodity.

"Of course I have," Michael said in the quick, light voice that never failed to alert the ever-vigilant Sylvia. "You know that," he continued. "Why do you ask?"

"I can't always tell how you really feel about things."

"We've been through this before. I'm quite reconciled to the place."

"Reconciled is not the word I want to hear."

"What do you expect me to say? You know I was against it at first. I told you right up front that I wasn't the type to go frolicking off into the woods."

"But I want you to be more than reconciled. I want you to like it."

"And I do."

"'What in Jesus' name would I do in the country?' I remember you yelling."

"I didn't yell."

"Your voice got awfully loud." Sylvia heaved a rather loud sigh. "Maybe you were right. Maybe we should have bought the yacht."

"No, you were right. As you pointed out, there's a lot of upkeep to a boat – scraping and painting and hosing down."

"But all that work would have been relaxing. I mean, physical labour is *so* relaxing, so different from the brutal life of an actor, the competition, the personalities, the stress of performances."

"As you also pointed out, yacht club annual fees are atrocious."

"You're right. And they're always increasing. It would have been an anxiety, never knowing what they were going to be in the future."

As it had happened, Michael, whose visions of being a yacht owner had not gone further than sitting on a deck chair in the sunshine, hat pulled low, beer at side, line cast, on which, hopefully, nothing would bite, after discussions with his wife, had started to see the truth of such a purchase. He hated physical labour. He reasoned that such labour at the acreage would be Sylvia's responsibility. If differences of opinion on the subject arose, he could remind her of whose idea it had been in the first place. For anything beyond her physical capabilities, she could hire someone. As it turned out, there was very little that Sylvia could not do, from shingling the roof to nurturing goats to whomping up incredible meals, the vegetables grown organically in her own garden. Michael also figured that he would not have to actually go to the country that often. He would have commitments, meetings, auditions in the city. He had reminded Sylvia of that fact – his profession demanded that he be very much present in the theatre scene. Her answer had been that it was only a five-hour drive to the city. Well and good. Let her traipse off and play Pocahontas. He looked forward to being on his own in town once in a while. He could relive some of his bachelor days. He had liked being a bachelor. If Sylvia was not such an adorable person, he doubted that he would have ever given it up. And with these parameters in place in his mind, he had, at times, during the past few months, come to enjoy their little place at the lake, although he had not yet admitted as much to his wife. He knew from long experience with women that there was mileage to be gained by withheld information.

"But you're sure?" said Sylvia.

"What?" said Michael.

"You like it here?"

"What could be greater than this?" replied Michael, with an expansive gesture of his arm towards lake and trees and sky.

Sylvia put her hands in her lap. She looked down at them and, at the same time, her watch. The morning was half over and she had a million things to do before her guests arrived. Along with preparations for their visit, she must get in a practice, at the very least, do her scales. But she hadn't yet discussed with Michael what was wrong with him. Or, she had, and it hadn't. Been wrong, that is. But if it wasn't this place, what was it? His career was going well, she knew that. Well, then, if something is wrong with a husband and it's not his home or career... what else could it be but... *There must be someone else.*

She raised her head and opened her mouth in surprise. She didn't know what to say. What she said was, "It's amazing that Pamela was attracted to Dobbin. She's so intense. He's so easy-going."

"They say opposites attract," answered the unsuspecting Michael. "But they're both intelligent."

"He's so cerebral. Did he fall in love with her?"

"I don't know. Dob's a funny old stick. But I'm sure he loves her in his fashion."

"How about Jack?"

"What about Jack?"

"What's he like?"

"Jack's a great guy. Give you the shirt off his back."

"But how about *love*?"

"Oh, Jack. Jack's a dentist."

"You say that as if the words 'love' and 'dentist' are incompatible."

"It's not a romantic occupation. Dentists have the highest

rate of alcoholism and divorce of any group of people in the country. And no wonder. Imagine staring into people's open jaws all day. The crooked teeth, rotting fillings, bad breath. Dentists must view the whole world as one big open mouth festering with canker sores. They must see the planet as a loose rotten tooth wobbling in the jaw of the universe."

"Ugh. Sounds awful. No wonder Jack is constantly seeking diversion."

"Diversion?"

"You know, the opposite sex.

"Oh yes, he does tally them up rather quickly. I lost count a long time ago, and those were just the serious encounters. I'm sure Jack himself can't remember the number of one-night stands in his life."

"How terrible."

Michael said nothing.

"He must be terribly unhappy. Apparently that Don Juan complex is caused by all sorts of twisted emotional baggage."

"I wouldn't put too serious a connotation on it. Maybe he just likes to have fun."

"But is that fun? Constantly going from one to another? Never settling? Never having anything lasting?"

"Maybe he hasn't met the right one yet. He's only thirty-eight. Many people don't meet the right person until later in life."

"Let's hope that's it. Well, it will be interesting to see who he brings this time."

"She's sure to be into hiking and swimming. All Jack's relationships are physical."

Michael took a third muffin. Sylvia had barely touched hers. She had been busy manoeuvring a path through trivia to arrive at her destination. By talking about their friends' relationships, she could now lead the discussion into theirs. But she must be tactful, diplomatic, must make it seem like a casual comment. "What kind of relationship do we have?" she said.

Michael's hand froze in midair as it reached for the coffee

pot. Sylvia's words seemed to be an escaped thought rather than a question seriously demanding a response, but he knew better. He should have seen where the conversation was heading. He should have kept up the idle chatter and not given her a chance to voice this subject. He hated these discussions which women insisted on having at regular intervals. However, he'd been married long enough to know that he must say something. Otherwise, he'd be accused of not communicating. "What?" he said, stalling for time.

"We were talking about the relationships of your oldest and dearest friends, so I wondered. What kind of relationship do *we* have?"

"What kind of relationship does any married couple have?" Michael hedged.

"But what about ours?"

"All relationships are different. I think we have a pretty good marriage."

"You make it sound mediocre."

"I don't mean to. Compared to some marriages in the theatre community, it's a huge success."

"Oh great! Marriages in the theatre crowd. What sort of comparison is that?"

"I said we have a good marriage."

"You meant so-so."

"What do you want it to be?"

"Extraordinary. Romantic."

"After all that romance on stage, perhaps I'm tired of it. Or just plain tired. It takes a lot of energy to be romantic."

Sylvia knew that romance on the stage, far from being glamourous, was hard work. Michael had told her this often enough. The poor man, she thought. He's trying to relax after months on the stage and I'm on his case. "All I mean is," she said, "are you still in love with me?"

Michael smiled across the table at his wife. "Who wouldn't be in love with you? You are Sylvia. All your swains adore you."

Sylvia found herself being annoyed, if only slightly, by that smile. Smarmy, smirky, it seemed to contain something not quite right, not quite straightforward. "That's not an answer," she said.

"Isn't it? I thought it was."

"It's an evasion."

"It's an answer for me." He drew back. His voice grew tight and cold.

She knew that when his voice took on that tone, she might as well give up. She could not penetrate his aloof mode, he had it practiced into an art form. She hoped he was not going to get into one of his theatrical moods for the weekend. She said as much.

"I'm not in a mood. I'm just tired of these inane conversations, which, by the way, you seem to wallow in. And then if I won't join you in your masochistic exercise you accuse me of not communicating. I wish you'd stop badgering me."

"I don't mean to badger you. It's just that you haven't been yourself lately."

"Who have I been?"

"I don't know. You seem preoccupied. Like you're not here."

He kept his gaze level with hers across the table. She realized that she was never sure of the colour of his eyes. Bluish green? Greenish blue? Greyish-blue? Whatever the colour, she thought he had to make an effort to keep them from shifting. "But I *am* here," he said.

That's true, Sylvia told herself sternly. And knowing Michael, he would not be here if he did not want to be. Still, she had a right to her feelings, didn't she? She had a right to her thoughts. "It may be silly," she said, "but at times during the last few months I've thought there might be someone else."

"You're right, it is a silly thought." With an abrupt movement, Michael reached for the sugar, ladled three teaspoons into his lukewarm coffee, stirred vigorously and set his spoon down onto his saucer with a clatter. "Can't a person be preoccupied once in a while without his wife accusing him of having an affair."

"Affair! I didn't mean an affair. I know you wouldn't do that. I just meant that maybe you were doing a little flirting. Or fantasizing."

"What an absolutely asinine idea."

"So are you?"

"Am I what?"

"Having an affair?"

"Jesus. What is this? The Inquisition?"

"You were the one who said the word. I wouldn't have even thought it."

"This is the most stupid conversation I've had in a long time," Michael shouted. He threw his napkin onto the table. "If you're going to lower it to semantics well, then, 'someone else' usually means 'affair'. How else am I supposed to interpret it?"

"What's wrong? Why are you acting this way? All I want is some reassurance of my husband's love. You act as though I'm being entirely unreasonable." Sylvia's blue eyes proclaimed nothing but sincere appeal.

"I won't have these accusations, that's all. This is complete nonsense. And while we're on the subject how about our next-door neighbour?"

"Next-door neighbour?"

"The guy who's constantly over here drooling all over you."

"He's not drooling."

"Are you kidding? I can recognize lust when I see it."

You should be able to, you see it often enough with your theatre friends, Sylvia felt like saying. But she decided that she had better nip this disagreement in the bud before it spoiled the weekend. "He's lonely, that's all," she said. "He's a writer. He doesn't have many connections to the real world. I think I'm a connection."

"That's no excuse for his salivating. He knows you're a married woman."

"Maybe he does have a little crush on me. But I don't encourage it. Anyway, it's all perfectly harmless. He just likes to talk. He's in love with his own words."

Michael said nothing. He sat with glum countenance which he managed to infuse with accusation of something... anything.

"I'm sorry," said Sylvia. "I'm just trying to communicate. All the articles say that the greatest threat to marriage nowadays is lack of communication."

Still, he said nothing, allowing his wife, in the silence, to create a scenario in her own mind in which she was entirely to blame and owed him an apology.

"It's just that...," Sylvia hesitated, "well, sometimes you seem to be worried about something. I only want to help."

"No, there's nothing. I'm not worried about anything," Michael answered in his light and airy voice.

She smiled across the table at him. "Well, that's a relief."

He did not erase the sour look from his face, knowing that, with women as with theatre, timing is everything.

"You're not mad at me are you?" she appealed with soft eyes.

He looked at her with only a little frown. "No, of course not. No, not at all. I'm glad we had this talk. Got things out on the table. Cleared the air."

Michael lifted his head and turned it toward the green growth and the warmth of the morning. He breathed in a long breath of fresh country air. He went back to his muffin and coffee. He felt fine. Now that he had the communication thing out of the way, he could relax and enjoy his weekend.

As for Sylvia, she felt thoroughly upset and agitated. Nothing had been said. Nothing had been resolved.

Robb Goodfellow put down his glasses. An enigmatic smile curved his thin lips. Things seemed to be progressing nicely, the universe once more resuming forward motion.

iii

"The major necessity in living a good life," said Dobbin Davenport, "is to get beyond personality. To give up the mean, dreary, despicable little self for something better, higher, something that connects to a transcendent cause or system. To get rid of our egos, that is what we should be striving for. Self as object rather than subject. And yet our contemporary focus is the opposite. Our contemporary gurus and advisors stress self-actualization. Self-fulfilment books stock the shelves of bookstores, self-realization seminars are rampant. It all leads to the most appalling selfishness and egomania. It's amazing how we think our petty miserable little selves that important. How we constantly go around from day to day with our minds full of a firmly implanted image of the self. We must learn to think of ourselves merely as part of the river, and I should not use the term 'merely', for being part of the river, part of the whole, is the most noble existence to which we can aspire."

Get real, thought his wife, who was sitting beside him in the passenger seat of an ancient yellow Dodge sedan that was rattling along the Coquihalla Highway in the interior of British Columbia. She was not in a good mood. She was doing this for her friend Sylvia. Personally, she would rather be jogging

"Reality is outside of us, not inside," Dobbin continued, stretching his upper body and pressing his spine into the upholstered seat back, stretching his right ankle up from the gas pedal. He was wearing a light cotton blue plaid shirt, one of six he had got on sale, three cellophane packages, two to a package.

He had been pleased with the purchase as it allowed him the advantage of having to think no longer about his summer wardrobe, thus leaving more time to think about what really mattered. Although it was hot in the car, on his head was his old beaten-up khaki hat, which he always wore on summer motor trips to remind him that he was supposed to be relaxing. Because he was perspiring, his spectacles were slipping down on his nose. With a practiced gesture, he adjusted them and went on. "We must learn to think of reality as being the larger picture and we must meditate on how we best fit into that picture, rather than constantly conniving to alter the picture to suit ourselves. We must question not how can we manipulate the whole to suit our own ends but how can we best serve the whole. We all carp about wanting to be happy but we do not accept that to be happy we must be good. We think happiness is satisfaction of our wills, whereas it is the exact opposite. We know the difference between right and wrong. We know what we ought to embrace and what avoid. We know the rules to live by. Our sins are to be avoided, not to be explored, even glorified. We should consider not what makes us happy or unhappy, but what is right and what is wrong, and as C.S. Lewis points out in his excellent little book, a book I encourage my students to read, by the way, all human beings, in all parts of the earth, have a clear idea of what this is. We know the rules of decent behaviour, the laws of nature, even though we constantly break those rules and laws. We know, for instance, that honesty is the law, that to work to relieve suffering is the law. We know that deceit and causing suffering are forbidden."

His wife kept silent. She knew that to do otherwise would only encourage him. If she did not respond, he might eventually peter out, aloud at least. Likely, he would ruminate the matter until their arrival at their destination, at which time he would not forget about it but, rather, put it temporarily on hold. She looked at the map in her hand, neatly folded into the rectangle pertinent to their situation at the moment. They had passed Merritt some time back. Kamloops was the next large black square. From there they would travel east.

Pamela Davenport was a tallish woman in her late thirties. She had a rather bony face, a large resolute mouth, a prominent though well-shaped nose, straight brows above snappish brown eyes and black, straight hair, coiffed to slightly turn under. Her makeup was ample but so subtle its application was not evident. Although not fine-boned, she was slim and looked terrific in a green and white sports outfit. She exuded energy and when forced into idleness, as now, was like a female tiger tensed for the leap. 'Relax,' her friends, who sometimes found her tiring, would say. But she could not relax, perhaps because, deep down inside, she loved her stress.

Dobbin Davenport was a substantial man of forty. Composed, staunch, sustaining, his friends and colleagues, like Michael Wilde, would have chosen him to be in their corners in a time of crisis. A slow thinker, yet precise and thorough, he had a problem-solving thrust of mind. Although young for such a role, he had already become a beloved uncle figure to his students, perhaps because there was something naive, even something of wonder, in his manner, perhaps because he genuinely liked them, perhaps because he was a kind man, and they knew it. Also, he looked dependable. As someone once said, 'Dobbin is so *there*.' Large and broad, with blond lank hair, he had a fair pinkish complexion and mild blue eyes. He never got steamed up about anything, which was the precise trait that drove his wife insane.

If they had been taking the Trans-Canada Highway Pamela would not have had to consult a map. That was their usual route on their jaunts to visit the Okanagan wineries. Dobbin considered the wine-making process to be complex and challenging. Chemical balance of the elements involved was one of the topics he felt should be fascinating to the wine and cheese reception crowd. Dobbin preferred the Trans-Canada to the Coquihalla, which he thought brutally hard on a vehicle, carved as it was through rock. Confrontational, he called it. In his opinion, it attacked the landscape rather than attempting to cooperate with it. Pamela preferred the Coquihalla. It got you there quickly, which was why they were on it today. The teaching assistant who was to supervise the final exam in Dobbin's Friday morning environmental ethics class had thoughtlessly got the flu. When a substitute could not be found, they'd had to put off their departure until noon.

The high road arched before them. The car wheezed up hill and clattered down dale. Dobbin had insisted on taking his old clunker. He said that with a gear-stick vehicle, you knew that you were driving. On either side of the highway, forbidding concrete barriers had been erected to keep travellers from flying off into the oblivion of deep gullies. The cold stone of nearby mountains, the regimental stiffness of parading pine trees, surrounded them. Pamela was not unaware of this hostile environment. She was not insensitive to the differences that the other route offered, the friendly valleys, the small farms, the gardens, the foliage and trees, the hazy tangle of the human landscape. It was, rather, that she did not wish to get caught in that landscape. She preferred the thrusting assertiveness of the mountains and their unchanging definition. There were no two ways about them. She supposed, also, that she was destination, rather than journey, oriented. She did not like to be out of commission the length of time it took to get from one place to another. She had no trouble living with this facet of her personality. She did not know why other people sometimes did.

The major necessity to living a successful life, decided Pamela, giving the map a snap to straighten it, is to know when to move on. When to get out. When to leave where you are and go to where you should be. Most people stay too long. Most people are cowards.

Pamela had no intention of being a coward and every intention of leaving her husband. She had been considering doing this for several months, but something always intervened. She was too involved with her career as an administrator with the regional health system to contemplate an upset at that particular time, or the two of them were having an immensely pleasant evening and she did not wish to spoil it, or what with committee meetings, the Royal Astronomical Society, the Philosophy Club, the University Nurses'

Alumni, and personal friends, she and Dobbin were not alone for a long enough stretch of time to set up the discussion. However, the present state of affairs had been going on long enough, much too long. She meant to tell him this weekend. It had occurred to her earlier as she had climbed into the car that this would be both a propitious and appropriate occasion.

It was not that she did not love Dobbin. Perhaps she loved him, she wasn't sure. She admitted that she did not know what love was, she did not seem to feel in these matters as other people felt, certainly people in romantic movies or novels. But she was wise enough to know that movies and books were not real life. She discussed the matter with female friends but they could not come up with clear answers, either. 'Wanting to be with a person more than with anyone else,' one said. Well, she didn't mind being with Dobbin, in fact, she rather liked his company most times. 'Having fun together,' someone else said. Again, they certainly got along in their fashion. They liked the same foods, fresh products, French cuisine. They liked the same decor in interior decorating, clean lines, nothing pretentious. They were both astute in their spending habits, although Pamela believed it was false value to purchase an inexpensive item that would soon become shabby and need replacing, while Dobbin believed the cheaper the better since he didn't see shabbiness and he never replaced anything until it obviously functioned no longer. They shared season's tickets to the symphony, the opera and the theatre. They never missed one of Michael's plays or Sylvia's performances with her chamber group and the VSO. They could easily discuss ideas and concepts, if not emotions. They could not discuss emotions because Dobbin didn't have them.

Their relationship resulted in a congenial existence. However, Pamela had to admit that she wanted more. What else could explain that, lately, she had found herself answering the intimacy and relationship quizzes in the magazines and tabloids at the checkout counters of drugstores and supermarkets. 'My marriage is not a perfect success.' True or False. She answered true, which turned out to be the right answer. 'Nobody's relationship is perfect so if you're being honest with yourself, the answer is true.' 'Despite being married, I often feel lonely.' Again, she had the right answer – false. She had to admit that when with Dobbin she was seldom lonely. They always had something to talk about. She supposed they actually were well suited and quite liked each other. How about sex then? 'Sex with my spouse has never been as exciting as in my fantasies.' Again, she struck the right answer, false, but not for the right reasons. She did not have fantasies, sexual or otherwise. She could not imagine wanting to be in a sex scene with Pierce Brosnan. Sex was all right, but she did not know why people made such a big deal about it.

Thus, according to the tabloids her marriage was, if not excellent, good. So what was wrong? After giving it a great deal of thought, she finally concluded that what was happening, and what she could no longer put up with, was that she was losing herself in the relationship. She was losing that ego which Dobbin liked to prattle on about getting rid of but which she found essential to her existence. She was, quite simply, an ego-driven person. She made no apologies for this fact. As she had said many times to many people, if it were not for her ego she would not be where she was with her career, and she liked being there. But more and more over the years, slowly, like some creeping paralysis, she could feel her personality, a personality which she happened to like very much, thank you, being invaded by another's influence. She fought against this, to the point of deliberately acting against his mind. But she feared that she was losing the battle. Dobbin's mind was proving stronger than her ego.

Dobbin lived in his mind. He was always processing an idea. She had nothing against thinking. She liked to think. But ye gods! Dobbin was too much. Give it a rest, she wanted to say. Give me a break. She was being dragged down. She was losing her joie de vivre. Before marriage she had perceived herself as a fun-loving, energetic, bright, vivacious person. She'd had a reputation for being the life of a continuous string of parties that she'd attended first as an undergraduate and then as a registered nurse. She'd had a few quite serious relationships with young doctors, who on the face of it seemed as irresponsible as she. Then she decided to do a master's degree in medical behavioural science because her friend was and it seemed like a good idea since she was becoming bored with her nursing and current male companion. At the same time, she and Dobbin, whom she'd known casually for years, became seriously involved and the long usurpation of her mind began. In the same way that some women are overpowered and destroyed by a man's physical nature, she was being destroyed by her husband's intellect. His influence, either by word or deed or implication, implied that she must give up her former self. Rigorous structured analysis took the place of sloppy hazy thinking and now, after ten years of marriage, she felt that she was anxious, morose, overly serious, in short, not herself.

Early in their relationship, it seemed that she might help him to lighten up, to sometimes get out of his mind. That was when they were in love, or, as she analyzed it later, when they were carried away by the phenomenon whereby two people, through the force of coming together, are shocked out of themselves and for a time become free spirits. Inevitably, the shock wears off and they settle back into themselves. But why had she settled into Dobbin's influence rather than the other way around? Why had she done all the adjusting in their marriage? On the face of it, she seemed the stronger personality. But Dobbin had more forbearance, he was more unyielding, and he was more consistent. He was like a steamroller, slow but steady and unwavering. He practiced, insofar as any one could, what he preached. He never, outwardly at least, considered his personality. He did not seem to have a strong, or indeed, any, sense of himself. He appeared to be unconscious of himself, and it never seemed to occur to him that he should or might change or that he should do or be other than what he did or was. While mindful that no one fell short of the mark so far as he, he lived by the rules of decency and the laws of conduct as best he could. Pamela knew all these things about her husband, and she admitted that he was a principled man, but she was sceptical about the virtue of his principles because there was no struggle. He could not think to do or be other than the way he was. He was a man without imagination.

By now they had left the Coquihalla and had connected with the Trans-Canada where it became the main street through Kamloops. To one side of them stretched a series of gas stations, fast food outlets and motor hotels. On the other, small industries and businesses flourished. The afternoon sun beat down on the car's metal. Pamela thought of her car at home in the garage, a zippy Toyota with air conditioning. She rolled down the window, which helped the temperature, but then the dust swirled in. This was desert country. Except for brief periods in winter when snow damped down the terrain, the area was always dry and dusty. South of the highway was a ridge of brown hills, north was flat barren land cut by the sharp banks of the Thompson River. Scrub and weeds were the only natural flora, although floating like balloons over the town were blobs of green, trees planted by homeowners and the municipality. Colourful flower gardens ringed the fronts of businesses as well as dwellings. As the Dodge sedan rolled along a straight section of road, through the town, and emerged the other side, it left the gardens behind.

Pamela found this part of the journey dull and uninspiring. If they were in her car, she could be driving, but since Dobbin would not give up the wheel of his pride and joy, she settled herself down to organize her day. She looked at her watch. Three-thirty. They could be there by four-thirty. She would have time for a jog before dinner. She wouldn't mind helping Sylvia with the dinner preparations but, likely, Sylvia would have been puttering away all afternoon in her slow steady way and would have most of it done. Just as well, thought Pamela, since she found it somewhat frustrating to slow her pace to that of her friend. Anyway, she had brought work to do. She always had reports to read, committee agendas to prepare, research articles to write, for she was conscientious in the extreme about her board positions, meticulous in her research and precise in her writing.

She looked out her window. The landscape was becoming

more encouraging, the barrens turning into fields dotted with wild
flowers. Small farms and orchards appeared at intervals along
the highway. The houses were fronted with lawns of green grass,
their windows bordered by boxes filled with bright pansies,
geraniums, chrysanthemums. Still, it was not a landscape which
appealed to her. Why her friends wanted to bury themselves
out here for months at a time was beyond her. Sylvia had even
gone into chickens and a goat! Ugh, thought Pamela.

The sky was blue. At their back was the late afternoon
sun. Pamela couldn't take any more silence. She had to say
something. "It's so hot," she tried. "I'll be glad when we get
there."

"Ummm."

After several minutes, she decided to use the direct
approach. "What are you thinking?" she asked, looking toward
her husband.

"What's that?"

Pamela felt like giving up, but she was not a quitter. "Have
you ever thought about what it would be like to be a bachelor
again?" she blurted out, quite loudly, and then thought, my god
what have I said? But he was so infuriating. She could not keep
her lips pressed shut. "On your own. To come and go as you
please. Eat what you want. Go to bed, get up when you want?"

A weighty silence issued from the driver's seat. Had she
actually managed to shock him? to make him think about concerns
of life as lived by human beings?

"Well, have you?" She raised her voice.

"Have I what?"

"Thought about being on your own."

"Why? Are you taking a trip?"

What's the use? she thought. Even when I tell him straight
out that I'm leaving him, he won't hear me. He'll just go on as
always. He won't even know I'm gone. "Why, exactly, are you
so distracted?" she said, meaning not only on this occasion but all
of his life, wondering it to herself, not expecting a reply.

"The negative dialectic," he answered. "Sometimes a difficult concept for students. I was wondering how I might present it to my new summer class next week so that they might better understand it. I look forward to this weekend. It'll give me time to think without distraction."

Oh, how I would love to tell him right now, seethed Pamela. She almost opened her mouth to do so. But, no, she did not want to spoil the weekend for Sylvia. Sylvia wanted to christen the new place at the lake and by god she would help her do it. She would not tell Dobbin until tomorrow night when they were getting ready for bed. By then the weekend would be almost over. They would only have to get through Sunday morning. She supposed she might tell him now and not the others until Sunday morning. But, no, likely that would not work. Neither she nor Dobbin were used to keeping secrets from these best friends. It would come out. In fact, she might not tell him until they were packing up after Sunday brunch. Sylvia had described the brunch menu on the phone during the week – muffins, cakes, waffles. Sylvia was so enthusiastic. That was one of her qualities that Pamela had immediately liked when Michael introduced her into their group. She was younger than Michael and rather childlike. She might be good for Michael. She might put up with his nonsense. How Michael might be good for Sylvia, Pamela did not know. She only hoped that Sylvia would survive. No, she did not want to spoil Sylvia's brunch. Yes, she would tell Dobbin Sunday morning after brunch and the others as they were saying their good-byes in the driveway. But, no, that would not work, either, because then the drive back to Vancouver would be insufferable. A long discussion with their friends would be necessary to bring the matter into perspective and create a comfortable atmosphere around it.

Pamela sighed at being so put upon by circumstances. She supposed, too, that she'd have to deal with Michael this weekend. God, why did she have to take care of everything?

Thank heavens they were nearly there. From the elevation of the highway, lakes and beach properties came into view. Retirement homes and tourist accommodations became prevalent. Bed and breakfast signs, restaurant advertisements – only 5 km to the biggest burger in the west – dotted the road. The growth was greener, almost lush, nourished as it was by underground arteries extending from the many small surrounding lakes. Fruit stands with colourful signs to attract customers announced apricots, cherries – the first fruits of summer. Within a few hours, thought Pamela, we've come through green rain coast, grey stone, brown desert and now this valley paradise.

Paradise for others, but Pamela would never choose to live here. If her friends wanted to hide themselves away all summer, that was their business. The landscape was too casual, too careless, for her taste. She preferred manicured lawns to random grass and orderly gardens to clumps of tangled colour. Here, the weeds and nettles grew waist high, the birch and aspen groves were not thinned and so produced spindly growth. However, she could appreciate that these untidy roadways and meadows suited Sylvia and Michael who, perhaps because they were artists, preferred things to sprout at will, without restraint, at any and every angle. Sylvia raved about the freedom of the country, but any time Pamela had been pressed into spending time *a la pastorale*, she had felt forcibly confined until she could get back to the city, to her regular gym and jogging path, to her word processor and her daily routine.

The car slowed. Dobbin turned the wheel and they crossed a log bridge that spanned a shallow ditch between the road and the property. Pamela jumped out to open the gate. They could see the house through the trees. The land had once been cleared to accommodate barns and sheds, fences and corrals. But that was near the beginning of the century when it had been a working farm. Now only a couple of small structures, besides the house, remained. Now, grass grew randomly upon once-ploughed earth and sprang up in clumps around trunks of second-growth willow and poplar.

The yellow Dodge bumped along the rutted lane, making a great racket and disturbing the country quiet. Up ahead, Michael and Sylvia appeared and stood waiting and waving. Dobbin braked slowly and circumspectly beside them.

"Hi. Hello. How're y'doing? Made it okay, I see," called Michael and Sylvia. "We heard you turn in at the road."

"Hello. Great. Yes." The other two had climbed out of their car. Cheeks were presented. Hugs were exchanged all around. "We had a fantastic drive," said Pamela.

"We had a relatively good trip," said Dobbin, straightening and stretching, rocking back on his heels a bit to limber up his glutes. "On a scale of one to ten I'd place it at six."

"What happened?" Sylvia's voice rose in alarm.

"Oh, nothing happened," answered Dobbin rounding to the back of the car and starting to remove luggage. "However, I hesitate to use terms such as fantastic or tremendous. One needs to keep things in cautious perspective. Life has taught us that the most we can ever expect is transitory contentment. You never know when the blow will fall."

Michael went forward to help Dobbin with the luggage. "Here let me get that bag," he said.

"Careful of that box there," said Dobbin. "That's the wine. I've brought you several bottles of my latest effort."

"Wonderful," chorused Sylvia and Michael, Michael's enthusiasm lagging only slightly behind Sylvia's.

"A cabernet sauvignon. It turned out rather well this time, if I do say so myself. Here, I'll take that. It shouldn't be shaken up."

Michael, with suitcases in both hands, fell in beside Pamela who was carrying several small packages containing gifts of chocolate, rare deli items, expensive cheeses. Pamela moved quickly forward to walk alongside Sylvia. "I knew better than to bring you flowers," she said. "That would be like carrying coal to Newcastle."

"I warn you, I'm here to think," said Dobbin to Michael. "The negative dialectic. Things are not what they appear to be."

"Sounds like theatre," murmured Michael.

"Yes, the concept is used in theatre and literature. It's supposedly a post-modern idea but of course it's always been around. Just with different names. Essentially, if a is not a and b is not b, there can be no c. The order of the entire cosmos is thrown into doubt."

"Let the comedy begin," murmured Michael.

The four friends entered the house.

Meanwhile, across a space of fifty yards, through a tangle of saplings and shrubbery, two shiny circles appeared. They were attached to a human forehead. Robb Goodfellow was again busy with his glasses.

iv

The red Mercedes convertible was rushing northward along the sun-drenched highway between Kelowna and Vernon. Like a huge bird of paradise it swooped and glided and soared down the hills, along the straightaways, and up and around the many curves. The road had been built between Lake Kalamalka on the east and a high ridge to the west, its parameters strictly drawn by nature and adhered to by engineers. On this day, the lake was a sheen of silver in the afternoon sun. The ridge to the west gave way at intervals to areas of weeds and wild grass and shrubs. The sky was without a cloud. *Moondance* was blasting forth from the CD player.

"I trust you like Van Morrison," called the driver to his companion.

"Oh, yes." The words were immediately ripped from the speaker's lips by the rush of wind and disappeared in the expanse of landscape.

Candice Patterson hunched down a bit lower in the passenger seat. Her hair, an indeterminate shade of brown streaked with orange, was spiked with gel into rigid spears that even the whip of the wind could not dislodge. On her face was a pair of enormous sunglasses. Candy hoped the weekend would not get any sportier than this. Weekends in the country could be a bit of a challenge in that regard. People expected you to hike and bike and play tennis and get all sweaty and enthusiastic.

"The way he combines that improv jazz style with a clearly defined rock base is pure genius," called the driver.

"Good rhythm."

Once again the words disappeared. Since both the wind and the music discouraged verbal interaction, the couple lapsed into silence, which was fine with Candy. She felt extremely unsure of this venture and was starting to wonder why she had agreed to come. What had ever possessed her to think that she could get through a whole weekend with her boss, a man not only fifteen years older than she but who was a professional? The word 'educated' came to mind, but she was not sure that dentists were educated in the strict sense of the term.

She scrunched her pretty forehead in thought. Why *had* she agreed? What *had* she thought? She hadn't thought. "Say," he had said in a low intimate voice, leaning over her desk in the reception area, "friends of mine have just bought a place in the country. They're having a little housewarming weekend. Would you care to come?"

"Yes, thank you very much, that would be lovely," she had said, without removing her fingers from the computer keyboard. Why did I say that? she had asked herself as Dr. Tzvetkov returned to his operating theatre. What if he makes a move on me? she asked herself now. She had to admit to an exciting little thrill at the thought. He was so experienced. But it would be unimaginably awkward, although she *did* like Dr. Tzvet... him. Jack. She must get used to calling him Jack. She couldn't very well go around all weekend calling him Dr. Tzvetkov. What would the other people think? And that was another thing. The other people. Dr... Jack, had told her a little about them. One was an actor. She hadn't heard of him but that didn't mean anything since she was not exactly travelling in the professional crowd yet. But they were all highly educated and accomplished. They all had interesting careers and were involved in exciting projects. And here she was, still a student!

Her teeth began to chatter, and not because she was cold. Her stomach had that hollow feeling it always got at times like this. The Christmas pageant, singing recitals, class presentations, from childhood on, anytime she was called upon to perform, her stomach felt like it was eating itself. Strangely, this feeling had not assailed her when she had been employed as an exotic dancer. But that was different. She did not have to speak. And dancing was so impersonal. When she was dancing, she was pure movement. She gave no thought to anything but physical sensation.

Candy clamped her teeth and tried to control her stomach. Grow up, she told herself. This is a problem you have to conquer. If you want to become an actor.

She knew people who always threw up before they went on stage, who regarded being sick as part of the process. She had read that Laurence Olivier suffered from stage fright all of his life. But she was not sure that she had that kind of strength.

She knew full well that she had only herself to blame for what was turning into a weird experience. She was the one who had said yes without thinking. She was the one who had been flattered and excited by the attention of this totally cool guy, a man completely sure of himself, a man in control – of all that complex dental equipment, of all those teeth that came under his arrogant appraisal, of his female staff of two nurses and two receptionists, herself included.

Part of the reason she had got herself into this mess was that she hadn't had anything else to do this weekend. Candy was a girl who hated to be at loose ends on a weekend, which happened more often than the ordinary person might think. She was an exceedingly attractive, well-proportioned young lady of twenty-two. Besides that, she was personable, a great dancer, and expert at shmoozing amongst her own crowd, the other dance students at Jeunesse Classique and the art students at the next-door College. Everyone assumed that she would be busy on a weekend, so a lot of people who might otherwise have called her did not.

She looked at her companion out of the corners of her eyes, which, because of her sunglasses, was easy to do without being detected. He, too, was wearing sunglasses, although not as large as hers. His were narrow with rectangular black frames. He had on a peaked cap and driving gloves. Deep in the low-slung seat, he appeared to be part of the car, part of a well-oiled machine. He seemed to be smiling but she could not be sure. He might be grimacing because of the wind or the sun's glare. Besides, he had the sort of face that seemed to be smiling even when it was not.

Candy noted how his quick agile hands manipulated the wheel, the same way they managed all that complicated equipment in his office. He seemed to be a man who liked gadgets, liked pushing levers, popping buttons, turning wheels, smoothly and precisely as now. She had first encountered him as a torso bending over her in the dentist's chair. She had been cranked back into a horizontal position by his assistant and felt like a slab of meat in a plastic foam tray in the supermarket. He marched in from behind her head, pulled up his stool and seated himself. He adjusted a mask across his nose and mouth and demanded that she open wide. She waited for him to pronounce 'utility', 'domestic', or 'first-grade' through the cloth. As he completed his investigation, she could not help but notice abundant black hair, trimly barbered, bushy eyebrows, thick curled lashes. When he lifted his head, the flecks of gold in his brown eyes flashed a moment into her blue ones. "Great teeth," he said, approvingly. And there was, in those two little words, a suggestive quality in his voice which made her tingle.

It was on her way out that she had noticed the sign that said 'receptionist, part-time'. It so happened that at that very moment Candy was wondering how she would make it to the end of the month, a state of mind which, as she so often viewed her life, seemed to be her default position. Her student loan money was gone and it was only early spring. She had been looking for something to tide her over until summer when she could look for a more substantial position. She could always go back to her job at Roxy's. He had said that he would take her back any time. She hadn't minded Roxy's, the clientele there was decent enough thanks to Roxy's rules, and the girls there wore costumes, but she was trying to change her life into something she did not have to lie to her mother about. Even though the dancing was all quite innocent on her part, her mother would never believe that.

She filled out an application form then and there, standing at the counter, and handed it to the then-receptionist who, she noticed, was so pregnant she looked like she might drop the baby on the floor at any moment. Candy did not expect anything immediate to happen. Job applications were like that. You filled something out and then waited days, even weeks, for the big N O. To her surprise, the receptionist, a person about her own age, asked her to please have a seat, she'd be back in a moment. She then disappeared, application form in hand, into the nether regions of the sacred chambers. When she returned, she ushered Candy into Dr. Tzvetkov's office. There Candy remained for a further fifteen minutes. She was starting to wish that she had brought a magazine from the reception area when the door opened. She looked up and there he was.

"Hi," he said, "we meet again." His voice was friendly, although his manner was businesslike, even abrupt. He strode into the room and across to his desk, energy exploding from his well-built compact physique. He was shorter than she had thought. She sat up and took notice. She liked a man who moved well and in her experience tall men seldom did.

As the weeks passed and she watched him daily, from two to five, from her reception area, she liked his style even more. He oozed male power. He was achingly suave. She began to understand how Sean Connery could be voted the sexiest man in the world, a concept that before then had eluded her entirely. But, take now, for instance. Dr... he looked so hip behind that wheel in his *Armani* sunglasses and those gloves with little holes at the knuckles.

The thought of sleeping with him was both exciting and frightening. She had never been with anyone that old. Truth be known, she'd never been with *anyone*, not all the way. People, men, had expectations, especially because of her exotic dancing, although Dr... didn't know about her former employment – she had not thought the fact relevant to her application as a receptionist. But she was quite used to putting off men and remaining friendly, that is, men her own age. Most of them were fellow students and really sweet guys. But what would this doctor... dentist... Jack, this *man*, be like? He had a reputation. Women called, they met him for lunch. One, in a temper, burst through the outer door and marched into the inner sanctuary before anyone could stop her. Those in the reception area, waiting with baited breath and her lingering perfume, could hear her loud accusations. Then Jack appeared, escorting the woman politely but firmly back out into the corridor. It was after that, the other receptionist had given her the low-down on Dr. Jack's adventures.

The virgin and the playboy, thought Candy. Weird. Still, she supposed, she'd have to lose it sooner or later. Maybe a man who'd had a lot of practice would turn out to be a good choice. Her stomach began to hurt in earnest. Get a grip on yourself, she told herself sternly. But what it came down to was that before today she and Dr. Tzvetkov had never discussed anything besides teeth. And not even teeth per se but, rather, appointments for teeth.

Candy figured she was about average when it came to socializing, hanging out, making conversation, whatever you wanted to call it, but that was with ordinary people, clerks at the supermarket, customers at Roxy's, her buds at Jeunesse Classique. It had not occurred to her until the actual moment of departure that she was in for trouble. Jack had knocked on her door at seven this morning, having arranged the details with her the previous afternoon. "Let's get an early start," he had said. "We'll go the southern route. It's more interesting. We can make a day of it." It was when he placed her one piece of luggage beside his in the trunk, her backpack beside his *Coach*, that a wedge of doubt was driven into her expectations. When she climbed into the Mercedes and settled herself into all that soft leather smelling so spanking clean and new, the crack opened wider. As they headed into the sun between Vancouver and Hope and Jack started telling her about his friends, the crack turned into a chasm. She could see clearly then that the situation was ludicrous. She was out of her league. She could not function in this new place. She could not move. She was struck dumb.

The first hour, Jack took up the slack without appearing to

be conscious that it was necessary for him to do so. He was voluble about the day, the sunshine, the fields, the mountains, this great province they lived in, and his friends. "You'll like Sylvia," he said, "she's a musician." Candy's interest increased. "Plays cello." Candy's interest decreased. She knew what that meant. Classical. No beat. Nothing you could move to.

Hope was a disaster. That was the town where they stopped for breakfast. That was where Jack stopped talking. He had to because his mouth was full of the hungry man's special and he was not one to talk with his mouth full. As she watched him devour hotcakes precisely placed one on top another with carefully spread butter between and syrup poured over all, she sipped a cup of weak tepid coffee. As he cut a square of stack and one-sixth of a sausage, speared the two together on his fork and popped it into his mouth, her throat closed up on her. Her thought processes shut down, nothing was transmitted from brain to tongue, and even if it had been, her throat muscles were as paralyzed as if she were having an allergic reaction.

Back in the car, she pretended to sleep. That got her as far as Osoyoos where they stopped for lunch. Jack chose a delightful lakeside restaurant. By this time Candy, a girl with a normally healthy appetite, was ravenous in spite of herself. She perused the menu looking for something she could eat without losing her dignity. She would love to have an overstuffed fajita but she had visions of her cheeks bulging because of having to take big bites so as not to lose it all. She saw her lips smeared with salsa and her chin with guacamole. And chewing was so unglamorous. She chose a soup. Maybe she would be able to manage some conversation through something as uncomplicated as soup. As it turned out, she spooned the soup silently into her mouth while Jack ate what looked like an absolutely delicious fat fajita, lifting it to his mouth, the juices oozing through his fingers. "I'm going to need a bath when I get there," he announced cheerfully, leaning back from his small orgy, wiping himself down with handfuls of paper napkins. "How about a bit of a stroll before we get back in the car?" The stroll turned out to be a route march and was especially uncomfortable because she was wearing high-heeled sling backs and pants so tight they cut into her crotch. Lucky I'm a dancer and used to physical torture, she reflected, as she stepped, thankfully, back into her side of the car.

As the journey progressed, Candy could feel herself slipping further and further into her own silence. She knew what would happen, it had happened before. She would slip so far in, she wouldn't be able to get herself out. Someone else would have to get her out, by saying something, a magic word, or by doing something, a magic act. Someone would have to say something kind to her or put an arm around her shoulder. Then the dam would burst and she would be all right. But unless something or someone happened to cause the dam to burst, she was in for a totally miserable, uncomfortable weekend. She drew her feet up on the seat, being careful to first remove her shoes, and hugged her knees.

The convertible was running along now at lake level. The strip of land between the highway and the water widened. Unbroken fields, wild grass and weeds and low shrubs lined either side of the road. Acreages and fruit farms populated this area. Towns were sliced in half by the highway. Speed limits were posted, pedestrian crossings marked.

Just before Vernon, the lake came to an end. Twisting her torso, Candy looked back from a rise in the road. She gasped. The length of the lake stretched into the distance, a shimmering sheet of bluish silver. Rising out of it on the east was a ridge of low mountains, greenish silver in the light. The sky was composed of layers of hazy silver at the horizon rising to cerulean blue. It was a picture of perfectly balanced shades of colour and texture in water, stone and air. It was magnificent. It was so perfect, so pure and cold in its beauty, it appeared unreal. Candy found herself longing for the city with its imperfections. This morning she had looked out her window and seen the merchants three flights down on the street hosing down the pavement before setting up their sidewalk stalls. She had heard them calling out to each other in various dialects and intonations. By mid-morning the street buskers would be out. She could have gone down to the corner grocery to have a donair. She could have felt the cracked pavement beneath her feet as she walked through the familiar dirt and noise. She would have been able to smell the wonderful grease of french fries, the spice of curries, the cinnamon sweet of bakeries, even stale smoke and beer through the open doors of pubs. On a warm summer evening such as today's promised to be, those doors would be standing wide to the pavement. She turned forward in her seat. She felt like crying. Even if she had not had a date she could have gone down to the Lucky Duck and met some of her friends.

As for Jack, he *was* smiling. He was smiling because he was looking forward to the weekend and because he was happy in the moment. Ah life! Great day, great driving conditions, a powerful, precise machine that responded immediately to his smallest command, and, by his side, a beautiful girl. He had hired her for her looks. Why not? An attractive girl in the front office was a good thing. Brightened the atmosphere, cheered up the patients, cheered him up when he came out of his cubicle and saw her at her desk. She was too young for him and too flashy with that hair and the eyeliner and those thick lips that were popular these days, but all he was doing was looking – until two days ago. He was not sure what impulse had inspired him to stop at her desk day before yesterday and invite her for the weekend, except that he was at a bit of a loose end since Maeve, jealous, volatile Maeve, had stormed into the office. That was the end of Maeve, as far as Jack was concerned. If there was one thing he would not tolerate it was a public display of any kind and especially one which made him appear at a disadvantage.

Jack busied his mind with tallying up the pros and cons of his weekend date. She didn't seem to have much appetite – he liked women who weren't afraid to eat. But she looked to be in pretty good shape. He'd bet she didn't have cellulite, not with all that dancer's training. He had to admit that when he'd picked her up this morning, at the top of three flights of firetrap stairs, he'd been surprised by her costume – low-cut toreador pants that displayed the stud in her navel, a high-cut top that revealed her trim midriff, and dangerously high heels. She looked all set for a rave concert rather than a weekend at the lake. And then there was her general air of untidiness – her hair, her bag, her worn-down heels. Jack realized that he was on the fastidious side, perhaps because of being a dentist, but to him worn-down heels were tacky in the extreme. Why had he not noticed her lack of style when she was sitting behind her receptionist's desk in his outer office? The white coat that you insist all your employees wear, he answered himself.

Jack, however, was nothing if not optimistic. She seemed to be a good sport. She had readily agreed to the walk in Osoyoos. That was when he learned that the only shoes she had brought were the high heels. "What do you intend wearing at the lake," he had asked. "I'll go bare foot," she had mumbled.

Oh well, thought Jack, maybe she's not up to my standards but she's a real looker and it's only a weekend date. And maybe she'll be great in the sack. That she was not a great conversationalist did not concern him. He was not all that keen on women who talked a lot. Take Pamela, for instance. She never shut up. It became tiresome. For him, looks, a cheery uncomplicated disposition, these were what was important, these were what oiled the makings of a good time. And this weekend should be just that. He was looking forward to getting close to something warm and fuzzy. It had been three weeks since the Maeve incident.

Jack was aware that he was one of the blessed. He truly lived the good life. Good job, good money, great digs (he had just bought into a high rise condo), great health, not bad looking, at least not such a dog that he scared away the women. Yes, he had exactly the life he wished. Some of his friends wondered when he was going to get married but, as he viewed it, a married man is one in solitary confinement where the prison warden strips him of human dignity and individuality by trying to fit him into a mould of rules and regulations. It would be sheer madness to put himself voluntarily into that position. No sane man would give up the life he was living for marriage, especially the part where you surrender your will to another person and become an item on their agenda.

He had seen it happen too often. Bright, energetic young men full of dreams and desires and opinions. Marriage. Pow! They became enclosed in the compound of the other person's goals and intentions, mere passive chess pieces in someone else's game.

On this subject, his thoughts turned to Michael and Dobbin, his oldest best buddies. He thought of their undergraduate days, Could it be nearly twenty years ago? After a time of freedom, a lot of laughs, a lot of hangovers, a fair amount of puking in the bushes, he had had to stand by and see them both go under. He had tried to talk Dobbin out of it. Not that he didn't like Pamela. She was a lot of fun, she was bright and attractive and good at parties. But did she have to be so in-your-face? Did she have to be such a control freak? "She won't let you be your own man," he had warned. Dobbin hadn't listened. Ten years later, he had changed from an erudite, brilliant free spirit with a great, although complicated, sense of humour into a dull, boring, pedantic university professor who spouted the most astonishing gibberish and had lost the ability to seriously consider anybody else's opinion on any matter. He was so enamoured with his own thought processes that he did not allow anyone else a turn. Meanwhile, in her frustrated attempts to intervene in Dobbin's love affair with his own mind, Pamela had become shrewish. Her sharp wit had become acerbic, her keen observations critical, her vivacity forced.

Jack traced the progression of what had happened. From the beginning, Pamela had not allowed Dobbin his thinking space. She always had to know what was in his mind. She seemed to take it as a threat if he had a private thought. Dobbin reacted by quitting his thought processes. For a while it seemed that he couldn't think at all. He became unglued – nervous and jittery. However, after a couple of years of that, he settled down. He returned to his senses. He did so by turning Pamela off, as neatly as he might have switched a radio button. At the time, Jack saw that as a good thing, it might lead to his friend's survival. But later he realized that the turning-off process was dangerous. Now, Dobbin did it with everyone. He was so damned irritating. The way he droned on with his intellectual exercises, he was a pain in the ass. As for Pamela, she had become compulsive in her habits and obsessive in her behaviour.

Michael, on the other hand, unlike Dobbin, had not lost himself in marriage. Jack had to admit that. Michael had retained not only his imaginative brilliance, his charm, his capacity for having a good time, but also those little quirks of character which made him somewhat despicable even to those who loved him. The way he took snide jabs at people, wielding that sneering, ironic wit, slashing hither and thither at any available object in sight. Was it being an actor that caused him to be bitchy? Or had Michael chosen acting as a career because of his natural aptitude for being nasty? No, Michael had not changed much, but, then, Michael had affairs. Jack was pretty sure of this, although Michael had never confided in him. Michael knew that Jack did not approve of affairs. In Jack's opinion it was all right to play around if single, but once married, that was it. Otherwise, what was the point of being married?

But when Jack thought about Sylvia, he almost did not blame his friend. For, while Sylvia was attractive enough if you were into organic, and while she did have a certain charm, she had no flair. Her personality lacked bite. She never had anything surprising to say. She might have a nice body, but beneath those layers of droopy skirts and shapeless tops, all in dull shades of browns and burgundies, who could tell? If her performance in bed was as uninspired as her performance in daily life, no wonder Michael strayed into extramarital territory. And now, as Jack understood it, she intended sticking herself out there on five acres all summer baking bread and hoeing a garden, no doubt without makeup. Such a woman had to expect dire consequences. Especially when her husband made his living romancing hot chicks. Okay, so Michael was a spoiled brat and a bully, but why did she let herself be bullied? Why did she wait on him hand and foot? Why did she smile at every goddamned thing he said? How's Sylvia? he had asked Michael just last week when Michael had phoned him with the invitation. She's up shingling the roof, had been the answer. What are you doing? Jack had asked. Besides phoning you, I'm having a gin and tonic and watching TV, had been the answer. It wasn't good for Michael. He needed someone to make him into a better person, someone who would not let him get away with such nonsense. And now that they had bought this country property, things could only get worse. In the city, Sylvia was stimulated by friends, interests, her music. She was busy with practices, recitals, lessons. Between plays and performances, she gave intimate little dinners. Jack and various women friends had been the recipient of several. In his mind's eye, Jack saw Sylvia's warm, lazy wide-mouthed smile. She did have a lovely smile.

It seemed to Jack that his two friends, each in his own way, were in destructive relationships. Why anyone would get into or stay in such a relationship was incomprehensible. But were there any constructive relationships these days? Were there any good marriages? Were there marriages where the two people involved brought out the best in each other, encouraged each other to be better people, helped each other to grow?

The red convertible had left the main highway which had forked off onto a secondary road. "The junction is just up ahead!" shouted Jack.

Candy, who had lapsed into a state bordering on comatose due to gloom caused by fear, lifted her head from where she was resting it on her drawn-up knees. "What?"

"What?"

"What did you just say?"

"Won't be long now! The junction is just ahead!"

She stretched her neck higher and peered ahead down a narrowing tunnel of green pine, so tall they threatened to block out the sun. She turned her head quickly to her right. There, a thick green wall slammed into her face. She looked left, across Jack's hairy brown forearms, only to be met with another impenetrable wall of green. She could scarcely breathe.

"I didn't know it would be like this," she murmured.

"What?"

"There are so many trees!" she shouted.

"Smell that pine!" Jack shouted his enthusiasm.

Candy considered flinging herself out of the moving car, but then the trees ended and she could see across a green stubble field, blessedly flat and open. More trees appeared but they were a mixture of various types and not so thick. Then there was the junction Jack had mentioned, which led into a small pretty town on a lake, and then they were flying low along water again. Jack explained after much shouting and repeating of himself that this was the southern tip of one arm of a large lake to the north. After the highway left this stretch of water, fields appeared on both sides of the car, green fields with cows grazing in meadows and houses with brightly coloured window boxes in neat yards with vegetable gardens.

There was less wind. She heard Jack clearly the first time when he said, "We're just about there. According to Michael's instructions. He said there's a great view of their lake from the next rise."

"Their lake?" Candy tensed.

"Manner of speaking. They're actually on a small bay on the lake. Great swimming."

Candy had not considered that she might be expected to swim. She did not swim. She hated water. Cold water. She was afraid of water. As a child, she had nearly drowned once in the local swimming pool when some playmates, who had thought it great fun, had pushed her under. Then, when she had seen the movie *Jaws* on a TV rerun a couple of years ago, all of her fears had been confirmed. For several weeks after that she had felt queasy even about getting into the bathtub.

The car mounted the rise and part of the bay came into view. It was nestled into a gently rolling contour of low hills and surrounded by what appeared to be a tangle of wild natural growth. Candy thought she could see a peaked roof, the rest of the house hidden by trees, and over there, to the left, was that another roof? a lower one? She could just barely make out the corner of it through some willow branches before the car descended the hill and cut off the view.

"I didn't bring a bathing suit," she called.

"Quite all right. Someone will lend you one."

Just when Candy felt that she might actually throw up all over Jack's soft leather upholstery, the car turned in at a private drive with a sign devised from driftwood and sticks which stated, *the Wildes*. Candy had almost hypnotized herself into thinking that they would never arrive, that she would not have to face a houseful of new acquaintances, a lake where she would be expected to swim, and Jack, this stranger sitting beside her who was becoming more of a stranger by the minute. As they bounced across a log bridge, she felt a further drop into the black pit of herself.

Jack hopped out, ran forward, lifted a pole out of its wire slot, folded back a gate of barbed wire, hopped back in, drove through, hopped out again, reinserted the pole, and hopped back into the car. He accelerated along a gravelled lane bordered on one side by a dusty hedge that brushed his side of the vehicle as it passed. On Candy's side was a meadow, a grove of trees and then the house. She could see it – tall, narrow, yellow with white trim. Soon she would have to meet Jack's friends. She would have to speak. Her mouth felt dry. Her throat was sore. She could not find enough saliva to swallow.

Jack drove into a wide gravel space, swung the wheel suddenly to the right and, squirting up the small pebbles, slid to a sudden precise stop beside an ancient Dodge sedan.

"Dobbin's beaten us to the punch," he shouted gleefully, vaulting out of the car.

Candy unglued herself from the hot leather upholstery and climbed out of the car, slowly, stiffly, like an old woman. Her top and toreador pants were sticking to her back and bottom. She could feel drops of sweat trickle between her breasts and settle in a ridge just beneath them. She reached an arm into the back seat and hauled out an enormous overstuffed Mexican straw bag embroidered brightly in primary colours. Jack was collecting their luggage from the trunk. Candy turned. Emerging from the back door of the house was a woman in long skirt and tunic top in woodsy tones. Shit, thought Candy. She had brought shorts and jeans and a few tops. She had not brought a long skirt. For formal wear, just in case, she had thrown into her bag a short black leather skirt, a new purchase with which she was very pleased.

Candy mustered all the strength that was left in her long legs and went forward. Her worn-down high heels sank into the gravel, the insteps cut into her feet, swollen from the heat. Pebbles found their way between her toes and the shoes.

She could sense, behind her, Michael's eyes on her legs and tight pants. She was familiar with that kind of appraisal. Oh, shit, she thought, for the second time in as many minutes. That's all I need to make the weekend complete.

She had a sudden urge to turn around. She was not sure why, except that she felt a pair of eyes other than Michael's. For an instant, she was blinded by a flash of light through trees, like the wink of a glinting eye. It came from the direction of a cedar cottage on the neighbouring property. The sun reflecting on glass, she concluded, but did not stop to wonder what glass it might be.

PART TWO

VENUS ASCENDING

i

Robb Goodfellow stepped out onto his back deck. The screen door shut softly behind him. Clearly, on the soft and warm night air, from the direction of the Wilde's, came the sound of violins and a cello. He stood a moment rolling his shoulders first forward then backward, rolling his head on the stem of his neck, first one way, then the other. He raised his arms high into the air, pulled his left wrist higher with his right hand, then performed the same action on his right wrist with his left hand. It was nearly eleven o'clock in the evening. He'd been working all day. Until midmorning it had been tough going. Then, after a foraging trip to the kitchen, on his return to work, he had happened to look out his window, the one facing his neighbour's property, and spied Sylvia having breakfast. A shadowy figure sat across from her. When Robb plucked up his binoculars from the window ledge, he could see that the figure was the husband. The tranquil domestic scene loosed in Robb a surge of motivation so powerful it had kept him going all day. Only the last half hour had he run out of steam. In order to take his plot development further, he needed to go out on a prowl for more inspiration.

Mentally and physically, he needed a break. He glanced at his watch, nearly eighteen hours hard at it, with time out only for essentials such as bathroom trips, quick snacks and a little afternoon caper involving Michael which had been necessary to further his own personal plot. About two o'clock, during one of Robb's breaks, through his trusty binoculars, he had spied Michael down on the beach in a lawn chair. The actor seemed to be reading something hidden in his lap. Robb clicked 'Save' and strolled down the path to the beach. In what he had planned, he would have to use considerable skill, for, except for one occasion of great hilarity fuelled by much imbibing, the relationship of the two men up to now had consisted mostly of dancing around each other like boxers. Robb perceived that Michael deliberately avoided him, that he felt uneasy in his presence, as though Robb's keen wily gaze might see the truth of his character, which was to say his lack thereof. However, this afternoon before the weekend of the blue moon, Robb must try and change that.

It turned out that Michael was reading a script, which was lucky because it allowed Robb to ask advice about problems he was having with stage directions. The actor was flattered to such an extent, Robb was able to lead him back to his house to show him the explicit problem on hard copy. This, naturally, led to a few beer to quench their thirst on a hot afternoon.

Tonight, the house next door was lit up like a carnival. Throughout the evening, Robb had heard and seen his neighbours and their friends at play. On the terrace, they had set the round table with cloth, flowers and candles. They had barbecued some sort of meat that had permeated the air with delicious odours. They had filled and refilled their wine glasses. They'd talked a great deal of nonsense. Wit was batted back and forth like a ping pong ball. Their voices had trilled melodiously as evening robins, their laughter had flown on wings through his open window. Their antics had not interfered with his work but, rather, had excited his imagination and buoyed his inspiration.

Robb looked out over the lake which the moonlight had turned into a shimmering silvery expanse. Deciding to get some fresh air and to exercise his stiff limbs, he descended the few steps to the path that led down to the beach. Soundlessly, he threaded his way through the trees. He stood at the water's edge and let the night, calm and still, enclose him. From the water came the splash of a fish, from a distance the bark of a dog. Across the lake, a campfire darted flickering shafts of red and gold into the water. The voices of campers echoed in the resonant air, creating a human dimension in the scene which was both lonesome and companionable.

From his neighbour's house, the violins and cello of a Haydn concerto were working toward a crescendo. Looking across his shoulder, Robb turned from the water. The house glowed through the darkness with an air of self-containment. It seemed to be its own planet, its own universe, as if it were both the light and the centre of that light.

Robb stood completely still, poised on one foot, the other barely touching the earth. He might have been a creature from another world, so lightly did he stand, as though merely pausing to rest a moment before going on his way. Then he stepped softly toward the music. Keeping himself low on the grass as he neared the house, bending still lower as he traversed the gravel, tiptoeing the last steps, he settled beneath an open sitting room window. Like an animal peering out of the woods, he slowly raised his eyes to the level of the sill, and inspected the room.

Small and boxy, it was cluttered in an old-fashioned way with bulky chairs and sofa, doilies positioned on chair arms and backs and end tables, fringed lampshades, pictures and photos on the papered walls. In one corner was an upright piano, in another a modern sound system. The wood floor of rich brown planks was scattered with colourful patterned rugs. The low lights gave the room a hazy atmosphere. Boxes of chocolates and slabs of cheeses, the delicacies provided by Pamela, lay partly consumed on end tables along with liqueur glasses and a nearly empty bottle of *Courvoisier*, one of a variety of brandies provided by Jack. People were strewn about in various postures and poses. It seemed that the music had cast a spell upon the room and its occupants.

Robb's eyes found Sylvia sitting cross-legged on the floor against the sofa, skirt tucked around her ankles. Her hair was gathered at the nape of her neck in a large bun, her bent head seemed weighed down with the volume of it. One shoulder was leaning against Michael's right leg, clad in a grey material.

Michael, his hand arrested in the act of stroking her head, as though
she were his favourite hunting hound, was staring across the room
in the direction of a very attractive young lady who, Robb knew,
was Candy. She had been uncommonly quiet during the evening
meal, but he had heard the introductions when she and Jack had
arrived. Through his binoculars, he had caught Michael's leering
interest, and it appeared that Michael was at it again. Robb
pronounced this as good. For his purposes, he needed Michael to
be elsewhere directed.

Beside Michael, on the sofa, in an evening pantsuit, was
Pamela, legs twitching with the strain of having to sit still. It
appeared that, at any moment, this strain might become too great
and she would explode in an eruption of fervent activity. Robb
had no difficulty knowing who she was, he had heard her strident
voice and infectious laughter throughout the meal. Dobbin, too,
had spoken often, in a dry lecturing mode. Now, he was sitting
forward in an easy chair, elbows on knees, hands like a goalie's
mask protecting his face. His right hand left his face a moment to
probe in the pocket of his blue plaid shirt. It returned to his face,
empty. Candy sat curled in the other armchair, opposite to Dobbin
and near the window. She was wearing a brief tight leather skirt
and a loosely crocheted top the same orange colour as the streak
in her hair. Her lovely long bare legs, ending with the same high
heels in which she had arrived, were drawn up onto the chair in a
fetal position. One hand dangled languidly down across the
rounded upholstered chair arm. Her eyes were staring vacantly at
a spot on the floor. A little worried frown appeared from time
to time between her eyes, as though sporadically she remembered
to give the impression that she was listening intently and
appreciatively to the music. Jack, in *Ralph Lauren* shirt and pants,
was sitting on the floor, leaning against her chair, surreptitiously
rubbing his hand from time to time along her inner arm. His head
was thrown back in shameless, almost smiling, enjoyment of the
good life – good wine, good food, good friends, good music.

For some minutes, Robb watched Sylvia clasping and
unclasping her hands, weaving her fingers together, releasing them,

stretching them, those fingers clearly itching to perform the music themselves. When his eyes managed to detach themselves from her to resume spying on the others, he discovered that Candy was missing.

Candy could not stand it a moment longer. The music did not seem to be going anywhere. It just went on and on without arriving at a conclusion. Its meaning, if it had one, must be in its meaningless pattern, much like improvisational jazz, which she could not stand either. And then there was Jack, who, like the music, was becoming more disturbing by the minute. He had told them about her connection with Jeunesse Classique but omitted mentioning the fact that she worked in his office as a receptionist. Of course, he could not tell them about the exotic dancing, since he himself did not know, but she knew that, if he had known, he would not have disclosed that information, either. Then, since their arrival, instead of keeping by her side and helping her to ease into the situation, he'd more or less abandoned her to the group. He seemed to assume that she could manage on her own, whereas if he had any sensitivity at all, he would have seen that she was nervous and uncertain. And now after ignoring her all evening, here he was making up to her, getting all cozy, likely in expectation of bedtime activities. He was sitting against a corner of one of the arms of her chair, so that the back of his head was directly in her line of vision. A few minutes ago he had been playing with her arm but his hand had fallen away. She wondered if he'd fallen asleep. His head was back. Were his eyes closed? She looked around at the others. They all appeared to be either asleep or completely engrossed in the music. Reaching down, she removed one shoe, two shoes. She did not want Jack to follow her.

Out on the porch, she felt a great freedom and sense of relief. She stood a moment, breathing the fragrant air of the warm evening, feeling giddy at her release. She went down the steps and carefully crossed the crunchy gravel, sharp on her bare feet, breathing easier when she reached the refreshingly cool damp grass. She found herself tiptoeing and told herself not to be silly. She could leave the room and the music if she wanted to. She was not in a prison. When she reached the sand, still warm from the day's sun, she dug in her toes and crossed to the water's edge.

Candy was not in an optimistic frame of mind. The prognosis for the weekend was becoming more gloomy by the minute. After arriving, she had been shown to her room by Sylvia. She had stayed there as long as decently possible. Thank heavens for the goat. Before dinner, he, along with the chickens, had provided her with companionship. A suspicious cat joined them. Like her, he didn't seem to belong. He seemed unused to human company. Her heart went out to him. He let her pick him up and stroke him, and before long he was purring like a well-oiled motor. At least, she thought, I'm a hit with the animals.

During and after dinner she had scarcely said 'boo'. She knew that she must appear totally boring and stupid, but she found it impossible to reveal to them her true nature, which was actually outgoing and voluble. Why could she not forget herself and act natural? They were all older than she but, normally, that would not be a problem. She was used to talking with all sorts of people. She thought of the dinner table, the conversation, quick, darting, over her head. Yes, that was it. They were all so verbal, so articulate, so up on everything, so cliquey. They had years of shared experiences behind them. Oh, they tried to include her, filling her in on pertinent background information when they remembered. But, after a few attempts, involved in their own high spirits, they simply forgot. Candy realized that it was not their fault. It was Jack's fault. A more thoughtful, considerate person, would have helped her bridge the gap. But he was so goldarn self-centred, he did not see that she had a problem. He was having a good time, he was completely relaxed among friends, so he could not conceive of her feeling otherwise. He had enjoyed the drive, the dinner, the wine and liqueurs, the music. He had a great-looking weekend date whom he would soon get into the sack.

And then and there, nearing midnight at the edge of the

lake, Candy vowed and declared that that would not happen. What had been an exciting possibility in the car was now out of the question. She might be merely an object, but she refused to be a sexual one.

She contemplated some kind of unannounced escape before she would have to deal with the sleeping arrangements. At least it was not assumed that she and Jack would be sharing the same bed. Candy recalled how Sylvia had subtly given her the information that Jack was to sleep downstairs in Michael's study. "I hope you'll be comfortable up here," was all she'd said. Sylvia did seem to be a very nice person. However, Candy was quite certain that Jack had the intention of coming to her door. To hell with him, was her inner pronouncement. She considered going out to the road and thumbing a ride into the town. She didn't have much money on her but she supposed she could use her credit card for a bus ticket. Why hadn't she thought of this when it was still light? It would be scary thumbing a ride this time of night.

Feeling alone and dejected, she threw back her head and looked up. How the stars could be seen so much better, so much more clearly, in the country! The sky was awash with them. No wonder they called it the milky way. She stood for some moments, letting herself be enveloped by the night, letting herself be carried away by the night sky. She could feel herself being lifted upward in an ecstasy of transcendence of earthly cares. Then she heard a step behind her. She turned quickly.

"Oh," she said with relief. "It's you. You... left the room, too." She had nearly said 'snuck out'.

"Yes," said Dobbin. "I hope I didn't frighten you."

"No... well, just for a minute," she replied, simply happy that it wasn't Jack.

"I'm afraid I'm one of those people who clings to an increasingly socially unacceptable addiction."

"Really?"

Dobbin drew a package of *Export A* out of his shirt pocket. "Would you care for one?"

"No, thank you. I don't smoke. Because of the dancing.

You have to be able to breathe if you're a dancer."

"Quite."

"But I don't mind if other people do," she added quickly.

Dobbin put a cigarette in his mouth, lit it, returned the package and matches to his pocket.

Candy turned back to the lake and prepared for an uncomfortable silence. They had, of course, met earlier but had not spoken directly to each other. The nearly full moon cast a silvery patina across the surface of the water. The campers on the opposite shore had gone into their tents, their fire now only a pinpoint of light. To Candy's surprise, the silence felt friendly and reassuring. Her body relaxed.

"Do you like that music?" she said and found that she did not choke on the words.

"Yes, I'm rather fond of Haydn. It's not that I'm more fond of my cigarettes. But I have heard that particular piece dozens of times. And it is a remarkable evening."

"Yes."

"Why don't we walk along a bit? There's a path, over this way. I was on it earlier. Watch your step now. Here, let me take your arm. There we are."

They walked in silence but, again, it was not strained. The act of walking provided an activity which filled a space that might otherwise have been socially awkward. And there was something about the darkness, too, although it was not really dark since the moon was like an immense round light bulb in the sky. But the night and the obscurity allowed anonymity. Candy felt less concerned with herself, and she was not at all frightened by the shadows or scurrying noises in the brush beside them or sudden splashes from the lake as some creature dived or surfaced. There was something reassuring about the physical presence of this man beside her. She glanced sideways at him but he was not looking at her. He seemed to be involved with thoughts of his own. In fact, it appeared that he had forgotten all about her. Far from being insulted, Candy was relieved. She felt a sort of solace in his disregard. Nothing was expected of her.

After some minutes, Dobbin stopped. Candy halted beside him. "How are you doing?" he asked, turning toward her.

"Fine. Great."

"The path goes into the wood here." He looked forward, toward the path. "And becomes narrow. You can't see it so well in the dark. Do you want to turn back? or shall we keep on?"

"I can go a little farther."

"Do you want to try to make it to the point? We're halfway there."

She hesitated.

"It's up to you," he said.

"How far is it?"

"To the point? About a mile from the house. Before dinner, I walked it in half an hour. And we've already done fifteen minutes. How about it?"

"Sure."

He looked down at her feet. "Perhaps you'd do better with shoes." He looked at the shoes dangling from her hand. "What are those things?"

She held up the sling backs.

"You can't walk in those things."

"Yes I can. I'm used to it." She bent to slip them on.

"Not much good for hiking are they?"

"Oh, they're all right. This isn't exactly a hike." She thought of her earlier march through Osoyoos with Jack. "I've been on worse."

"Well, I suppose if they're all you have. Perhaps they're better than nothing." Again, he looked down at her feet. "If I recall correctly, the path is uneven. I'll lead the way."

"All right."

"Tallyho then!" and so saying Dobbin strode forth.

Again, they walked in silence. Because of the path and the shoes, Candy was not entirely sure that she was enjoying herself but anything was better than going back to the house. Anything was better than facing Jack. Perhaps by the time she returned, he would be fast asleep in Michael's office.

After several minutes, they came out of the trees onto a grassy bank at the water's edge. Dobbin halted again and inquired about her comfort. "Do you want to stop a moment?" he said. "I'm about ready for another nail in the coffin."

He lit a cigarette. They sat on two large rocks and watched the moon on the lake, a brilliant effusion of molten silver. For several minutes, Dobbin was silent. He seemed to be deeply considering something. Then he seemed to remember his social manners. "Tell me about yourself," he said, rousing himself and looking toward her. "You're a dance student?"

"Yes. Although I'm really an actress." Candy was aghast. Had she really said that to somebody? Only a few of her very best friends in the city knew that she was attending the dance studio to improve herself until the big break came along. "But dancing is a good thing to have," she went on, "for movement on the stage and all. And it makes you more versatile, too, in getting work. The more skills a person has, the better. I did go to university for a couple of years, right after high school. But it wasn't doing a thing for me, so I took some time off to find myself."

"And did you?"

"Did I what?"

"Find yourself?"

Candy thought a moment. Certainly, her life as an exotic dancer had decided her as to what she did not want to be. But even though she wanted to be an actress, she was not sure that she liked acting. Perhaps she only liked the idea of being an actress, a successful one. And there was that thing about stage fright. She did not know if she could put up with that. The problem was that she had not had enough roles so far to know whether or not it was going to work. "I'm not sure," she said.

"No one is," he said.

"I guess I'm still looking."

"That's the main thing. To keep looking." After a moment, "Maybe you'll find yourself in the acting."

"I don't know. Right now, all I know is I like to dance.

And I like being a student. I mean I totally like the life. I like the other students. My mates. I seem to have found my niche. I totally like arriving at the studio early in the morning in my leg warmers and doing bar exercises. I don't know. There's a certain smell to the studio. Do you know what I mean?" Candy thought a moment. "Maybe I like the role of a dancer," she said.

"That's very astute. You are an astute young woman. And what kind of dance do you do?"

"It's more a modern dance. Expressionism. Movement. Of course, ballet training is a great benefit. I took ballet when I was a kid. Years of it. My mother thought I would become the next Karen Kain. Maybe that's why I can't stand classical music. You know, rebelling against parents."

"That's insightful of you."

"Oh, that's one thing my generation is good at. Analyzing ourselves, blaming our parents."

Dobbin thought of all the little girls struggling through all those years of ballet. "I'd be interested in seeing you dance sometime," he said.

"You would?"

Dobbin considered the question. He had said that to be polite, an automatic response to encourage a student. Still, he decided he was on safe enough ground here. Likely, he would never be called upon to visit one of her performances. But he should not tell a lie, either. Dobbin tried not to tell lies. He turned toward her and for the first time noticed her. He looked at her eager upturned face. Her skin appeared luminous in the moonlight. It crossed his mind that she was an extraordinarily beautiful creature, in spite of hair which looked like the result of a disastrous mistake at the hair salon.

"Yes," he said. "Just having this little talk with you, you seem to be a young woman who has something to say."

"I do?"

"Something to express, for are not all art forms born out of a need for self-expression. They merely take various forms in music or painting or dance."

They were silent a moment. "I wonder if dentists need self-expression?" Candy wondered out loud.

"You mean Jack," Dobbin said. "He goes on those adventure trips. Maybe that's his way of expressing himself."

"I work part-time in his office." Candy had decided that she could trust this person with the information. "To support my dancing. Oh, I'm not a dental assistant. You have to be trained to do that. Besides, no way I'd want to work with teeth. Ugh. I work in the outer office, making appointments. You'd never guess how complicated it is. People are always cancelling. I'll bet more people cancel out of dental appointments than any other thing. I mean, everyone hates to go to the dentist. No one wants to go and see Jack. I'd much rather be an actor. Like Michael. People *want* to go and see him. They're out for an evening of fun. But it's all gloom and doom when you're off to see your dentist."

"You're perfectly right. Hadn't quite thought about it that way myself."

"You all seem to know each other so well, I mean you and your wife and the others. You seem to be such good friends."

"We go back a long way. Pamela, Michael, Jack, me. Then Michael married Sylvia, about five years ago now. I'm quite fond of all of them, actually."

"It's a lovely spot they have here."

"I suppose. I must admit, I find it all a bit too pastoral."

"You do?"

"I'm afraid I'm essentially a city person. The corner grocery if I run out of cigarettes or a carton of milk. That sort of thing."

"I couldn't agree with you more," said Candy fervently. "What do people find to *do* in the country?"

"Well, there's swimming. They're great swimmers. They're very sporty, the others, especially my wife and Jack. And boating. Michael likes boating. They plan to buy a boat. Windsurfing. I expect they'll do a lot of water stuff."

"That's not for me. I hate water. I mean lakes. They're always so slimy and weedy and cold. Ugh."

"This one's not bad. It's quite clean, actually."

"The fact is, I don't swim," Candy confided. "I haven't told Jack, he seems so keen on it. I'm sure he expects I'll join in tomorrow. I didn't even bring a bathing suit."

"Likely Sylvia has extra suits around the place. But I wouldn't worry about it. If you don't swim, you don't. That's that. No one will force you to swim."

"No... but it's just that I'll feel so totally out of place with everybody else swimming."

"I'll bet you could swim."

"How could I when I hate the water?"

"You could learn to like it. You're a dancer. You must be coordinated. That's about all it takes. That, and remembering not to breathe in when your face is beneath the water."

"I don't know..."

The teacher in Dobbin rose to the surface. How he would like to show this child the rudiments of the back stroke, the front crawl. What a sense of achievement he would feel if she caught on. "Too bad we don't have our bathing suits," he said. "I could give you a lesson."

"You mean now?"

"Certainly."

"Isn't it too dark."

"With that moon! and stars! Why it's nearly as light as day."

Candy looked out at the moon and stars reflected on the water. For a moment she wavered. "I hate cold water," she said.

"It wouldn't be cold. Not after a day like today. Likely, it's as warm as bath water."

"I'm afraid of deep water."

"Of course you're afraid of deep water if you don't swim. You'd be a fool not to be. But if you learn to swim, your fears will disappear. And, according to Michael, this is a very friendly lake. The water doesn't become deep for a good twenty-five metres and it's all a gradual slope."

The glitter of lights on the water made Candy think of the lights at Roxy's, the way they had flashed and sparkled, reflecting on chrome and glass. That was one thing she had liked at Roxy's. It had been like dancing among revolving planets and shooting stars.

"Are you sure it's warm?" she asked.

"We could dip in our fingers and see," he replied.

Candy had an impulse which, later, she attributed to moon madness. She felt the need to break free of the constraints that had been placed upon her personality throughout the late afternoon and evening. She wanted to do something totally unruly. "Why don't you give me a lesson," she said, sitting up straighter on her rock. "Right now."

"Now? We don't have swim suits."

In this area, Candy, uninhibited as she was about her body as long as her emotions weren't involved, had the advantage. "We don't need swim suits."

"Oh, I don't think... I didn't mean..." Dobbin being a member of a university academic staff was very much aware of the repercussions of leading young women astray. Also, he was not sure that he wanted to bare his white fleshy body to this nubile slim brown nymph.

"Come on." And, with the encouragement of a force larger than herself, Candy bounced off the rock on which she was sitting and started disrobing. She kicked off her shoes, flung off her crocheted tunic and started to skin down her skirt.

Dobbin, too, jumped off his rock. In alarm, he started to pick up her discarded clothing. "No, stop, don't," he urged, trying to press the skirt and top back around her, supplicating her to take them in her hands and put them back on. Instead, ignoring his protests, she stepped out of her panties, a narrow rectangle of cloth strung on a bit of elastic.

And then, both Candy and Dobbin found themselves acting out a farce. As he came near her, she grabbed his shirt and proceeded to undo the buttons.

"You mustn't do that." He caught her hands.

"What's the harm?"

What *is* the harm, thought Dobbin. What she proposed was

only what they used to call skinny-dipping. When he was young, they used to do it all the time, without ulterior motive or thought. For a lark, just a lark. He was being prudish and irrational. Nothing unmanageable was about to happen. They were mature adults, at least he was. He would preserve his dignity. "My dear young woman," he said. "I am quite capable of taking off my own clothes."

He unlaced his oxfords and placed them side by side near the rock. He removed his watch, waterproof but why take a chance, and placed it inside one shoe. He took off his socks, folded them into each other, and placed them on top of the shoes. Trousers and shirt were folded on top of this. He put his thumbs into the top elastic of his boxer shorts and hesitated. He might leave them on, wear them in place of swimming trunks. But no, that would be cowardly. Lastly, he removed his spectacles and put them neatly on top of the pile. He turned toward the water where Candy was standing at the edge, prettily dipping in first one toe then the other. He did not let his eyes focus on her body, although he could not help but notice that it was very lovely indeed. But she was the student, he the teacher. Those must be their roles.

"The first lesson," said Dobbin, "is to get wet quickly. It's a little like removing a bandaid. One rip and you feel no pain."

"I don't know if I can do it," said Candy, looking out at the expanse of silver-tipped soft ripples. "It's not *that* warm."

"Of course you can," said Dobbin. He took her hand. It felt small, like a child's. "One, two, three." She gripped his hand tightly. With little yips from Candy protesting the cold and calls of encouragement from Dobbin, they ran jumping and splashing into the water.

After their first immersion, they danced a little victory jig by the light of the moon. In knee-deep water, they held hands and turned round and round in a circle and then fell down, purposely, plunking their bottoms into the water. Kicking and splashing, whirling and hooting, they righted themselves and repeated the procedure, singing ring-around-a-rosy.

Above, la Luna smiled upon her children, blessing them with

her silver light.

Cavorting like two water sprites, said children were oblivious of their surroundings until they were brought back to reality by a sharp voice from shore which could only be Pamela's. "Dobbin, is that you out there? What in the world are you doing?"

ii

As the strains of the Haydn concerto drifted into the evening attracting Robb and repelling Candy, Pamela was glancing surreptitiously around the little group gathered in the boxy living room. She hoped that her announcement would not change things. It must *not* change things. She couldn't stand it if it changed things. Oh, she was a wreck. Now that she had made her decision she would be on pins and needles until the deed was accomplished. She *should* have told Dobbin on the journey here. She could have sworn him to secrecy so as not to put a damper on everybody's weekend. She didn't think that she could wait until they were leaving on Sunday morning. She would tell him tomorrow after all. That had been her first plan. First plans were often best. Tomorrow night. Late. So as not to spoil the day. She thought she could manage to hold out that long. Tomorrow promised to be full of activities. She would be too busy to think about it much. She would tell him when they were getting ready for bed. After they were in bed, both of them lying on their backs staring at the ceiling. That was when, by habit, they discussed the next day's events. One of the next day's events would be her leaving him. But then they would not sleep. Well, likely Dobbin would sleep. Likely, he would direct himself not to think about it, and then he would not. He would tell himself that there was no sense thinking about something about which he could do nothing. But *she* would not sleep. Better to save it for morning. She would tell him first thing Sunday morning. She thought again of Sylvia's brunch. She didn't want to ruin Sylvia's brunch. But it need not ruin brunch. In fact, it need not ruin anything. That's how she would put it to the others. They could all go on as before. She and Dobbin would still be part of the group. The only difference was that they would arrive and depart separately. Of course, she and Dobbin would remain friends. She could not imagine a world in which she and Dobbin were not friends. They had been friends forever. There was nothing for anybody to get steamed up about. Of course, there was the alternative of telling him when they went to their room after breakfast to pack. Then there would be only a short period of discomfort before they went downstairs and told the others. Then the scene with the others would not, could not, last more than a few minutes.

Obsessively jogging the treadmill of her thoughts, she noted only vaguely Dobbin, then Candy, leave the room, and when the last note of the concerto was struck, she was caught off guard. Without thinking, she jumped up from her corner of the sofa and announced that she was going for a run before bed.

"I'll join you," said Michael, standing also.

"Where's Candy?" asked Jack, opening his eyes and looking around the room as one returning to the land of the living. "She must have gone off to bed," he answered himself.

"We're going for a walk," Michael said to Jack, who had hopped lightly up from the floor. "Want to come?"

"You two go on ahead," Jack said, casually, although he squared his shoulders as if preparing for the energy required of a root canal. "I think I'll turn in early."

"Let's go," said Michael to Pamela.

Pamela's mind did a quick survey of possibilities for a way out. She really did wish to jog. But, more importantly, she did not wish to be alone with Michael. "How about Sylvia," she said. "Maybe she'd like to come."

They all looked down at Sylvia. Her head was lolled back on a cushion. Her lips were slightly open. Her eyes were closed.

"Is she alive?" questioned Pamela, for it seemed to her that Sylvia was uncommonly still and that no breath was passing in and out of her mouth.

"Her chest goes up and down," said Jack.

"Her eyes are moving beneath her eyelids," said Michael. "She must be dreaming."

"Wake her up," directed Pamela.

"You're not supposed to wake a person in the middle of a dream," said Michael.

"What if it's a nightmare," said Pamela.

"Let her sleep," said Michael. "She's had a busy day."

Pamela could have kicked him. If he had any sensitivity, he would have observed the fact that all evening she had avoided being alone with him. She did not wish to play games with him here. A liaison in town was one thing, but being boinked by her friend's husband while under their roof, partaking of her friend's hospitality, even eating the food she had slaved over with her own two hands, was another. After all, she had her principles. Michael, on the other hand, had been making suggestive comments to her all evening, rubbing up against her, patting her arm, putting his arm, albeit a casual one, around her shoulder. If he had any decency, he would know better than to make obvious their relationship before their friends and, especially, before Sylvia.

With the excuse of changing, she left the two men standing over Sylvia debating whether or not to put another cushion behind her head. While Pamela was donning leotards and jogging shoes, her mind was busy trying to think of a way to lose Michael before or after they got started.

By the time she returned to the sitting room, Jack had discovered that Candy was not in the house and so was going with them after all. This was both good and bad news for Pamela. She would not now have to be alone with Michael but she wanted, needed, some real exercise, which might be difficult with these two clowns in tow. "Why don't you guys go together," she tried.

"Don't be silly," said Michael. "We don't mind including you."

Trekking along the path which led to the point, Pamela was

working herself into a foul temper. The path had been Michael's idea but, although the moon was bright, the ground was so uneven, if she didn't watch every step, she might wrench an ankle, and then where would she be? Laid up for months, possibly. What a terrifying thought. If it were not for Michael, she would be flying along the road instead of stumbling on a treacherous path. She was not getting her heart rate up which meant that she would sleep badly which meant that tomorrow things would not go as she had planned. She had done it all wrong. She should have quietly retired, changed into her joggers, then slipped out on her own, climbing through a window and down a drainpipe if necessary. Instead, when the music ended, she had reacted, rather than acted. She did not like herself when she did that. She did not like to do things wrong. She liked to do things right.

"This is stupid," she snarled. "Why did I let you talk me into taking this path instead of the road?"

"You can walk on a road any time," said Michael. "Look at the lake through the trees. Look at the stars."

"Fuck the stars," she said. "I want to stretch my legs. This is what I get for letting myself be influenced by others."

"Oh, stop your bitching," he replied cheerily enough. "Look, we'll head off through the trees here and connect with the road and you can jog to your heart's content. Will that satisfy you?" Without waiting for her reply, he turned sharply in the opposite direction of the lake.

After a few minutes of dodging branches and stepping into holes that were even deeper than those on the path, Pamela wanted to turn back.

"It's not much farther," Michael called across his shoulder. "Only a hop, skip and a jump."

Pamela suddenly realized that behind her where there should have been noise was silence. She turned but could see nothing but bush. "Where's Jack?" she called, plunging through an entanglement of branches through which Michael had disappeared. She did not wish to lose him also.

"I thought he was back there with you."

"No, he's not here with me."

"He probably went back to the house. In search of Candy."

Michael let go a branch prematurely.

"Christ!" said Pamela. "You just about took my eye out."

"Sorry."

"Maybe he went ahead," Pamela persevered. "Back there where we turned off."

"No. I don't think so. Maybe he stepped into a large hole and disappeared. You know, like Alice."

"Don't be funny. I'm not in the mood for it."

"Obviously."

For a few minutes, Pamela's efforts were directed toward the tangle of bush ahead of her. She had the feeling that she was being dragged through this ordeal by a hand larger than hers. She did not like that feeling. She did not like to think that in the universe there might be a hand larger than her own.

"Are you sure this gets to the road?" she called, as much to hear a reassuring human voice as anything, although she would never admit that she might need to hear such a voice.

"It should. The lake and the road run parallel."

"I don't hear any traffic."

"There wouldn't be traffic. Not this time of night. You're in the country. Remember?"

"How could I forget?" Then, after a few more minutes, "You call this a path?"

"I *thought* there was a path here."

"You wouldn't know a path from your arse."

While a few such additional rude comments were exchanged, the bickering was kept to a minimum due to the fact that travelling single file they could not hear each other. Also, they were preoccupied with watching the ground beneath their feet, a mixture of fallen brush, logs, sudden drops and exposed roots. At face level was the hazard of branches. Michael did try to hold them back until Pamela was safely through, but their efforts lacked coordination.

In spite of Michael being so annoying, Pamela did not now

wish to lose him. She knew how people can wander around in circles, without direction, becoming confused. She had read of people starving to death within a stone's throw of sanctuary. Oh, she knew that would not happen. In daylight, she would easily be able to make her way out toward the sounds of the road or the lake. But she had no desire to spend a night alone in a creepy crawly wood. She kept her eyes solidly on Michael's heels. And that was another thing. He was still wearing evening loafers. Why had not that fact alerted her when still back at the house? A man does not have serious exercise in mind if he's wearing loafers with decorative tassels. But, then, Michael had planned this whole farce to get her alone. She supposed that when she announced that she was leaving Dobbin, he would be egotistical enough to think it had to do with him, which of course it did not. He was, if anything, the symptom, but certainly not the underlying cause. The very thought of leaving Dobbin for Michael was ludicrous. Michael was an actor, for god's sake!

Michael's heels stopped so suddenly, she slammed into his back. She looked up as he turned. Their faces were close in the moonlight. Another time, Pamela might have felt the pull of Michael's attraction, but now she took a step backward and nearly fell over a log. He caught her arm. She shook herself loose. "What now?" She put as much weary sarcasm into her voice as possible.

He was gazing upwards. "Look at that full moon. Isn't it incredible?"

"It's not full until tomorrow night."

Michael gave a short laugh and brought his head down. "Oh, Pam, you're hopeless."

"What do you mean?" She was genuinely puzzled.

"Don't you have any response to the beauty of nature?" He lifted one arm and struck a pose.

"Not when I'm stuck in all these trees."

"Where is your romantic side?"

"Fuck romance. Give me intelligence and common sense."

"Oh, Pam. Put away your logic and reason. Let your

imagination have a good romp. It's a full moon, a blue moon according to Sylvia who keeps track of such things. It's a time when all sorts of magic things might happen."

"What nonsense you actors talk."

But Michael was not to be stopped by Pamela's lack of enthusiasm. Raising his right arm and holding out his left, he burst into song... "'give me a June night, the moonlight, and you...'" Pamela was not to be moved. "Oh, never mind." He lowered his arms. "Here, let me help you over that log."

"It's quite all right. I can manage by myself. I'm probably in better shape than you."

"No doubt."

And then she could see the reason for his stopping. Before them lay a grassy area which, in the light of the enormous moon, appeared to be enchanted. The edge of a small pond was heaped with wild flowers of all description – daisies, bluebells, columbine. She became aware of their perfume mixed with the dry herb scent of the grass and a sort of green apple smell from the trees. She also became aware of trickling water, the chirp of crickets and the far off hoot of an owl. For a moment, Pamela was transported by the beauty of the scene. Then, like an abrupt snapping of shutters, the wood enclosed her in a claustrophobic circle. She could not *move.* All she could think of was escape. She felt herself becoming frantic. In an attempt to control the feeling she pushed it down inside herself, allowing a kind of horridness to surface which expressed itself in sniping remarks and sarcasm.

"If you have any ideas about getting cozy, you're a man suffering from delusions."

"Oh come on Pam. Can't you see little elves and fairy sprites dancing about in this glade?"

"You've had one too many brandies."

"Three too many, to be precise." Michael stepped forward into the open space, lightly positioning himself. "But that's beside the point."

"I don't see how." Pamela, too, stepped into the clearing.

There was nowhere else to go.

"The point is," he said, sitting himself down on a fallen log like an actor in a drawing room comedy, "it's no good trying to avoid each other. We can't do that for the whole weekend."

"You've brought me here on purpose," she accused, standing over him. She had her hands on her hips and was facing him squarely.

His eyes travelled up her shapely legs encased in tights. She was wearing a light jacket. Her hair was caught back with a band. "Don't be absurd. But I've been trying to have a private word with you ever since you arrived."

The idea that she had let herself be manipulated into a trap by Michael infuriated Pamela further. She paced back and forth. "I have to hand it to you," she said. "You're not inept after all." Her pacing took her up against a wall of bushes. She turned. "You are certainly ept at being deceptive." Five strides took her across the clearing where she was met by another such wall. Again she turned.

"There's no such word."

"What?"

"As ept. It's apt."

"This is no time for a lesson in vocabulary. I'll make up words if I feel like it."

"I would remind you, then, that we share the same eptness in that regard."

"What's that supposed to mean?"

"Surely I don't have to remind you of your deception with your husband."

"Oh, that. At least I don't lure people into a secluded rendezvous against their wishes. I suppose Jack was in on this, too. Men always stick together."

"Jack knows nothing about us."

"Really? I thought men told each other everything. Details in the locker room."

"Men can be quite discreet on the subject, believe it or not. No, I wouldn't tell Jack for many reasons, one being that he would be disappointed in us. In Jack's mind we are, each of us, a certain way and he wouldn't want that to change. It would disrupt our circle if we changed. And he does not approve of married people having affairs. He's quite old-fashioned, actually. Not like us. *He* would find deception difficult. He's quite a moral fellow."

"That's more than we can say for you." Pamela's agitation mounted each time she encountered a tangle of brush.

"I don't pretend to be a moral creature. But I don't believe I'm a villain, either. I'm just a tawdry character of the moment, who believes that this life is all we have or will ever have and so tries to have fun on the passage through." Michael waved his hand as though it contained a martini glass full of gin. He had always wanted to say those lines, which he had heard another actor say once. He couldn't remember who.

"Well, I do pretend to be a moral creature. I'll have you know I consider that I have high morals."

"And yet, to use the euphemism currently in vogue, you sleep with your friend's husband."

"That has nothing to do with morals."

"Really?"

"We've always liked each other. Sex is merely doing another activity together."

"I see, like tennis."

"Or good stimulating conversation. I've always thought the physical thing incredibly overrated anyway."

"Perhaps our mental activity is immoral," mused Michael. "Perhaps it is exclusive, snobbish, supercilious. I thought that at dinner when we were all madly engaged in it leaving Jack's new girlfriend quite bewildered."

"Is *that* why you were staring at her so intently."

"Don't be silly."

"I'm on to you. Don't forget I knew you back in our student days. I saw the way your eyes raked up and down that Candy person."

"I'm not blind. I hope I'll always be able to appreciate great legs."

"Aren't we the wild stallion? Wife, lover, and now the young ingenue?"

"Of all the preposterous ideas. I merely sensed that she was uncomfortable. We might have involved her more."

"I wouldn't worry about it. Jack's girlfriends come and go."

"Still, it opened my eyes a bit."

"Well, perhaps it was thoughtless. But I wouldn't call it immoral."

"I would be interested in knowing just what you do consider immoral."

"Lies, deception, betrayal," said Pamela.

"I hope you have the decency to squirm a bit under that definition."

"I never told lies, either to Dobbin or Sylvia. When you and I went out to dinner, I always told Dobbin where I was going. I'm going out with Michael tonight, I'd say. Have a good time, he'd say. Sometimes I asked him if he wanted to come along, but he never did. He always had to mark papers or some damn thing. That time, that first time, at the closing party of the Molière play, I told Dobbin all about it the next morning. Not what happened in that pile of coats on the bed, but everything else. It was his fault it happened anyway. He was too tired to go to the party with me."

"So you tell Dobbin everything except you just happen not to mention that you're having an affair with me." Michael's voice dripped with amusement.

"I'm not having an affair."

"What are you having?"

"I'm not a married woman having an affair."

"Oh Pam, you're priceless."

"I'm simply using your definition of Jack's definition of affairs."

"Whatever do you mean?"

"I mean..." Pamela stopped. She mustn't speak too soon.

"What I think is, you feel guilty. You want to pretend that it's not happening."

"And I tell you that we're not having an affair."

"What in heaven's name are we doing?"

"Having a bit of diversion."

"So now that you have our little affair organized and categorized in your own mind, now that you have intellectualized it, you feel quite comfortable with it, is that it?"

"What other way is there to look at it. Any other way, one becomes involved in a whole lot of emotional mess.

"Perhaps you're right."

"Of course I'm right."

"The other way would be to let oneself become involved in an emotional mess. Let oneself feel fear and guilt and remorse. Admit one's weaknesses, one's lapses of morality. One could say, I've done wrong but I'll try and do better in the future. Perhaps an aspect of morality is accepting suffering as the consequences of our actions."

"This is quite hilarious. You defining morality."

"Why can't I define it? I don't have to live it to define it."

"I don't see any point in staying here any longer debating the issue. It can't be that far to the road." Pamela stomped to the edge of the clearing, raised her arms and clawed at the branches.

If you'll give me one moment more. I wanted to talk to you about..." Michael hesitated. Earlier, when they had been listening to the music, two things had happened to Michael. As he gazed across the room, his eyes had fastened on Candy's legs, the shape of her torso rising from black leather, her nipples, beneath a revealing top, standing out like raised buttons. He realized that she wasn't wearing a bra. Earlier in the evening, she had shyly confessed to him that she wanted to be an actor. Ah, yes, he had thought, she'll fall like a ripe plum into my experienced hands. As for Jack, at this stage of the game, the first date stage, it was every man for himself. Then, as Michael's eyes circled the room, they had landed on Dobbin. I'm despicable, he thought, I must end this thing with Pam. For that very purpose he had insisted on joining her for a walk. While Jack had briefly disrupted his plan, losing him and stumbling upon this glade was fortuitous. It almost made him believe in Sylvia's moon and stars. Still, it was damned awkward. He and Pam went back a long way. The situation called for the greatest tact and diplomacy. "What I'm trying to tell you," he persevered, "is that even though I'm not a moral creature, I'm feeling uncomfortable with our situation. I mean, while I'm married to Sylvia. Perhaps I should set it right."

Pamela stopped clawing. "You mean you're leaving Sylvia?"

Michael was awestruck at the misinterpretation of his words. "Pamela, you know that I am and will always be extremely fond of you, but..."

Pamela did not hear the 'but' nor the formal 'Pamela'. She spun on her heels. "I wasn't going to tell you right now. This is terrible timing, but the fact is..." she took a deep breath and plunged on, "the fact is, I'm leaving Dobbin."

Michael was so stunned by this information, he almost forgot to act like an actor being stunned by information. "Leaving Dob! I don't believe it."

Pamela was almost as shocked as Michael. By speaking the words she had made them real. "Don't you dare tell the others," she appended.

"You can't toss Dob out like an old shoe," Michael spluttered. His mind was reeling with the thought that Pam was leaving Dob because of him when he was planning to get rid of her in favour of Candy. "How did he take it?"

"I haven't told him yet."

Ah, thought Michael. All is not yet lost. "When do you intend telling him?"

"Sunday morning. I know it will be a blow. But it doesn't have to change anything. We can continue as we are. I'll simply come by myself and Dobbin will come by himself." In the confusion of the moment Pamela forgot that she had just heard that Michael was leaving Sylvia and, in that case, there would be nowhere to come to.

"This whole thing is ludicrous," stated Michael emphatically. "You can't break up with Dob. He's my oldest and dearest friend."

"How about me!"

"You, too. You're both my oldest and dearest friends."

"What I mean is, how about *my* welfare, *my* survival?"

"Of course, there's that, too," said Michael distractedly. Then with more force, "Look, Pam, what did poor old Dob do?"

"Don't say it that way. You'll make me feel sorry for him."

"I can't imagine what Dob would do that would offend anybody."

"That's just it, he never does anything. It's enough to drive a person mad. He's emotionally challenged. He wouldn't know an emotion if one sprang up and struck him down. You can't communicate with that man. No normal person could. All he ever talks about is what he reads in books."

"That's just the teacher in him. There's more to Dob than that."

"If there is, I can't discover it. After ten years of trying."

Now that Michael had gotten over his first shock, he thought about Dob being free, being able to make his own decisions, to live his own life, without the dominance of Pam's personality. He thought of what it might be like if Dob met a *nice* person, an amiable person, a sweet woman who would not make his life such hell. "Maybe it is for the best," he mused out loud. "Perhaps he'll find someone else."

"Dobbin? You must be joking. I can't imagine Dobbin with anyone else. Who would put up with him? No. Dobbin in his own stolid way can be absolutely infuriating. Dobbin..."

"Shhht!"

"Don't shhht me!"

"No, listen..."

"Don't tell me what to do!"

Michael put his finger to his lips. "Do you hear something?"

Pamela kept silent a moment. "I hear voices and splashing." Pamela's voice rose in disbelief. "I thought we were near the road!"

"Shhh. So did I. But we must be near the lake. It must be just over there. Come on, if we get down to the beach we can follow it back to the house."

"What about my jogging?"

Michael didn't answer. Already, he was on his feet and was heading in the direction of the voices. Pamela sighed. There was the odd time when even she had to admit defeat. She supposed that she would have to give up her plan of exercising this night. Once again, she found herself stumbling through the bush following Michael.

After only a few minutes, using the voices as a guide, they could see through the trees ahead of them the sparkle of the lake in the moonlight. "Stop!" called out Pamela.

"What?" Michael looked back. "Something wrong?"

"Shhh. Listen!" Pamela stood still. Michael followed suit.

"That's Dobbin's voice," said Pamela. "I'd know it anywhere."

Michael plunged through the last few bushes between them and the beach. Pamela was close behind. Michael was bent low. Pamela could see across his shoulder. As they emerged from the growth, she pushed Michael aside and strode forward onto the sand. "Dobbin, is that you out there?" she called. "What in the world are you doing?"

Dobbin and Candy rose up from the water, their bodies white in the moonlight. They were holding hands. They were both stark naked. As Pamela attempted to comprehend the situation, her amazed eyes became rivetted on Dobbin's endowment, a fair-sized one, standing at rigid attention, forming an alarming angle to his body.

iii

Meanwhile, back in the living room, Sylvia slept on, oblivious to the fact that she had a watcher. Robb had climbed through the open window. Indeed, he appeared to spring or leap, so agile was he and so filled with motivational energy at the opportunity which lay before him – to gaze at his lady love to his heart's content and at close range.

As he stood looking down at her upturned face, his passion responded to her beauty. Each strand of hair, each curly tendril softly reflecting the light, was perfect and unique and contained her mystery. And her hairline was so cleanly defined, the line so charming and graceful, the way it curved and swept down into the delicate hollows each side the classical bones of her brow. An inner energy glowed from her face. Her whole being seemed to serve, to feed, this glowing energy.

But what about the person behind that exposed face, lips slightly parted, so unselfconscious in sleep? What were her thoughts, her concerns? What forces gave her direction? He must try to understand her. He must try to decipher her inner being. Until now, he had not considered her character. He had not cared a fig about her character, or whether or not she had any character at all. Robb knew this about himself – sometimes he got so carried away with the image, he forgot the real person. Sometimes he was an irresponsible lover.

He must take a closer look. Binoculars brought the image of the subject close but permitted only an impersonal view. He must become part of her life, part of her story. He must put

himself where she was. Time was fleeting. 'Had we but world
enough, and time,' he recalled the Marvell poem. He had wasted
too much time. He had been such a coward about meeting her.
He had preferred to gaze from afar, to keep the dream aloft. If she
hadn't introduced herself to him they might never have met. It
happened in the supermarket in town. He was digging around in
the frozen food section when a fresh scent assailed his nostrils.
He raised his head and sniffed. He was reminded of a green wood
in spring. He turned and saw her. She was draped in some sort of
loose rustic looking garment. He moved behind a stack of tinned
chunky soup, meatball and tortiglioni, he would never forget. The
spirals of pasta became indelibly engraved on his mind, he stared
at them so intently, hardly breathing for fear of getting caught.
He picked up a tin and pretended to be reading the label, at the
same time straining his eyes sideways in her direction.

Her head was up, her glance travelling blindly across his face
to the shelves of soup selection. Then it travelled back. She looked
directly at his face. "Are you our neighbour?" she said.

Her voice was pure poetry – low, melodic, with a pleasing
resonance. And she had beautiful teeth, pearly white, even, and
just the right size.

"Neighbour?"

"On Blind Bay Road?" He watched her lips mouth the
words. He was particularly attracted to the 'o' in road.

He said yes, perhaps he was, he certainly could be since he
lived on Blind Bay Road. "In that lovely cedar cabin?" she
said. "Yes," he said. "We're in that old farmhouse next door,"
she said. "Really?" he said. "Yes," she said. "We live in
Vancouver but we plan to settle in here for the summer."
"Wonderful," he said. "You'll like it here." They spent an
amiable few minutes discussing the landscape, the weather and
the price of groceries. Robb could not remember the details.
He kept getting lost in the incredible colour of her eyes,
something between blue and purple, he had never seen that
colour before. He became entangled in the smile that lingered
at the corners of her mouth. He noticed that she had a dimple in

her left cheek. He staggered through the out door, after first trying to go out the in, and to his vehicle. He was all the way home, in the act of turning off the ignition, when he remembered that he had forgotten to buy groceries.

Still, he did not pursue her. Still, he viewed her from a distance as she planted a garden, staked a wire enclosure for the chickens, tethered the goat. A few times, when going in and out of their neighbouring driveways, they spotted each other and waved.

Then one Saturday evening Robb's telephone rang. "This is your neighbour." Her voice, sweet and low, sounded in his ear. "We're going to barbecue steaks," she said.

Robb said 'yes' before he properly thought about it. As he set down the phone, he had an uneasy feeling that cavorting with one's muse was likely a dangerous business. However, he changed out of his work denims into slacks and a shirt, grabbed up a couple of bottles of wine from his collection, and crossed the space between the two houses. He found himself stepping carefully, as though he were walking through territory seeded with land mines.

Sylvia met him at the door. She moved lightly and gracefully in a long skirt of leafy patterned material. How lovely she looked with her hair entwined with a ribbon the colour of her eyes. As he stepped through the door, he could feel her warmth, smell her perfume wafting up from the back of her neck. He thought he might swoon. He could not speak. He was afraid that his voice would squeak. He thrust his bottles of *Chateau de Gourgagaud* at her. He laughed. He noted that his laugh sounded forced and nervous. He cursed himself. She looked at the wine label. "Ummm," she said. "This looks like a nice one." She turned into the kitchen. "Should we open it now?"

"I suppose we should." His voice wobbled dangerously. Get a grip, he told himself sternly, or you'll be giggling like a schoolgirl. "They say it should breathe. Here let me do it." They both reached for the corkscrew at the same time. Their hands collided. His sprang back as though burned. They both laughed. She handed him the opener. He uncorked the bottle. Later, he had no memory of the act.

She took him through to the living room where Michael was watching himself on the television. Although he was dressed for the occasion in grey pants, shirt and patterned silk cravat, he was grumpy at being interrupted and rose only momentarily for the introduction. He went back to watching himself. Sylvia went back to the kitchen. Robb followed her. "Do you think it's breathed adequately?" she asked.

"Sure. Thirty seconds should be long enough."

Her laugh trilled up from inside and burst pure and clear from her throat. He poured their glasses almost full. "This way we don't have to come back for refills," he explained. They went out onto the porch to check on the barbecue. The evening was warm and fragrant with spring. The sun was low along the western edge of the lake. The trees were in new leaf. Chirpy sparrows and mellow jays gossiped amongst themselves. From somewhere came the drum of a woodpecker looking for his evening meal. In the air was a sense of promise, of life beginning yet again.

"It's my fault." Sylvia squeezed the potatoes wrapped in foil. "I double-booked, you might say." She put down the barbecue lid, removed a thick pot holder from her hand, and turned. She picked up her wine. "I forgot about that rerun of *Quincy* this evening. He had a part in that episode. He learns so much by watching himself perform. He's his most severe critic. He's always trying to improve his performance. And he hasn't done much on film. So this is a rare chance..."

Robb scarcely heard Sylvia's excuses. He watched her mouth, her eyes, as she spoke.

"Tell me about yourself," she said.

"Actually, I'm a pretty simple guy, live in the woods, spend most of my time with my head in a word processor."

"That must be a strange life. Writing. Living in your head."

" I occasionally come up for air. Go to Vancouver to help mount the play, do publicity, see friends."

"Have you ever had Michael in a play?"

"No. Of course, I've seen him. He's good," he thought to

add. At that moment, since he was in heaven, he could afford to be generous. "And how about you?" he asked. "Sometimes I hear you practice the cello."

Her lovely eyes clouded over with concern. "Oh, I hope I don't disturb you." He watched the movement of her lips. Had lips ever moved so provocatively? Had lips ever been so ripe, so luscious?

Michael took that moment to emerge through the screen door, his own glass of wine in hand.

"So you're Robb Goodfellow, the playwright," he said. He sounded sceptical.

Robb admitted that he was.

"Haven't we met?" said Michael, offering Robb a cigarette. Robb said no thanks and yes, they had met. He mentioned a few occasions – parties, receptions. Michael took a cigarette for himself and lit it with a gold lighter which he fished from his pants pocket. He then stood, drink in one hand, cigarette in the other, leaning nonchalantly against the deck railing smoking and frowning deeply, as though following a director's order to lean nonchalantly against a deck railing smoking and frowning deeply. "I saw that thing you had at the Pleiades last winter," he commented. "Venus Rising..."

"Ascending."

"What?"

"Venus Ascending."

"That was it. A good effort."

"Thank you," said Robb.

"I might have done a few things differently..."

"No doubt."

"That dialogue at the end of the second act," Michael went on as though he had not heard. "It's so necessary to have that sort of thing go quickly. Like a tennis match."

"It's written to go quickly. How it's delivered is out of my control. It's the director's job. And the actors'."

"Yes, I suppose. Except some dialogue is almost impossible to say quickly. Too many big words."

Luckily, Sylvia, who had gone into the house, came out again with a platter of steaks and saved Robb from saying, 'for an insensitive dull-witted boob with marbles in his mouth, perhaps.' He said instead, "Are you here for the entire summer?"

Sylvia opened the barbecue hood, lifted baked potatoes onto a rack and put the meat on the grill. Smoke and the smell of searing meat burst forth.

"Pretty well. I have to make the odd trip back for business. I'm already booked for fall and winter seasons. How about you? Do you stay here in winter?"

"Mostly. I like the solitude, for writing. But I'll be in Vancouver quite a lot this fall. My adaptation of Chekhov's *Uncle Vanya* starts October at the Arts Centre."

"So you're the one. I heard that someone was bringing that relic out of mothballs."

"I've tried to reclaim it for contemporary audiences."

"Personally, I've always thought Chekhov overrated. All that wistfulness and autumn leaves."

"I've exchanged that for a more robust atmosphere..."

"All that introspection, that pervasive air of futility," Michael went on, and then as though relishing his own rhetoric, "all that whining into their vodka."

"You don't think there's a texture and complexity to Chekhov that most modern playwrights can only aspire to?"

"Those period pieces are so outdated. Look to the present, I say. Give me a good Neil Simon."

"I have no quarrel with Neil Simon."

"I did his *California Suite* two seasons ago. Rita Stevens played Diana Barrie to my Sidney. God, what a disaster she was. Try pushing that cow around the stage for two hours every night. I had my work cut out for me. It didn't help that she invariably showed up drunk. But getting back to revivalist theatre, did you see Miranda Gale in *Easy Virtue* last winter?"

"Yes, I thought she was pretty good."

"She was terrible. I saw Jennifer Holmes in that role once and let me tell you, Gale was abysmal."

"That's a pretty demanding comparison. Holmes, I mean."

"Perhaps. But one must aspire to some sort of standard."

They carried the dinner inside and ate in the kitchen, which Sylvia had turned into a cozy cocoon. The oak floor and cabinets were finished in rich warm tones. The walls were papered a cheerful flowered yellow. "I hope you don't mind being 'family'," she said. Robb didn't mind in the least, and once he decided to go for the drink and let Michael's remarks roll off his back, he was able to view the other man as an actor, rather than as a human being who fell so far short of what one should be that it was a miracle he was allowed to live in a community of humans. Robb was happy simply to be in Sylvia's presence, and especially since she was proving to be what a muse should be, absolute perfection. In addition to her beauty, she was pleasant, demure, at the same time both shy and bold, a charming combination. As for Michael, he improved as the evening progressed. And he *was* witty, Robb had to give him that, although his wit often took the form of acerbic observations and poisonous barbs. Both men lifted their glasses again and again. Sylvia, too, was no slouch. Michael went downstairs to his wine cellar more than once. One of the times, he did not return. Sylvia sent Robb to look for him. Robb found Michael curled up on a rug at the door of the cold room. After trying to move the body, which flopped around like a one hundred and eighty pound fish, he found a blanket on a high shelf and placed it over the recumbent figure. He returned to the kitchen to help Sylvia with the washing up. Although it was a perfect opportunity to do a little romancing, since both of them were quite silly and giddy, Robb thought about it only in hypothetical terms. He would not be able to bear it if familiarity were to breed contempt. He needed his goddess to remain as she was, a source of inspiration. He said a reluctant goodnight.

"Don't be a stranger," she said, her syllables only slightly slurred. "Drop in when you get lonely."

"I never get lonely," he said.

"Oh, you poor man," she said.

After that, when they met on the street of the village, in the supermarket or hardware, or down at the beach, he would stop and chat. Gradually, Robb became more confident of his ability to retain the necessary aloofness and so became more adventurous. Once, when he saw her get into her car and turn it toward town, he waited a decent interval, jumped in his car and followed, then in town, 'happened' to run into her on the street. One afternoon, he managed to be down on the beach just as she was going for a swim. The resulting nervous excitement of playing this game fired him up, gave life a delightful edge, and heightened the joy of his daily existence.

Once, feeling particularly daring, after his writing stint was over, Robb ambled through the growth of willow and birch, through the field grass dotted with wild flowers, which separated the two houses. The day before, he had seen Michael throw a small overnight bag into the trunk of the car and drive off by himself. Sylvia invited him in and gave him herbal tea. "What else could I do?" she said later to Michael. They sat at the wooden table in her kitchen. The kettle hummed on an old-fashioned big black cookstove which had been converted to gas. A light breeze through an open window billowed the yellow gossamer curtain, bringing with it the sweet smell of honeysuckle.

As Robb made his way home, he felt light-headed. He wondered what had been in the tea. He thought about his earlier statement about never being lonely. Certainly, he never used to get lonely. He was not sure that he did now. He let himself think about being around another person every hour of every day. For the first time in his life, he was not struck with panic at the idea.

As Sylvia continued to sleep, Robb lowered himself to his haunches like an animal of the forest settling itself down to watch and to wait. He adjusted his perched figure, stretching himself forward until his face was within inches of hers. He breathed in her sweet breath as it left her mouth. He warmed himself in the light of her radiance. He could see that, beneath heavy veined lids, her eyes were active, a movement like the heartbeat of a bird beneath its tender feathered breast. She must be dreaming. What visions was she seeing? What music was she hearing? It would surely be something raised beyond the mundane level of mere mortals.

Sylvia was dreaming of chicken, frozen chicken, chicken that rose up, feathers and all, from its frozen condition, clucking loudly and furiously and pointing an accusing finger at her.

Then the scene flipped. She was staring down at her recipe book, one of several piled up and propped open in chaotic disarray on the end of the kitchen counter. 'Soak 12 bamboo skewers in water overnight.' The words leapt off the page. Large bold black letters circled her head like angry wasps.

Flip. She was behind the wheel of a car, swinging the wheel this way and that. The car was travelling at an incredible speed. Suddenly, from out of nowhere, a huge truck came straight toward her.

Flip. She was looking down, eyes wide with horror, into the black maw of the barbecue. Grotesque grease monsters loomed up, surrounding her with black clouds of noxious fumes. She staggered backwards choking, clutching her throat, choking... choking...

Sylvia, being an uncomplicated person, tended to have dreams that were straightforward expressions of her concerns. This dream was no exception. The morning's conversation with Michael had left her upset and jittery. After that, things had gone badly – the egg yield was down, the goat had got loose and eaten the lettuce she had planned for the salad. As the day progressed, things had not improved.

To start with, she had forgotten to take the chicken out of the freezer. Only a few hours before she had to present it as something edible to her guests, she was staring down at what appeared to be a block of solid ice. Then came the skewer complication. Drat! Why had she not read her recipe beforehand as Martha Stewart would have done? Where was Michael? She would have to send him into town. The little store at Blind Bay corner would not have skewers. But Michael could not be located. Sylvia found herself frantically careening the thirty

kilometres into town, clocking it at thirteen minutes. When she
returned, while waiting for the chicken to defrost in a pail of cold
water, she removed the tarp covering of the barbecue and lifted
the iron lid. Layers of black grease gobbed with lumpy stuck bits
of burned meat confronted her. Where was Michael? She had
told him about the barbecue! Oh, why hadn't she checked it sooner?
She got out pail and brushes, detergent and rubber gloves. But it
soon became evident that this was a job for something stronger
than detergent, which entailed another frantic run through the house
calling Michael's name, another quick trip, although this time only
a kilometre to the corner store and gas station at the head of Blind
Bay Road.

By three o'clock, Sylvia had the bamboo skewers soaking
and ready to proceed further. Back to the recipe book, then.
'Pour sauce mixture over chicken and marinate in refrigerator
overnight'. She experienced a moment in which she wondered
if she should give up right then and there on this particular menu.
But then she would have to replan the meal and that would take
longer than forging ahead with this one. The chicken would
simply have to do with a shorter marination, say half an hour.

She set her teeth and, while waiting for the chicken to
defrost, attacked the rice and salad dishes, all the while the
resentment inside her building. Why couldn't Michael appear
in the kitchen doorway, like some husbands she knew, and
cheerfully offer his services? As she attacked the chicken with
a cleaver, as she frenetically scraped char from grills, her
thoughts about Michael were as black as the barbecue monsters.
Where was he? her mind, on automatic pilot, repeated the question
like a profane litany. Lolling on the beach, reading, pretending to
read, one of his goddamned scripts, she supposed. Why could he
not chop some of these damned vegetables? Why did he hide like
some kind of rodent? Every time she needed him he had his nose
stuck in one of those scripts.

It did not occur to Sylvia that her husband might be at Robb
Goodfellow's in script consultation over a few beer. The two men
scarcely knew each other. The morning after Robb's dinner visit,

Michael had stated in no uncertain terms that he had come here to get away from the theatre scene, especially from people the likes of Robb Goodfellow.

By four o'clock she was in a fine frenzy of activity amid a clutter of bowls and blenders and mixers. The sink was piled with pots and pans. Peanut sauce for the meat and orange sauce for the crepes were simmering nicely. Marinade for the chicken was whirring in the blender. Yeast was frothing up in a bowl. Eggs were boiling gently. Crepe batter was resting. Then she remembered that she had to bring wine up from the cellar so that it would be room temperature. Then she remembered that she had to run out to the garden and try to salvage some lettuce leaves that the goat might not have eaten. And she had not touched her cello today, not even to do scales.

When Sylvia heard Pamela and Dobbin's car turn in from the road – by the sound of it they *had* brought the old dinosaur – she was wiping up the kitchen and feeling a fright. Sweat trickled down between her breasts and pooled above the waistband of her skirt. Damp tendrils of ticklish hair clung to her steamed face and crawled down her neck. As she hurried out to greet her friends, tripping and almost hurtling headlong down the porch steps, Michael appeared, sauntering over from the neighbour's, looking cool and relaxed. And why in hell shouldn't he be? He'd done nothing but relax all day! And the heat didn't bother him, he loved the sun and never felt fussed by hot weather. She contrasted her flushed swollen feeling with his unruffled demeanour and shot him an ugly glance. Then she turned with a wide smile toward her guests.

After showing Pamela and Dobbin to their room, she disappeared to have a quick shower and change her clothes. As she ran a comb through her hair and put on a dab of makeup, she realized that her state of equilibrium was pretty shaky, which explained, she told herself later, the scene before dinner. It was not so much the happening itself, which, after dinner was over and they were all sitting back in their chairs, she had to admit was minor, but what it represented. An illuminating moment in her marriage, it arrived at about seven o'clock when the company was gathered on the deck for drinks. After punching down her dough and shaping it into buns, Sylvia had picked up the hors d'oeuvres and whisked herself outside. She thrust the tray at Pamela, noting as she did so that Jack, standing next to Pamela, was holding an empty glass. Where was Michael? Could he not at least see to his guests? She turned to find him holding court, being charming and witty, preening and posturing for the benefit of Jack's date. He was speaking in his clipped stage voice, the one he used when he was being very clever indeed, and acting like a guest at his own party. Could he not act the part of a responsible host and pass canapés and refresh drinks? And the barbecue should have been lit fifteen minutes ago!

In that moment, Michael had been diminished in her eyes. In that moment, she had ceased to admire him or to respect him. No longer was he her hero or even a reasonable facsimile. He was a silly foppish irresponsible fool. The thought entered her mind like a poisoned dart and lodged in her brain.

The insight had left Sylvia profoundly disturbed, the disturbance had taken root in her subconscious and from there had filtered into her dream. When she awoke, before her eyes opened, she remembered the dream. She remembered what had brought on the dream. She felt a resurgence of her annoyance with Michael. She opened her eyes and saw what, in her present state, seemed to be a magical creature sprung from the woods and nature, a light-boned man with a thin face, a Renaissance face. She remembered that he was connected to the theatre.

Robb straightened back on his knees, shifting his upper body away from Sylvia and jostling a low table behind him. He was not certain what her reaction to him would be. He didn't want her to be nervous, but would she at the very least be startled? But no, his sweet accepting Sylvia was not the type to be easily startled, and she recognized him immediately. She brought her head forward and smiled her slow smile, which for Robb lit up not only her face but the room, the world, the stratosphere.

"Where did you come from?" she said. It was not really a question. She knew, of course, that he had come from next door. She might have said 'what a surprise' or 'what a pleasant surprise' but she did not seem surprised. It was almost as though she were expecting him.

"I saw the lights and heard the music," he said.

She looked at the tape deck. "The music's ended."

Robb noted that she seemed saddened by this, or perhaps it was just that she was not yet fully awake. She squeezed her eyelids tight, opened them wide and blinked several times. She looked around the room. "Where is everybody?"

"They've disappeared." He gestured.

She seemed to simply accept his words. She was staring at him as though he were a genie released from a bottle to grant her wishes and thus solve her problems.

In fact, Sylvia was thinking, 'my dream of one man was smashed this evening. My eyes opened and the first thing they saw was this man who kneels before me now.'

For Sylvia, who believed in signs, such a happening was loaded with meaning.

"Shall I help you up?" Robb held out his hand.

"Why don't you join me down here?" she said. He's very good looking, she thought. Why did I think his face was too sharp and rather crafty looking. How could I have thought that his ears were rather pointy?

Robb sprang to it and spread his length on the floor in front of her, elbow crooked, head in his hand.

"It occurs to me that I don't really know you," she said. She stared at him. She stirred. "Did I ever tell you how I met Michael?"

"You were a music student."

"Yes. He seemed like a girl's dream. He was so handsome, a perfect date. He knew all the good restaurants and wine bars. He had such a way about him. Such flare. Now, I think he was acting the part of a perfect date. I'm not sure there's anything to

Michael at all, anything real, I mean."

Robb said nothing. He was amazed. He had come with arguments and persuasions. He realized now that he didn't have to do or say anything. Sylvia and Michael's characters would do it all. Michael would betray Sylvia, he already had, because it was in his nature. Sylvia, because she was an intelligent woman, would eventually see him for what he was. All Robb had to do was let her be and she would end up in his arms. She'll figure out the ending for herself, he decided. She'll talk herself into it as the logical outcome of events.

Sylvia had been staring straight ahead at a spot on the far wall. With a little start, she seemed to come to and remember that he was there.

"Do you play any instrument?" she asked.

"Mandolin, ukelele, at university. I played the flute in the high school band but that was a long time ago."

"There's a flute over there on the piano. Why don't you play me something?"

Any ordinary man might have felt a tad out of his league trying his rusty musical skills before a professional musician, but modesty had never been one of Robb's weak points. He hopped up. He retrieved the flute from its case and after a few tentative notes struck on a jaunty five-note melody. Sylvia laughed a tinkling musical laugh. She jumped up and danced around him. She plucked a handful of daisies out of a vase. Quickly, with a few flicks of her wrists, she wove two garlands. She placed one on each of their heads. She took the pins from her hair, releasing it into a cascade of tendrils that caught the golden light. Robb tripped lightly about the room, around the stuffed armchair, the piano, the low coffee table. Sylvia followed after, arms wide and gesturing, making up a little song to sing to his piping. She sang in clear bell-like tones. She did not think about her day, the dinner, or Michael. In this moment, she was happy.

PART THREE

BERRY PICKING

i

Saturday morning, what the revellers called morning, Robb was delighted to find Sylvia on his step. He had already put in a day's work. Inspired by what had happened the evening before, he had jumped out of bed before the clock radio CD player came on and taken his first cup of coffee directly to the word processor. For an hour, his fingers had not stopped for breath. The words seemed to leap onto the page, real dialogue spoken by real people, dialogue which either revealed character or furthered plot. He spent the next three hours revising, honing and polishing. He had a scene complete, from beginning to end, in four hours. He could have yelped with joy. Any other day, to take advantage of the roll, he would have made himself a fresh pot of coffee and got back to it. But when he looked out his window and saw Sylvia leading a charge of berry pickers through the trees and tall grass, when he realized that she was headed for his porch, he knew that he would work no more that day.

As he approached the door, responding to her soft knock, Robb could see her through the screen. He actually felt himself to be a little nervous. Usually, his dealings with the opposite sex were easy. Usually, there was not a great deal at stake. It either worked or it did not. If it did not, he let it go. But last evening the eyes of his muse had opened and seen him. In the blink of an eyelid, they had seen the husband for what he was, a silly player, as she had confessed when, exhausted from their dance, they had collapsed on the sofa with a fresh bottle of champagne, which, Robb recalled, they had subsequently emptied. In the ensuing clarity of vision he, Robb, became the man of the moment. On the way home, after a night of what could only be called dallying with his lady love, he had fairly leapt upon the grass, turning in circles, swinging his arms to the sky. He had slept the sleep of those who enter heaven without going through the inconvenience of mortal death or the trial of having to present a resumé at the gates.

But in the instant before he opened the door, it occurred to him to wonder how Sylvia might feel about last night. Although nothing had actually *happened*, things had progressed into an intense session of heightened sensibilities. While his motives had been less than honourable, in her innocence she had not faltered. She had simply been sweetly flirtatious. Still, his lady Sylvia would not have dreamed of such trifling if she had not felt the weight of disillusionment and the effervescence of champagne, and, in the morning light, she might be embarrassed at revealing herself to a relative stranger. Yet, she was knocking on his door. She must not be *too* embarrassed. But he must be careful. It had taken him longer than usual to ignite that spark of interest in her, that spark so fragile, so precariously balanced against reality, it seemed it might disappear as quickly as it had come, dissolve in a puff of smoke, leaving him with a blank page.

He opened the door. He felt a sudden shock at the meeting of their eyes. Hers regarded him with a level sober honesty. He tried to shut his so that she would not see into his mind, but he could not. Her eyes held his open. He could hide nothing from her. She would know if his intentions were not honourable. What was even worse, she would know if he was lacking in both talent and skill.

What was she saying? Something about berries. She was wearing loose slacks and a long-sleeved blouse of soft light material. On her head was a wide-brimmed straw hat. It had a purple velveteen ribbon around the crown and chiffon ties beneath the chin. To get a grip on himself, Robb moved his eyes across her shoulder to where the backs of the others were going on ahead, disappearing into the trees.

"You mentioned a berry patch..."

What a miracle it was that those lovely lips could open and close like that and such a melodious sound issue forth. What a miracle was a human smile lighting up eyes, face. Robb drew in his breath. He must pull himself out of this rhapsodic state of mind. He must stop seeing her as a goddess beyond earthly seduction. He must remember that seduction was the answer to his problems. Consider what he had accomplished this morning merely by taking the first step. Seduction was his means to survival. And as he thought thus, before his eyes, Sylvia changed from an aloof princess unattainable in her tower to Little Red Riding Hood carrying her basket of goodies through the dangerous wood. Robb grinned a wolfish grin.

Yes, he vaguely remembered offering her his berries, telling her of their superior quality. "I never use them," he had said, "they just go to waste."

Robb detested picking berries. Of all the useless, senseless, time-wasting activities! If one wanted berries why did not one simply purchase them at the supermarket? What possessed people to voluntarily place themselves in a position of such discomfort where hordes of insects attacked every available bit of skin, where bushes prickled the back of your neck and poked at your arms and legs and perspiration tickled your chest and armpits. For no one ever picked berries in the rain or the cold. No, it was always hot and sticky and buggy.

Robb's grin widened even further. "Okay if I join you?"

The berry patch was a hum of activity. In the lazy heat of the late morning sun, flies droned, bees buzzed, mosquitoes whined. Luckily, Pamela had thought to bring insect repellent. Amongst the thick green, like scattered blossoms hiding, were parts of the berry pickers – Jack's smile, Michael's slouchy khaki hat, Sylvia's purple ribbon, Pamela's scowl. Candy had stayed behind. As she explained, she was not into berry picking. Dobbin had also begged off, to mark papers. 'I'll just bet,' Pamela fumed, slathering herself, face and hands, the back of her neck and her ankles. To mosquitoes with a yen for rich simmering blood, Pamela's at the moment was a fatal attraction. This was because Dobbin, as she put it in her mind, was a crazy old coot into premature male menopause. Cavorting with females half his age! Next thing, he'd have a heart attack and expect her to look after him!

The patch was on a slight rise facing east where it caught the early sun and yet was protected from the late afternoon heat that would have withered the berries. Certainly, there were other patches around. The whole area was dotted with saskatoon bushes. The road allowances were spilling with them, but those berries were smaller, shrivelled and dusty. The Goodfellow patch was far superior, both for size and juiciness of the berries and for density and productivity of the bushes, which had been tended and groomed by one of Robb's long-forgotten ancestors into a fertile stand where the pails seemed to fill themselves.

As Robb, jam tin slung around his neck, searched for clumps of berries in the bushes, he watched through the branches. He must keep everyone in his sights, so that he could take advantage when the opportune moment arose. If he knew anything at all about human nature, it would be only a matter of time until he could be alone with Sylvia. He knew of last night's skinny-dipping episode. He had been with Sylvia when the others returned, Dobbin strangely elated, Michael strangely quiet. He had been surprised, Dobbin and Candy seemed like an unlikely pairing. And if Dobbin and Candy ended up together, where did that leave Michael? Where did that leave Pamela? The answer to the latter was – affronted by a new side of Dobbin that had emerged without her permission. Robb decided that she would have to slip away to see what her husband was up to.

As for Michael, he didn't seem himself this morning. At times, he actually seemed to be seriously thinking. After what Robb had seen of him ogling Candy the day before, he would have predicted that he would be off in search of that young lady, but Robb had to admit that he was no longer certain what his arch rival might do next. He did know that Michael hated berry picking. That much was clear, since Michael was not one to be a silent martyr. Likely, then, he would not hang around long. And what of Jack? In Robb's pairing of Michael with Candy, he had left Jack dangling. Indeed, while he had been busy with Sylvia, he had entirely forgotten about Jack. But, as Jack kept mentioning to the disinterest of everyone, he had spent the night on the beach, alone and uncomfortable. All right, then, Jack would have to go off in search of a little comfort. The only question remaining in Robb's mind was who would be the first to leave. He flipped a mental coin and came up with Pamela.

Pamela was picking berries furiously, filling her small jam tin, dumping it into a large plastic pail provided by Sylvia, turning to fill it again. She did not care that she was mashing her berries as she stripped them from branches with clenched fingers. She had not slept well the night before. She had tossed and turned, heaving her body first one way and then the other. She had not cared if she disturbed Dobbin. She hoped she *was* disturbing him. How dared he sleep like a baby when she could not sleep at all. She jumped out of bed and switched on the bright light. She went into the bathroom. She ran herself a glass of water, jerking the tap shut, which caused it to squeak. She thumped back to the bed and flung herself in beside the oblivious Dobbin. Of course, he hadn't offered an explanation. It would not occur to him that the situation needed explaining. Pamela knew her husband's reasoning – all he and Candy had done was go for a midnight swim. As for his physical condition, that was just a logical physical reaction to the situation. Pamela lay rigid on her back and stared at the ceiling. Who did he think he was? What the fuck did he think he was doing anyway? She'd show him. You wanta see what a fling is, baby, she had thought as once more she leaped out of bed, this time to grab a cigarette, one of Dobbin's, she'd quit years ago, I'll show you what a fling is.

Savagely, she stripped down another branch of berries, seeing in them Dobbin's bland cheerful face as he announced that he would mark papers instead of picking berries. His voice had definitely been shifty. That he could be so audacious, so blatantly deceptive! So careless of her feelings! After she had been so careful not to hurt him by not letting him know about her and Michael. Flaunting his indiscretions! Looking everyone, his best friends for Christ's sake, in the eye and telling a lie, without so much as the twitch of a facial muscle. Of course, those glasses helped. You never could really see Dobbin's eyes behind those glasses. Maybe he had been lying to her for the past ten years. He *had* been lying to her for the past ten years if you counted lies as being when a person is not open and honest and sharing, when a person holds back themselves. For that *was* what Dobbin did, held his mind apart from her, as if his thoughts were too precious, too private, too superior for the likes of her. It was as though all these years he had been having an affair with his own mind, a sort of mental masturbation. The lying, sneaking, snivelling, pathological degenerate!

And where was he now? Marking papers, my foot, she seethed. Rocking on the bed with that Candy person right this minute, was her bet. Enjoying himself, having fun, while she was stuck in a dusty old berry patch. Suddenly Pamela was struck with an irresistible impulse mounting to an obsession to return to the house. She could easily slide away, pick farther and farther from the others, fade into the bush, then make her way down the rise, off the main path. She imagined the surprise and dismay on Dobbin's face as she threw open the bedroom door and caught him in his act of betrayal, not only of her but of their friends, of the house itself. And Jack. What about Jack? Poor Jack, who had spent the night on the beach while his date was two-timing him. Thus, Jack, whom Pamela had always privately thought of as a brainless womanizer and a cad, became a sympathetic character – Jack, who for the past half hour, had been cheerfully popping berries into his mouth, unaware that he was being deceived by his best friend and that lollipop female.

When she lifted her head, Pamela could see Jack through the bushes, or at least part of him. She could see the back of his forearm. Sturdy, muscled, covered with fine dark hair, the tips of which the sun burnished into gold. It was in a horizontal position, poised amongst the greenery. It stopped her still. Possibly her eyes were affected by the heat or the sun's glare, but she saw Jack's arm as a thing in itself. She saw its beauty. It was like gazing on a Greek statue, like seeing the detail of a Titan. It was like seeing these wonders for the first time, coming upon them unexpectedly in a green magic wood. It was the same feeling she had had when she had first visited the Rodin sculptures in Paris. On an ordinary street, in an ordinary square, there they were. Here is something perfect, she had thought then. Here is something detached from life, untouched by human emotions and attitudes, untouched by human greed and covetousness, pride and malice.

Jack moved his arm. His hand moved from the branch it had been holding, which sprang back into place, and he stepped around the bush. But Pamela's epiphany had been indelibly inscribed on her brain as an image is held by the eye's retina after the reality has disappeared. She stood staring at the place where Jack's arm had been. Although her revelation had lasted only a few moments, she knew without question that her happiness resided with Jack.

Jack, oblivious that his arm was the object of Pamela's vision and thus elevated in her thoughts to an intensity bordering on religious mania, was giving the clumps of berries the same attention he gave to the open jaws of his patients. In a posture of superb attention to the task at hand, he removed the berries skilfully, with scarcely any movement of branch. Rather than pulling on the berry, which tended to bruise it, he clipped its stem with his thumbnail, thus causing little trauma to either berry or branch. Jack's movements were precise and efficient as in everything he did. Besides being trained that way, it was his natural bent. However, on this particular morning, while focussing on the berries, he was also giving some thought to the previous night when he had been following a rustling in the bush ahead of him. He had thought he was following Pamela and Michael, but, then, he had come out onto the Wilde's beach and a small deer had appeared before him, dashing at once back into the trees. He had sat down for just a minute but had immediately fallen into a deep sleep. When he had woke up some time later and stumbled up to the house, all was dark and quiet, too quiet to start anything with Candy. In any case, chilled and cramped, one side numb due to loss of circulation, he had not been in the mood. Yes, last night was a write-off. Last night was neither his idea of a good time nor his intention for the weekend. He meant to revise his strategy for the coming night.

Sounds penetrated his thoughts. The throb of a distant outboard motor arrived from the lake. The chirp and twittering of birds descended from the tall branches of trees. Voices came from the other side of the bushes.

"These young playwrights are appallingly serious," Michael was saying. "It's so tedious."

"You prefer farce?" That was that other fellow, the neighbour.

"I prefer irreverence."

" Which is often insincere."

"To quote another Wilde, insincerity is merely a multiplication of the personality."

"I'm surprised you agree with another actor," said Robb.

"It's playwrights we never agree with," answered Michael.

"Oscar was also a playwright. How can you let yourself defer to him."

"Oh, I can defer to brilliance. It's the mediocre, unfortunately more commonly met, which I must resist."

"Still, we know people by their quotations. Oscar may be witty but he's entirely frivolous. No substance," Robb stated.

"Is that so?" Michael countered. "I always find him a breath of fresh air after O'Neill or Miller. If we want to be depressed, we can always go to real life. We attend the theatre to be lifted out of our humdrum, sordid little lives, not have them smashed in our faces."

"Judging from the popularity of O'Neill and Miller, I'd say a lot of people are mature enough to take on real life drama," contended Robb.

Sounds and conversation faded back into the background of Jack's consciousness. Into the foreground sprung thoughts of Candy or, more precisely, Candy's body. He recalled her slim waist and well-developed bottom. He liked that, liked a bottom that was there, so to speak, and it was firm, he supposed from all that dancing. The dancing may explain, too, her erect figure, such a compact body, such a light yet decided walk. She moved like... Jack's brow furrowed... like a slightly swaying willow. And those breasts! Not overly large, he supposed large breasts would hinder a dancer. You couldn't have a whole lot of weight swinging around on the stage. Might do someone an injury. At the very least, they would get in the way. No, Candy's breasts were not melons, not cantaloupe. They were more like oranges, large oranges, or grapefruit, small grapefruit. Jack frowned slightly. He didn't like the idea of comparing any part of Candy to acidic fruit. What was his favourite fruit? Plums. But, no, plums were too small. Peaches, then, large peaches, ripe for the plucking, downy and warm in the sun, cream-coloured with just a hint of blush. The perfect size. Oh, some men may go for huge knockers but, truth to tell, he preferred them medium-sized. They didn't draw so much attention in public. It was embarrassing to be with a woman who aroused the stares and lust of every man in the place.

And where was this downy ripe peach this very minute? In a hammock? Reading a book? Had she fallen asleep, book in hand, the book falling to the ground? He could see her waking up, her eyes slowly opening to him, like two blue cornflowers opening their soft petals to the sun. And her face when she first woke up would be soft and giving. He knew it would be, she was so young, so tempting. Yes, she would be warm, her skin would be warm, all the parts of her would be warm, warm and moist.

Caught up in his fantasies, Jack felt stirrings below. He looked down. This heat not only made him hot and sweaty but also horny as a toad. He had a sudden enlightenment. Candy had begged out of the berry picking, hoping that he would return. She was back there waiting for him, this very moment. She had not said anything to him, but she hadn't had an opportunity. They had not been alone this morning. When he had appeared for breakfast, groggy from lack of sleep, he had joined the men who were drinking coffee on the terrace, Michael nodding absentmindedly at Dobbin's expounding. Michael greeted him enthusiastically, perhaps hoping for a way out of the negative dialectic, but Dobbin, after glancing at Jack, steamrolled on. Through inserted comments whenever Dobbin stopped for a breath, Jack learned that Sylvia had already had her morning swim and was collecting tins and pails and Pamela was off jogging. He tried to impart the information that he had spent most of the night, neglected, on the beach, but the other two didn't seem to care. Feeling slightly piqued at their disinterest in his discomfort, he turned his attention to Candy's movements who, in full makeup and hair gel, leotards and bare feet, was performing warm-up exercises on the grass. Damn, he had thought, how could I have fallen asleep and not taken advantage of that. He had made a vow to himself regarding tonight's activities.

Now, he realized, he wouldn't have to wait until tonight. Jack glanced across his shoulder. To get to the main path he would have to cross a short space of open ground, the others would see him leaving. He turned. He could instead slip away through the thin growth between him and the lake. He dropped back two bushes and pretended to pick a few moments longer before discerning that no one had noticed. Darting a glance toward where he had heard the voices, he turned and made a dash for it.

Pamela saw Jack leave. Since the moment that her eyes had been opened to the wonders and beauty of his arm, she had not let him, or some part of him, out of her sight. Peering through the screen of bush, no longer even pretending to pick berries, she stood, mesmerized, watching the place where he was, where a bit of his outline was evident, or a snippet of his shirt, or the edge of his sunglasses. When she saw him drift off towards the lake and disappear, she knew that she must follow. She edged herself around so that there were several bushes between her and the other three berry pickers. She then turned and fled, making her way through bushes and trees. She could not see Jack ahead of her. She concluded that this was because of the foliage. Also, his few minutes head start would give him an advantage. She assumed that he was headed for the house. Where else would he go? She veered toward the main path and slowed down, forcing herself into regular breathing.

Since seeing Jack's arm, Pamela had been in a state of euphoria transcending thought. When she saw him leave, she did not think to wonder why. When her action was slowed, her mental process kicked in. Why would Jack leave in such a stealthy manner? It was not like him to be secretive. Usually, Jack, warts and all, was an open book. He was like a child, a precocious doted-on child, who knows that he is adorable and, therefore, loved. That quality in Jack was one of the things that made him rather appealing.

And then she knew and a pang pierced her heart. He must be looking for Candy. Could they have prearranged a rendezvous? No, for how could Candy be rendezvousing with two men at the same time? But Jack would come upon her and Dobbin! Pamela became alarmed. Would he be insane with jealousy? Would he challenge Dobbin to a fight? Pamela did not want Dobbin to get hurt, even if he was a stupid person. And she had no doubt who would win in such a confrontation.

Don't be silly, her rational self said. Jack and Michael and Dobbin had been through a lot together. In their youth, they stole each other's girlfriends, borrowed each other's booze, traded each other's vehicles, always being open and honest about their underhandedness.

Pamela arrived at the house without seeing hide nor hair of Jack or anyone else. No one was about. Well, Dobbin and that girl would hardly be doing anything on the driveway. She tiptoed up the porch steps and slipped in through the screen door. The house smelled of warm wood, baking plaster, dry crisp wallpaper, all the smells of an old house on a hot summer noon. She paused. She listened. All quiet. Dobbin was supposed to be marking papers in the study. She tiptoed to the study door. Again, she paused and listened. She put her hand around the doorknob, turned it, and pushed. Just as she had suspected. Dobbin was not there. Ever so quietly, placing her foot carefully on each step before allowing her full weight to fall on it, she made her way up the stairs and down the hall to their bedroom. The door was closed. She stood a few moments outside listening. She could hear nothing. Again, she put her hand on the knob and turned it. It did not squeak. Good. Then in a quick burst, she thrust forward her arm. The bed lay before her, pristine and empty, the corners tucked up neatly. The student papers were in a neat pile on the desk, untouched.

As she stood in the doorway, uncertain of where next to look, through the open window came sounds from the lake, motors ripping the serene air, voices calling across the water, laughter lifting up from the beaches. Of course, people were outside on such a lovely day. Dobbin and Candy would have found some quiet spot, some grassy hideaway. She did not think they would be at the beach. Dobbin hated lying around on beaches, all that sand getting into his papers and books. She decided to go down and scout out the area.

Pamela let the porch door slam behind her. She made her way along the path that wended through willow and scrubby pine. As she neared the lake, she heard voices, close, immediate, voices which did not call attention to themselves, which were meant to be heard only by each other. One of the voices, a woman's, had a drawling seductive quality. The other voice, a man's, was murmuring encouragements of some kind. Pamela could not make out the words, but the tones were obvious.

And there, to the side of the path, a dark figure was crouched peering through the bushes toward where the voices were coming from. Pamela saw immediately that it was Jack. She came up behind him and stood still. He did not hear her approach. She tried to see what he was seeing, but the growth was thicker at her eye level. Again, came the voices. She could hear, now, what they were saying.

"Ummmm," said the man. "Do that again."

"Like this?" asked Candy.

"Yes," answered Dobbin. "That's perfect."

ii

Meanwhile, in the berry patch all was still. All was quiet except for the thrumming of insects and the audible sun, its rays humming like electrical wires.

"Oops," from out of the bush came a male voice.

"Damn," came another.

"Did I step on your foot?" asked Robb.

"No. But you jostled my berries," returned Michael.

"Sorry."

"I didn't know you were picking this side."

"I didn't know *you* were picking on this side."

Robb and Michael were bumping into each other because Michael, with an eye to an escape route, had moved around into Robb's territory. There, he noted, as had Jack before him, that to get to the main path it was necessary to cross an open area in which he would be visible. But while Jack had not wanted to field questions from the group, Michael's situation was more specific. He did not want to be questioned by his wife. He started moving in the other direction, back toward the lake. Perhaps he could get down to the beach. Then it would be only a skip and a jump to the house where he was sure Pamela had headed. He was well aware that she was no longer in the berry patch. He had been keeping a vigilant eye on her. She must have disappeared when he had been distracted by that stupid conversation with Robb about tragedy versus comedy. Why he had tried to penetrate the thick skull of a playwright, why he had tried to illuminate that abysmal dark ignorance, he did not know.

The voices of Michael and Robb lost impetus and conviction with each volley. Both minds were marking time until they could get to the real business of the day, in Robb's case, the seduction of Sylvia, and in Michael's, contrary to Robb's brain child of pairing him up with Candy, the convincing of Pamela to stay with Dobbin. For, since Pamela's declaration of the night before, pursuing Candy had been replaced in Michael's thoughts with schemes to get his two friends back together.

From the beginning, Michael had been uncomfortable with his and Pamela's situation. While he felt it his duty to assert his creative spirit even if it meant fooling around on his wife, or even with one of his wife's best friends, he did draw the line at fooling around with his best friend's wife who was also one of his best friends. And yet that is what he had been doing. Ironically, this thing with Pamela would not have started if he had not, in his own little way, been trying to do his friends a favour. Pamela had needed to be seduced. She had been on edge, very tense. One evening the four of them had been dining in a restaurant and Pamela in surly, hostile tones had spat at her husband, "why don't you quit talking, you talk too much." True, said husband had been involved in a lengthy explanation of Boethius' theory on the life of pleasure, making the whole business of pleasure sound dreary, but a tactful person, a thoughtful wife, might have redirected the topic and the man in a more kindly, even loving, manner. While Pamela's comment had scarcely made a dent in Dobbin's consciousness – he had paused only briefly, regarded her with calm eyes as though trying, but not very hard, to remember who she was, then had gone on with his dissertation – it had thoroughly upset Michael to hear his friend, whom he respected, spoken to in this manner. Michael had looked at Dobbin. Poor Dob was not much of a romantic figure. He had looked at Pamela. Poor Pam looked like she needed a bit of romance in her life.

Still, Michael had not planned the seduction. Fate took over when Pamela showed up at that party without Dobbin. Michael was without Sylvia. With Pamela's eagle eye on him, he could not flirt with any other woman in the place, so he flirted with her.

But a situation that was meant to last only one night had now been going on for five months. Michael's instinct, and in such matters his instinct had been honed to perfection, told him that if he and Pamela continued, it was only a matter of time before Dobbin or Sylvia found out. Michael could not bear the thought of losing Dobbin or of destroying the friendship between the two couples – that Sylvia might have some objection to the situation did not occur to him. He had decided some time ago that he would straighten out the mess this weekend. Stumbling upon that glade last night had seemed fortuitous, a perfect opportunity to resolve things. And then Pamela had dropped the bombshell about leaving Dobbin. She must be leaving Dob because of him, was Michael's conclusion – what other reason would she have? But that was ridiculous! It was unthinkable that his friends should break up because of him. He could not let that happen. He must break up with Pam before she blindsided Dob. She must be brought to her senses. And yet, after Dob's revelries of last night, things looked dark indeed.

Bad luck that, he and Pam crashing through the bushes and into the middle of a compromising situation. Although Dob had not seemed to feel compromised. He had splashed out of the water, up onto the beach, calling to them, "Come on in, the water's amazingly warm." When they didn't take him up on the suggestion, he and Candy found their clothes. He did not seem to notice his nakedness. He was like a babe in Eden, washed pure by the warm waters of the lake, and perhaps the presence of Candy. Pam, however, had been less than enthusiastic. "Don't drip all over me," she had said in that ugly impatient tone she got sometimes. "Sorry," Dob had said and stepped back a bit.

Michael was also a little surprised by Candy's reaction to being found sans clothing with the husband by the wife. She had seemed so shy and reticent at the dinner table and throughout the evening. However, he concluded, she *was* a dancer. His experience with dancers was that they ran around naked backstage half the time. And why would a Perfect Ten be embarrassed at being caught unrobed?

When Michael first noticed that Pamela was no longer part of the berry picking group, he felt alarm. Because of several sarcastic comments which she had ground out between gritted teeth on the way to the berry patch, he knew that she suspected Dobbin of contriving a rendezvous with Candy. The very idea was ludicrous, but Pam would see what she wanted to see. He must keep her away from Dob. But she had disappeared. She must have gone back to the house to spy on him. What other explanation was there? Why else would she leave the berry picking and so unobtrusively? He would have predicted that she would be gung-ho about berry picking, measuring her accomplishment against that of others, making it into a contest which the others would be entirely happy to let her win.

Michael knew what he had to do. He must sabotage Pam's mission. Further, he must confront her with the subject of last night's interrupted talk. He must get their awkward situation straightened out. He must try and talk sense into her about Dob. He had his work cut out for him. He'd better get on it. She couldn't have much of a head start.

The berry patch became very still, literally baking in the midday sun. "Michael," came Sylvia's call, clear and melodious as a meadowlark. And again, from out of the green growth, "Michael?" And then, "Jack?" Then, "Where's Michael?"

"I don't know," came Robb's voice. "Isn't he there?"

"Michael!" and after a pause, "No, I don't think he is."

"Perhaps he went back to the house."

"Why would he do that?"

"Maybe he had to go to the bathroom."

"He doesn't usually. I mean, he's pretty good at planning things like that, being an actor. And Pamela! Where's Pamela? And Jack? Jack! Don't tell me he's gone, too. Where is everybody?"

"I don't know." Robb's voice had an artless quality that might have alerted a more sophisticated damsel.

"I don't see how they can all have gone. Oh, Michael's not

much for something like berry picking at the best of times. But I'm surprised at Jack. He's usually such a good sport. He played football at university."

"Did he?"

"Yes. He's bursting with team spirit. And I'm surprised at Pamela. She makes everything into a challenge. I thought she'd try to pick more than anybody."

"Everybody has disappeared."

"Where have they gone?"

"Back to the house most likely. Maybe they were thirsty."

"But I brought drinks. Or, rather, Jack and Michael did. They carried the cooler between them. They'd know about the drinks. Now all those drinks will go to waste."

Robb's brain was a whirl of activity. Slow down, he told himself. This must be done meticulously, adeptly. "Why don't we sit down and have one?" he suggested.

"Now?"

"Right now."

"It's too soon. We've just gotten started."

"Are you serious? Look my tin is full."

"But we're supposed to fill the pail."

"What pail?"

"That plastic pail."

"We can do that after we have a drink."

"I wonder what they did with their tins? I hope they didn't lose them. It's hard to find the right kind of container for picking berries. And I made holes for the string. I had to look high and low for that ball of string. The shed's such a mess. I really do wish that Michael would straighten it up."

"Where *is* the cooler?"

"There, under that tree. You'd think after carrying it all this way, Jack and Michael would have stayed for a drink. Maybe they'll be back. Maybe we should wait."

"I'm parched. I think we should rest a moment. Dehydration can have serious effects."

"It does appear that the others have deserted us. Perhaps I

will sit a moment."

"Not over there in the sun. What are you doing over there in the sun? It's cooler in the shade."

"I like the sun. Mmmm, the grass is so nice and warm. I may fall asleep."

"You'll get sunstroke. Come over here in the shade of this elm. See how it fans its leaves above, providing a canopy just for us."

"Oh... I don't know."

"That's better. But you seem tense. Why are you so tense? Are you all right?"

"Of course. Why wouldn't I be?"

"I don't know. There's certainly no reason for you to feel tense. Why don't you lie down? The grass is warm here, too."

"Mmmm, yes it is warm. And soft. But what are you doing? Don't sit so near."

"Why not? I swear my innocence. I just want to be near you."

"If you are really that devoted, sit a little farther away."

"You know I would never do anything to harm you."

"Perhaps. But you're just about on top of me."

"What's the harm in that. I'm not a celibate bachelor."

"But I am a faithful wife."

"Here, look, it's columbine."

"They *are* pretty."

"Let me twine these blossoms in your hair."

"Mmmm. You really are very sweet. And gentle."

"And hopeful. Don't forget hopeful."

"I'm afraid that what you hope for will never come to pass."

"Why not? Where's the harm in a little hanky panky?"

"Even if I weren't a faithful wife, why should I give myself to a man who merely lusts after me?"

"What do you mean *merely* lusts?"

"Well, that's all it is isn't it?"

"Certainly not. But what if it was... I'm not saying that it is, but what if it was? What's wrong with lust? Lust is very important in the scheme of things. How else would the human race procreate?"

"In this situation lust is inappropriate."

"Lust is never inappropriate."

" I don't know. There's something not quite right about it. A woman is not supposed to give in to lust. She is supposed to give in to love."

"Do you think the two can be separate?"

"Of course. You can love someone without lusting after them."

"My Aunt Minnie perhaps. She's ninety years old and senile. Is there nothing I can say that will convince you?"

"Convince me of what?"

"To leave that imbecile husband of yours and fly away with me."

"This is so sudden."

"It's not sudden at all. I've been in love with you since the first moment I saw you."

"That time in the supermarket?"

"Even before. When I saw you from my window."

"How can one love so suddenly? You don't really mean that."

"Yes, I do."

"Do you really?"

"You doubt me?"

"It's just that, last night I thought we were playing a little flirting game. I never thought for a moment that you were serious."

"Look at me. That's right. Look me squarely in the face while I tell you. I am very very serious. I am not joking."

"It's just that I'm so used to Michael. He's always acting. I thought you were acting."

"I am not acting."

"But... Michael."

"He doesn't deserve you. You know that. You must know he..."

"What are you trying to say?"

"Nothing."

"I know what you're trying to say. You think Michael is unfaithful. But he just acts that way. It's his nature, the nature of any actor."

"Maybe. But how can a woman put up with a man who is so self-involved. A man who, every time he passes a mirror, stops and gazes longingly at himself."

"I know he's vain, he's terribly vain. But then he has to be to be an actor, doesn't he? He's a born actor. He can't help it. He's happiest when playing a role on the stage. That's when he knows who he is. But I keep hoping that he'll come to know who he is in real life."

"But do you want to spend the remainder of your life with an immature, thoughtless, insincere egomaniac?"

"Do you have anything better to offer?"

"Timeless devotion, at your beck and call, catering to your every whimsy."

"What if I interfered with your writing?"

"You wouldn't do that."

"What if I did?"

"I know you. You wouldn't do that."

"Maybe not. But what if I did?"

"I don't have to consider that possibility. I know that you would not."

"You're so free, Robb. That's what I first noticed about you. You are a free spirit. You don't want a woman, or anybody else, interfering with your freedom."

"Normally, I'd agree with you. But you're not just any woman."

"Who am I?"

"You're Sylvia. Entrancing, enchanting."

"Stop it now. You're going to turn my head."

"That's what I mean to do."

"What woman doesn't want to hear that she's beautiful and desirable. Any woman would be flattered by your words. But this can't be happening. We cannot be having a romantic tryst on the grass, especially in broad daylight. I'm in love with Michael."

"Don't say that. Don't be mean. Not after you made me love you."

"I didn't do anything. I'm still Michael's devoted wife."

"That doesn't mean you can't fool around a little bit."

"Yes it does. For me."

"Do you know the statistics on married people fooling around? If you resist, you're in the minority."

"Oh come now. That's as bad as the one that goes, 'it'll improve your relationship with your husband.'"

"You've heard that one, too, have you?"

"And, 'you'll never know what it might have been like with someone else.' Don't forget I travel with theatre people."

"It's true though. Just think, it might be earth-shattering with me."

"Stop tickling my arm. Oh, this is starting to sound like one of those romantic farces that Michael's so often in."

"Good God! I hope it's a cut above that."

"I don't know. We're being pretty silly."

"Maybe it does need some editing. I did want to get in though, that line of Marvell's, 'Had we but world enough, and time...'"

"Oh, now you've moved to my neck... Oh, I don't know. It's just that I can't."

"Yes you can. It's so warm here on the grass. I want so badly to kiss you. What harm can one little kiss do?"

"It can lead to something else."

"No. I swear it. Just one kiss. That's all. This will not go further than one kiss. Come on."

"Well..."

"We must seize the moment, the magic moment."

"Please don't think badly of me."

"How can I think badly of you? I love you."

"I don't know what I think. You mix me up so."

For a moment, there was silence in the berry patch. Then a mixed flock of chickadees and sparrows in the branches of a nearby tree set up a harmony of chirping and trilling. The clear robust song of one male sparrow stood out clearer than the rest. A flurry of chickadees provided cheerful backup. Two frolicsome squirrels playing tag spiralled around the elm's thick trunk, scooting up and down and thither and yon, darting and leaping from branch to trunk to branch, sure in their instinctive knowledge that they would not miss their footing and fall.

iii

Dobbin was lost in thought. He was standing in thigh-deep lake water, his right hand supporting his left elbow, his left hand supporting his chin. Pale blue boxer swimming trunks covered the lower area of his large pale body. He was watching in a detached manner what appeared to be a large fish thrashing the glossy blue-green water close by him.

The churning stopped and, after a wild flailing of slim arms, a bedraggled Candy emerged out of the subsiding froth and lurched to a standing position. She, too, was clad today, partially at least, in what was obviously something borrowed from a wardrobe not her own. A shapeless bag of faded large flowers, its elastic shredded, hung heavy with water down from her shoulders, obliterating her curves. The strap of one shoulder kept falling down onto her arm and she kept pushing it back up. Her orange hair, flattened into straight wet strings, revealed pale brown roots. She rather resembled a dunked poodle.

Dobbin's smooth face displayed bland amiability mixed with deep speculation. He seemed to be giving the problem of teaching Candy to swim the same concentration he had yesterday bestowed on the question of the negative dialectic. His face held steady in a pleasant expression. His blue eyes did not comment one way or another. He had found that being overly sympathetic with students weakened rather than strengthened their resolve. Supportive yet firm, that was his motto.

He was starting Candy off with the breast stroke. He thought that might be easier than the front crawl. Personally, he preferred the crawl, but it required more stamina and trickier coordination of breath and stroke. Candy, however, was not proving to be a quick study of anything, not even the dead man's float, mainly because she resisted the water.

"Go with it," he kept reminding her. "Think of the water as your friend. Think of it as a bed," he had instructed when trying to get her to float so that she could practice holding her breath.

Candy, standing before him in nearly waist-high water was shivering so violently she could hear her teeth chatter. The lake at midday in late June might be warm by local standards but to someone to whom bathing meant a long hot shower it felt like the Arctic Ocean. Her knees were knocking together and her mind was as numb as her body. She simply could not dredge up the true grit necessary for this venture.

In the light of morning and the clarity of sobriety, Candy had thought about her situation. Lying between the lavender-scented sheets in the sunny guest bedroom, she had stared at the small pink and purple flowers of the wallpaper and considered her escapade of the previous night. What would Dr. Tzvetkov think? Even though she was totally off him, she had come here as his companion for the weekend and the first night ended up romping around in the nude with another man! But when she thought about it some more, she decided that she didn't care what he thought. He was a jerk, the type who took you to a party and then ignored you for the entire evening while he dashed off to schmooze with everyone else. She thought regretfully about her job. It fit in so conveniently with her dance school schedule, being just the right amount of hours, and it paid well. Now she would have to go to all the bother of finding something else. Shit! That would teach her not to think things through before leaping into dumb situations. That would teach her to date the boss. Even if he did not fire her, she would feel so awkward in his presence she would have to quit.

As for the others, she had probably cooked her goose there, too. What must it look like, she, a total stranger to the group, being found without clothes with somebody's husband? The wife was certainly totally down on her. Walking back from the lake last night, she had felt hostility virtually oozing from the other woman's pores. On the other hand, there was a whole lot of mischief going on around here. Candy could sense it. Something was up between Pamela and Michael and right under Sylvia's eyes, which were totally closed. Maybe that explained why she hadn't had the trouble with Michael that she had anticipated upon arrival. He was busy elsewhere. Candy bestowed a moment's thought upon Michael. When Jack had told her about the well-known successful Vancouver actor she was about to meet this weekend, her interest had been roused. Then, during the evening she had discovered that he was one of those old farts who went around pinching the bums of young actors, probably of both sexes. Jerk number two. But what of Dobbin? Candy felt a pang of regret regarding Dobbin. What must he think of her, practically ripping off his clothes? And he couldn't know that, to her, taking off clothes was nothing personal. But when she thought about it, he had seemed to have fun, on the walk back going on about the moon and the stars and the night. And they hadn't done anything wrong, in spite of how it must have looked. Just a little crazy. And stupid, definitely stupid, under the circumstances. Oh, it had been a dumb dumb dumb thing to do. However, what was done was done. She could not turn back the clock. She'd stay in bed as long as possible, that way maybe she wouldn't have to face the others, especially Jack, at breakfast. Her strategy for the day was to avoid Jack as much as possible.

Candy was doing this swimming thing for Dobbin. After the others had left to pick berries, she was sitting on the porch listlessly swinging one bare leg and waiting for the weekend to be over. She heard the screen door slam behind her and then his "good morning." She gave him a quick shy glance, thinking he might be embarrassed about the evening before, but he didn't seem to be. He reminded her of her wish to learn how to swim. He wondered if she might like to give it another go in daylight. She looked at his reassuring bulk and thought of her teddy bear which sat in a corner of the couch in her place back in Vancouver. She had been clutching that bear in her arm the day she'd gotten off the Greyhound from Lone Butte, when she'd arrived in the city to seek her fortune. Looking up at Dobbin's kind smile, she did not want to disappoint him. People whom she liked and respected made her want to try her hardest. Sometimes this trait in her character led to her downfall. Sometimes she made errors in judgment as to who should be liked and respected.

Upon being reminded that she had not brought a swimsuit, he disappeared into the house. A few minutes later he returned with outstretched hands, holding a rag of something in them as though he were bringing her a gift greater than all the perfumes of Araby. So then her fate was sealed.

Although the bay was never as busy as the larger lakes around, those with public beaches and boat launching docks, it was fully mobilized on this beautiful last Saturday in June. The residents of the summer cottages, which were spaced around the shoreline like jewels in a necklace, were out in full force. Sunbathers dotted the sand, children paddled in the shallows, swimmers struck out from the shore. Canoes drifted lazily. Fishing lines trailed languidly. A motorboat dragging a water skier whizzed past, its wake causing Candy to sway dangerously on her unsteady limbs as she stood before her teacher waiting for instructions. Meanwhile, Dobbin was plodding through the cards in his brain filed under swimming – methods and techniques. There must be one in there which would appeal to Candy, which would inspire her imagination to visualize the procedure and thus help her to put it into action. "It's like the hopping about of a frog," he said in his slow thoughtful way. "Would you like me to demonstrate?"

Candy nodded miserably. She watched and shivered as Dobbin stretched his arms forward and effortlessly pushed himself off from the lake bottom with scarcely a ripple of the water's surface. With arms and legs outstretched, he glided for a long way. Then he drew his arms back and under his chest. At the same time, he bent his legs at the knees, kicked them briskly sideways, then straightened them together again. He raised his head to take in a breath. As he again straightened his arms into the glide, he lowered his head. Little bubbles appeared on the water's surface. He swam parallel to the shore, five or six strokes, then turned back and swam toward her in long slow coordinated movements. Like a dolphin, she thought. She admired the way he performed the exercise with confidence and sureness, the way he knew what he was doing and didn't make a big show of it. As he came toward her, he lowered his knees and scooped the water forward with his hands, settling lightly on his feet. He brought one arm out of the water. Droplets falling from it caught the sun. He held out his hand. She took it. "Why, you're a beautiful swimmer," she said.

Candy didn't know why this surprised her, unless it was because he was old and a little heavy, with shark's belly skin. Until now the subject of male attractiveness as it pertained to Dobbin had not been an issue with Candy. Until now Dobbin had been filed into that space in her mind which was populated with vague figures who were outside her deeply felt experience, people who had no relation to her and, therefore, in whom she was not interested. This included stuffy old professors. In short, she had not looked at Dobbin before. She looked at him now.

"It's your turn," said Dobbin. "It doesn't get deep, but swim parallel to the shore. That's always the best idea."

"I'll try." Candy sounded doubtful.

"That's the spirit."

Candy endeavoured to copy Dobbin's performance. Still she came up flailing, gasping and spluttering. She grabbed the water with her hands for something to hang onto. Dobbin caught her arm and steadied her. "Can you think how a frog moves?" he tried to explain. "You're a dancer. Imagine that you have to portray a frog. Think of the muscles in its body and how it would use them and then how you as a dancer would move to portray a frog."

"Maybe," said Candy.

"You've seen a frog leap forward," Dobbin expounded. "You simply imitate that in the water. Leap forward like a frog. Spring along the top of the water. Remember now, think frog!"

Again, Candy put herself to the effort. Her body parts were

better coordinated this time but, after two leaps, again she came up coughing.

"Don't breathe in," instructed Dobbin. "Remember what I told you last night. Cardinal rule. Don't breathe in when your face is underwater." He stopped and thought a moment. "Perhaps I should be teaching you how to blow bubbles. You put your face in the water, like this, and then you just blow bubbles out of your mouth. You lift your face out of the water, take in a deep breath, put your face back in and blow bubbles."

For several minutes they practiced blowing bubbles. "I think I can do that," said Candy.

"Very well, then. That's what you do when you're leaping about like a frog. When your face goes into the water, blow out bubbles. Then when you need to take a breath, lift your head up and breathe in. To lift your torso so that you can take a breath, bring your arms under you and scoop the water back and up."

"Okay."

"Right. So now we put it together."

Candy did not do so well this turn. In trying to blow bubbles, she forgot what her hands and legs should be doing. Again, Dobbin helped her back onto her feet. She looked so woebegone, he had a sudden urge to take her in his arms and comfort her. He shook himself violently. When he spoke, his voice was stern. "You could do a head-up breast stroke, I suppose. Try leaping like a frog, but keep your head out of the water at all times."

Once again, Dobbin demonstrated the procedure. Once again, Candy was enthralled with his smoothness. She so admired coordinated physical movement. You can do it, she instructed herself. This was no different than dance class. The instructor demonstrated the movements and the students copied as best they could. When Dobbin arrived back on his feet beside her, she set her teeth into resolve position and, like a trooper, gave it her best shot. And lo and behold it worked! Not perfectly. But she was able to keep herself on the water's surface for a few strokes.

Dobbin was pleased. "You have good floatability," he pronounced. "Now, try to go four strokes."

At the same time as a new experience was taking place for Candy, something was also happening to Dobbin. Up until this moment, while he had been finding pleasure in Candy's efforts, his delight had been that of a concerned teacher when confronted with a student who is genuinely trying. He had not been emotionally involved in the procedure or in Candy. His thoughts had been on the mechanics of the exercise, on how to present the problem to the student in such a way as to make the student understand it and rise to the challenge of solving it. And he had had to make an effort to keep his mind from drifting off toward the negative dialectic.

Then something, like a shutter in his mind, clicked, quite unexpectedly, and in watching Candy, he felt a different kind of delight. A surge of feeling rushed out from his chest. The feeling only peripherally involved Candy's efforts, good-spirited as they were. Rather, he saw her truly, he sensed and encompassed her as a person. At this moment, she was without ego, which for Dobbin was a state of grace. He felt tenderness toward her, tenderness and pure unqualified joy.

"Wonderful," he said. "Do that again."

"You mean like this?"

"Yes. That's perfect."

Jack, on the shore, had been watching for several minutes. After ducking out of the berry patch, he had made his way through shrubs and trees onto the beach where the going was easier. He had gone only a short way when he saw two figures in the water, a man and a woman. He was pretty sure the man was Dobbin. Good, that meant that Candy would be alone at the house. As he neared the figures, he tried to make out who the other person was, perhaps some neighbour who lived along the beach or someone out camping for the weekend. He darted back into the trees. He did not want Dobbin to see him, call to him, invite him to join the swimming. He wanted as quickly as possible to get back to the house and Candy before the others returned from berry picking. Then, when he was alongside the figures, he heard a voice issue from the female, a tinkling musical voice. He recognized it as

Candy's. He crouched low behind a tree.

At this juncture, Candy was at her most miserable. She had tried and tried again. She just could not get the hang of it. She stood in a stooped posture with her hands clasped before her chest, her shoulders hunched forward, as though by compressing her body, by holding it tight, she might hold herself together. The baggy swimsuit added to her lack of definition.

Jack did not recognize the pert, cheerful, delectable and very sexy young woman whom he had brought here to seduce. With her hair plastered to her head he could see that she had an oddly shaped skull, flat at the back and pointed on top. She looked like something newly born, wet and wrinkled. Her attempts at swimming were comic. Watching Candy shivering with cold and consternation and defeat, Jack felt something rise up in him. It was as though a balloon was expanding in his chest, a balloon that might burst and in so doing cause him to cry out in anguish. It was a terrible terrible feeling. It was frightening. He could not control it. It was actually physically painful to feel this thing that he was feeling, whatever it was, for this pitiful creature whom he was seeing as if for the first time. He could not stand the feeling. Luckily, at that moment, there was a movement behind him. Looking sideways and down, he saw five perfect toes – five toes in perfect slanted alignment banded by a strap of leather, brown slender small toes each one tipped with red. He saw toes that were a work of art, perfect in themselves. He did not have to feel sorry for such toes. They demanded nothing from him. To view such detached perfection, after having just been wrenched by human imperfection, to Jack seemed a miracle. His head continued in an upward swing and his eyes encountered Pamela. She was crouched slightly and was peering through the trees. He had never been so glad to see anybody. He could have thrown his arms around her. She, or more correctly her toes, was his saviour. Her presence allowed him to push the painful balloon back down inside himself.

Pamela became aware of Jack's gaze. She glanced down at him. "Why are you looking at me like that?" she said.

"You're a damned attractive female." His dark eyes snapped. "Has anybody ever told you that? Of course they have. I remember at university how the guys chased you."

Since Pamela did not know quite what to make of such a remark coming from Jack of all people who had never made anything but impersonal and platonic comments to her in more than fifteen years, and since her heart was beating loudly in her ears at being so close to him, to cover up her confusion, she lifted her head toward the lake. "Who's that out there with Dobbin?" she asked.

"Dobbin?" said Jack, completely addled.

"Out there."

"Where?"

"There. One of the two people you've been watching for several minutes."

"Oh, Dobbin." Jack faced forward again.

"But who's that girl he's with?"

"My date," said Jack.

"I didn't recognize her in that awful costume."

"Looks like it came out of the rag bag Sylvia keeps in the closet," said a voice behind them. Both Jack and Pamela turned their heads quickly to see Michael. He was standing, stretching his neck and squinting through the trees.

"It's Jack's date," said Pamela cheerfully. Now that she was obsessed with Jack, she no longer cared what Dobbin did. Oh maybe she cared just a little bit. Maybe she thought that there he was out there with his white complexion getting redder by the minute without her around to tell him to wear sunscreen and not to stay out too long. He wasn't even wearing his hat! Well, let him get sunburn! Let him get sunstroke! But it was just as well that Dobbin would be kept busy with Candy. She intended keeping busy with Jack. But what about Jack's pursuit of Candy? For a moment her heart plunged, but just in time, before it hit bottom, she remembered that Jack was never terribly serious about his girlfriends. Anyway, she'd think about that tomorrow. Right now, she was so elated she didn't care. She was willing to let everybody love everybody. Jack had told her that she was attractive. Her heart was singing.

"I didn't recognize her with her hair like that," Michael said. "What in the world is Dob doing with her?"

"Teaching her to swim."

"Can't she swim? After the skinny-dipping last night I assumed she could swim."

"Skinny-dipping?" inquired Jack.

"She and Dob. Last night. Didn't you know?"

"With Dobbin?"

"Yes, Dobbin."

"I don't believe it. Dobbin?"

"We came upon them, during our walk. After you got lost."

"What's she doing out there cavorting around in that old bag looking ridiculous?" snapped Jack. He could not believe that he had ever been attracted to this miserable looking person, that only a few minutes ago the thought of bedding her had filled him with desperate desire.

"You sound upset," said Michael.

"Of course I'm not upset. Why would I be upset?"

"Maybe you don't like Dob teaching her to swim."

"Don't be ridiculous. Why should I care who teaches her to swim? But one does expect a certain sense of decorum from one's date when one is presenting her to one's old best friends. And why would anyone come to the lake for the weekend and not bring a bathing suit?"

"Makes sense if you don't swim."

"Why would anyone not know how to swim?"

"Lots of people don't know how to swim."

"Everyone I know knows how to swim."

"They also know how to play tennis, golf, soccer, squash. They also jog and do aerobics. This girl is a breath of fresh air."

"People who don't exercise are disgusting."

"She's a dancer. She exercises all day long."

"That isn't exercise. That's her job."

"Anyway, looks to me like she wants to learn. What more

can you ask?"

"It's ludicrous."

"How can learning to swim be ludicrous?"

"It's not the learning to swim. It's that get-up."

"Oh come off it. I've got an idea. Let's go up to the house and get our suits and we'll all go for a swim."

"I don't feel like going for a swim," pouted Jack.

"Since when have you not wanted to go for a swim?" queried Michael.

"Lots of times."

"You're sulking. I don't believe it."

"I'm not sulking. I don't have to feel like going for a swim."

"I'm sure your young lady is not attracted to Dob. I mean, that's *Dobbin*!"

She's not my young lady. She's only the part-time office girl. I was doing her a favour. A weekend in the country."

"I thought she was a dancer."

"She is a dancer. But dancer's are always starving. I gave her a job." Jack suddenly stood up. "I'm going up to the house to get my swim suit."

"You're going swimming?"

"Yes."

"Just a minute ago you weren't having anything to do with swimming."

"I've changed my mind." Jack turned and started walking briskly toward the house.

"I'll go along with you." Pamela hurried after.

"Don't leave me behind," said Michael.

The three friends scrambled up the path to the house. When the path came out of the trees and widened, the two men fell into step either side of Pamela. Pamela, walking beside Jack, was happy. Above them the trees formed a lacy green canopy. From a high branch, a robin trebled an uplifting melody. Beside the pathway, lilacs bloomed, filling the air with fragrance, overwhelming Pamela with a sense of well being. What a beautiful wonderful day! she thought. She would always remember this day, the day her eyes had been opened, the day she had looked through leafy branches and known the true meaning of love. Michael was on her other side. She would have to do something about Michael, especially after his remark of last night about leaving Sylvia. She would have to tell him that it was over between them, not that there was much to be over, since they had not had a real affair, just occasional meetings. But they had enjoyed each other's company. They had had a few good times together. Certainly, at no time had she thought that their relationship was permanent. The only reason she had not broken it off before this was that she did not want to hurt his feelings. This new thing with Jack would make it easier, indeed, would make it necessary. Perhaps she would tell Michael later today, perhaps this evening after dinner. Or tomorrow. Maybe tomorrow. That way the evening would not be spoiled. Yes, she would tell him tomorrow morning. Before or after I tell Dobbin? she asked herself. Before, she decided. She'd tell Michael before breakfast and Dobbin after breakfast.

Having that settled and entered into her mental daytimer, she could relax and enjoy the rest of today.

PART FOUR

A PICNIC IN THE GRASS

i

They stayed in the water a long time. It was a perfect day –
cloudless sky, slumbering hills, serene forests, white sails drifting
lazily. The water was clear and sparkling, warmed by the sun,
without ripple except for the occasional wake of a motorboat.
Michael, Pamela and Jack swam far out into the lake.

Candy, standing tentatively in shallow water in her baggy
bathing costume, watched them start out. Pamela, who had
appeared in a form-fitting, navy blue suit similar to those worn by
swim teams, quickly dove in and set to it. Her strokes were sure
and efficient, used to greatest advantage to slice her body cleanly
through the water.

Then there was Jack. Candy tried not to notice him but she
could not avoid doing so since his *Nautica* swim trunks strutted
directly into her line of vision. She tried not to be impressed by
his caramel-coloured muscled legs and torso, by the patch of dark
hair on his chest. She liked hairy chests. She couldn't help it.
Even if she didn't like him. As she might have supposed, Jack
was a strong energetic swimmer, driving his body through the water
as though he were attacking a patient's tooth with his dental drill.

Michael, also true to form, swam with a great deal of dash
and splash as if to say, 'look at me, look at me.' This manner,
however, was habit rather than a display of his current attitude.
For, ever since hearing about his friends' plight, Michael was a
changed man. He had forgotten about the spotlight and being the
centre of attention, or at least he had put it on the back burner of
his mind for the present. His thoughts were too full of Dobbin and

Pamela to leave room for himself. Even on his way into the water, while crossing the sand, he forgot to expect that everyone was watching him. He forgot to impress Candy with his cartwheels and somersaults, his finning in circles and upside down. Michael's approach to swimming was like his approach to everything else. It was all a game, a bag of tricks, and anyone who thought it was more than that was only kidding himself. But today he immediately set out, following the other two. And while he swam, he attempted to sort things out. He still had not managed to catch Pam alone to tell her that they should no longer see each other in *that* way. He must accomplish that mission as soon as possible. But what if his breaking off with her was not enough? What if it did not change her mind about getting rid of Dob? Michael was convinced that the two still cared for each other. After all, they were Dob and Pam, his oldest friends. The marriage needed a shot of adrenalin. Whose did not? Romance, that was the thing. Thoughts of the glade popped into Michael's mind. Last evening, with the balmy air, the moon and the stars, it had been a perfect romantic spot. Tonight promised more of the same cooperation from the heavens. There was to be a full moon. Sylvia, who knew everything there was to know about moons, had said so. As Michael's brain started to formulate a devious plan, his splashing took on a merry tone. Tonight he would convince Pamela to meet him in the glade. Only, instead of him showing up, Dobbin would show up. Let the moon and the stars and the magic of a summer night do the rest. But how to get Dobbin there? Dobbin was not the sort to go traipsing off into the woods to have a rendezvous with anyone, let alone his wife. Well, he'd solve that problem somehow. For now, he might as well enjoy the rest of his swim.

When the group arrived back at the house, everyone ravenously hungry, they quickly changed out of wet bathing suits and convened in the kitchen. But where was lunch? Where was Sylvia? Candy hovered. Jack paced, lightly on his toes like a boxer. Dobbin stood irresolute, large and immovable, near the doorway. Michael perceived that he would have to do something. He would commission dependable Pam. Whatever was she doing standing in the middle of the kitchen with that stunned cow look on her face? Usually she was at the forefront, like a camp leader directing activities. "What should we do?" he appealed to her.

"I don't know," she answered, dreamily.

Michael could not believe his ears. Were those words coming out of Pam's mouth, emerging from between the lips of a woman who could take charge of every situation, or thought she could?

"What's in the fridge?" said Candy, who was used to dining impromptu wherever she happened to find herself. In her social circle, when people were hungry they simply opened the fridge door of whoever's flat they were in and extracted whatever was handy.

"Quite right," said Michael, doing a slow shuffle around the room. In the confusion of the moment, he forgot where the refrigerator was, or, more accurately, he could not remember where he was, at the country house or the town house. Candy stepped forward and swung wide the fridge door. She held it open while he rummaged inside. "Here," his voice emerged muffled from the interior. "This looks like potato salad. And here are cold cuts." He handed the items back to where they were taken up by an assembly line which had formed from fridge to counter.

"Are you sure Sylvia hasn't planned this for dinner?" asked Dobbin, having been married long enough to be apprehensive of interfering with a woman's menu plan.

"She wouldn't give us cold cuts for dinner," said Michael with great confidence. "She must have meant this for lunch."

"Perhaps we should wait a little longer..."

"You wait if you want. I'm starved. So's Candy. Aren't you Candy?" Michael handed her a jar of pickles.

"I am, a little," said Candy who thought she would faint if she didn't get some food into her stomach, having been immersed in frigid water for two hours and not having eaten breakfast.

"Sylvia won't mind," said Michael, straightening, kicking the fridge door shut with the toe of one beach sandal. Arms laden with yet more cold cuts, lettuce, tomatoes, cheese, butter, and mayonnaise, resembling a Dagwood cartoon, he staggered to the kitchen counter. Candy had found bread and buns in a tin and, although Dobbin had a little trouble making the leap, they all, even Jack, bent to the task of assembling a variety of sandwiches. As for Dobbin, the sight of the food caused his salivary glands to activate and it occurred to him that if he joined in he could snack as he worked.

Pamela was the only one who appeared unsure of how to proceed. It seemed that she did not know how to pick up a knife and butter a bun. What's wrong with the woman? wondered Michael, who did not usually wonder about anyone because he was too busy wondering about himself. But that was the old Michael. The new Michael thought that she must have had too much sun.

As the little group formed a jolly troupe of slicing, slathering, stacking and cutting, Candy so forgot herself that she slapped Dobbin's hand as he reached for an end of tomato. "You'll spoil your appetite," she said, smiling provocatively, or what Jack deemed provocatively.

Jack was standing the other side of Dobbin so that he was privy to all facial expressions which Candy tossed in that direction. And while he no longer cared what she did, especially since he had truly seen Pamela's toes, he had brought her here and the least she could do was refrain from making a fool of herself and him.

Dobbin, however, did not think Candy's manner unsuitable. Rather, he thought it delightful. A delightful, charming child, thought he, for it was impossible for Dobbin's mind to take the low road, to think of this child in a lewd fashion or even in terms of a romantic involvement. At the same time, he was discovering that being around her was a joyful experience.

Pamela did not notice the glance and was scarcely aware of the remark. She was standing to the side stacking sandwiches on a platter, having been assigned that job because she was not being much good at anything else. She had been bleeding on the food because she had cut her finger, which was now wrapped in tissue since Sylvia was the only one who knew where the bandaids were. She was taking directions from the others, without so much as a discussion about it, cheerfully doing what she was told. Michael could not fathom this change in her. Was it because of her decision to break up with Dobbin? Suddenly, he wanted the old grouchy Pam back.

They trooped outside with the lunch. Pamela was given the cloth to spread on the grass, the consensus being that she could not do too much damage if assigned that task. The others set down their bowls and platters and plates and cutlery and then themselves. Without preamble, they fell to the task at hand, grunting their approval as the food hit their taste buds. They tipped up steins of icy, foamy beer, the glass dripping with rivulets of condensation. The new Michael could not do enough for his guests. Instead of plunking himself into the middle of the picnic and seeing to his needs before those of anyone else, he tended to his company as though he were the footman. He hovered at the edge of the cloth, as if he were waiting in the wings for his cue. Could he fetch more sandwiches? Could he get anyone another cold beer?

"Sit down," Jack ordered. "You're making me nervous."

They ate and they drank, their voices and laughter mingling in the still air of the summer afternoon, until they fell back satiated. For a few moments, all was silent. Then, someone thought to wonder, "Where's Sylvia. Can she still be picking berries?"

"Yes," said Michael, who thought he knew his wife. "Sylvia *could* still be picking berries. She envisions quarts of the things gleaming like jewels on cellar shelves, or perfect gems in freezer bags. Bless her bourgeois hausfrau heart."

"I'd hardly describe Sylvia as being bourgeois," Dobbin spoke as though he had given the matter considerable thought. "She's a musician."

"She's very artistic," agreed Pamela.

"Can't one be bourgeois and artistic at the same time?" questioned Michael.

"It is unusual."

"Although many artists have emerged from the middle class," stated Dobbin.

"If she was bourgeois, would she have married an actor?" said Jack.

"She's certainly taken to this back-to-earth-and-nature thing," said Michael.

"Maybe she wants to live the artist's life," said Pamela.

"What's that like?" said Jack.

"You know. *La Bohème.* Wine, women, song. Or in her case, men and song."

"If you mean free sex, everyone lives like an artist nowadays," said Jack.

"A bourgeois existence is not incompatible with an artist's life. Bach is an example. Good steady family man," said Dobbin, who was sitting with his back curled into the tree trunk, legs stretched before him. He was dressed in a fresh blue plaid shirt and walking shorts of the British military variety.

"He was an exception."

"Name another."

"Yes do."

Their picnic was in the shade of the fanning branches of the elm tree. The cloth, a splash of bright yellows and reds on the green, was cluttered with the remains of the meal – mustard-stained plates, crumpled flowered napkins, a bowl empty except for scattered bits of red and green. The company, having consumed a good deal of food and beer, lay sprawled about in various attitudes. Stomachs digesting, senses dulled, they rested from the activity of eating, the exertions of the morning, and the enervating effects of an inordinate amount of sun and exercise.

"Nothing bad could possibly have happened to Sylvia," commented Pamela in a distracted tone due to the nearness of Jack. She was wearing a sleeveless pale green pyjama-type outfit, presumably Sylvia's, which she had found in the spare room closet. Because it was two sizes larger than what she usually wore, it was rather voluminous and gave to her a buoyant quality.

At the moment, she was sitting with knees drawn up and legs folded to one side, leaning on her arm and hand. Because her hair took on a natural curl when it was damp, her face was framed with soft fluffy hair. Ordinarily, she brushed and blow-dried her hair into straightness, but today, after she had towelled it, she looked in the mirror and was delighted with her new tender look. Following that, the denim pants she was about to don did not seem appropriate either to her hair or to her frame of mind. She wanted to be attractive to Jack. Evidently, she had achieved her goal, for he, stretched out on the grass beside her, was paying her a great deal of attention. Dobbin had not noticed her dress or her hair, but she no longer noticed him not noticing.

"Not on a day like today," she continued. "Nothing unpleasant could happen today."

"She's with that Robb fellow," came from Michael, who was lying flat on his back, looking up at the startling colour combination of blue blue sky and bright green elm leaves.

"Who is that guy anyway?" questioned Jack.

"The neighbour with the berries," answered Pamela.

"The playwright," said Michael. "He'll take care of her. He has a crush on her."

Jack moved his hand so that it collided with Pamela's.

On the other side of Pamela was Candy, looking like a newborn orange-feathered chick with her face clean of makeup and her hair fluffed and sticking straight out around her head and already dried in the sun. She was sitting cross-legged and erect in shorts and tube top. She was smiling. She was thinking about the swimming lesson and her achievement, the way that achievement had given her confidence and brought her out of herself, the way she had escaped from herself. She was thinking about the person who had made it happen, such a nice kind man.

"Sylvia loses all track of time when she gets into nature," said Michael, lifting his knees into a bent position because the dry grass was tickling the backs of his bare legs. "The way she's taken to all this gardening and cluck clucking the hens, it's unbelievable." Truth to tell, he was a little surprised at Sylvia's absence. It was not like her to disregard guests. It was not like her to forget about their meals. She was usually overly conscientious about such things. And so, as he half dozed in the droning heat of the early afternoon, the thought lingered in his mind, Where *is* Sylvia?

Robb, looking out his window, noticed that something was wrong with Michael. The afternoon, hazy with heat, was like a scene filmed through gauze over the camera lens. Was that why Michael appeared so different? Oh, he looked the same, same hairy brown legs emerging from khaki shorts and ending in sandals. Same shapeless hat he liked to wear in summer. Same virile good looks. But there was something wrong with his acting. He was not acting like Michael. He was not jostling for place on centre stage. He was at the edge of the picture, undefined. And he was not pairing up with either Candy or Pamela.

Robb frowned. This new Michael did not fit into his plan. This new Michael might appeal to Sylvia. Robb had a bad moment until the arrival of an inspired thought. The new Michael was not permanent! He was acting the role of a generous thoughtful human being to get himself out of a jam, to restore Pamela and Dobbin's marriage and thus get rid of Pamela so that he could romance Candy. But something was wrong with Pamela, also. She was acting in an absurd manner unlike herself, and it seemed to have something to do with Jack. Jack and Pamela? Give me a break, thought Robb. A more unlikely pairing, he could not imagine, unless it was Candy and Dobbin. And what of Candy? Even though things were rapidly deteriorating between her and Jack, she was not at all attracted to Michael. She could not be counted on to keep him busy and/or add fuel to the flame of Sylvia's suspicions. It crossed Robb's mind that, for the advancement of his own situation, he'd better keep a careful eye on these characters and what they were up to. Then he heard Sylvia's voice and he forgot everything else.

"Oh, what are they doing?" She was standing a little behind

him. She did not want anyone to know that she was at her neighbour's, although, as Robb had assured her more than once in the last hour, superman vision would have been required to spot her across the distance and through the walls.

Her head darted around his shoulder and back again. "I can't look. Tell me."

"They've taken care of themselves."

"Really?" She sounded a little disappointed. Again, she glanced around Robb's shoulder. This time, she did not pull her head back quite as quickly. "Is that my good crystal out there on the grass? Oh, I must go."

"But you haven't finished your tea." Robb turned and took her hand and led her back to the table. Sylvia in dishabille, hair loosed and untidy, lipstick smudged, shirt and slacks not quite together, he thought more charming, if possible, than ever before.

They were drinking a special tea made from hibiscus, rose hips, blackberry leaves and lemon grass. Robb had explained the restorative powers of such a tea. "I've just about finished," Sylvia replied.

"Here, have some more." He pushed her gently down onto a chair. "And you were eating an apple and cheese. You said you like that brie cheese."

"I do." She rose. "It's just that I really must be getting back to my guests."

"They don't seem to be suffering." Robb did not want to say, 'they seem to be managing without you,' however much that appeared to be the state of things.

"Still, they'll wonder where I am." She started back to the window.

Robb followed her. "How about cherries? I have a whole bowl full of cherries."

"No thanks. I'm really quite full. What with the biscuits and the greengages. I do hope they found the potato salad." She tried to see across the distance.

"I'm sure they did. Here, have a look." Robb set down the cherries and picked up the field glasses from their place on the window ledge where they were kept for immediate easy access.

"Thank you."

"This little knob here adjusts them." Robb had to put his arm around Sylvia's shoulder to show her how it was done.

"Yes, that's better. I can see everything. I can see their faces. These must be very good glasses. Yes, they do have the potato salad. I see the empty bowl. But I don't see the jellied salad. I made a lime pear jellied salad. I don't see it on the cloth."

"They'll survive without lime pear jellied salad."

"I suppose you're right. But when will I serve it?"

"You can serve it with dinner."

"No, I can't. It won't go with barbecued beef."

"You and Michael can eat it next week."

"Michael hates jellied salad."

"Give it to me. I love jellied salad," Robb lied, at the same time thinking, I'll find something to do with jellied salad. "Look," he advised, "let them take care of themselves. They *are* adults." At least physically, he thought, but again kept the sentiment to himself.

Sylvia was not being her calm relaxed self. Like Michael she was acting in a strange manner, but hers was due to receiving two equally opposite directives from her feelings. She wanted to go home and be with her guests. She did not want to go home because she felt so guilty about her dallying. She could not at this moment face her friends. Looking rumpled and tumbled about as she knew she did, she could not walk across that space with them all sitting there, all turning their heads toward her with inquiring looks. Even though all she had done was give in to a little spooning, well, and maybe a little fondling, she was appalled at herself. She would go beet red. She had not gone beet red for at least ten years but as an adolescent going beet red had been the bane of her existence. She knew the signs leading up to the condition, a state of great discomfort, a feeling that she was not in control of her emotions. And if she went beet red, they would know that she had been doing something that she should not have been doing and would guess that she had been doing even more than she had been doing.

Still, she could not stay at Robb's forever. Sometime, she would have to cross that space. She would have to face them. But perhaps not all at once, went her thought. If they would finish lunch, if they would go into the house or off to other pastimes, then she could go home. "Surely, they're not going to stay out there in the heat all afternoon!" she exclaimed, more to herself than to Robb. "Oh, maybe they are. Now Jack's girlfriend is chasing butterflies. She has that old butterfly net. Michael must have found it for her. I haven't seen that thing for ages. She's very attractive, isn't she – the way she dashes about, the way she leaps and floats? And Dobbin has jumped up and is leaping around after her. I'm afraid he looks more like the goat. Oh, she's caught something. Dobbin seems to be explaining to her what it is. I hope they let it go."

"They will," said Robb, who was also watching the butterfly catchers, although without the benefit of glasses. However, since his vision was excellent, he could still make out the gist of things.

"How do you know?"

"What else would you do with a butterfly?"

"Some people pin them to boards."

"Not these people."

"They've turned the net over... although it seems stunned... they're joggling it a bit... there, Dobbin has given it a nudge with his finger... it's coming to life... it's moving... it's lifting its wings. That girl, Candy, she's waving her hand at it. Goodbye, goodbye, she seems to be saying. There it goes. I'm imagining it's one of those yellow butterflies with amber-tipped wings. There's a lot of them around here. They flutter so prettily. Fly, fly away, little butterfly, she seems to be saying. Something has happened to that girl." Sylvia was still peering through the glasses.

"Who?"

"Jack's girl. Candy. Now she's dancing on the grass, whirling and leaping. Look how she lands so lightly. She's so graceful."

"She *is* a dancer."

"And now she's taken Dobbin's hand and he's dancing, too.

They're going around together in a circle." Sylvia watched a moment through the glasses. "She seems changed. Different than when she arrived yesterday. Different than this morning."

"How do you mean?"

"I don't know. Different. She scarcely said a word last night at dinner."

"She didn't know anyone yesterday. Perhaps she was shy."

"And yet she went swimming in the nude with Dobbin."

"Some people are uninhibited about their bodies. It's their minds that defeat them."

"I expect you're right. And how can I know what she's like since I only met her yesterday? She seems to be having a good time now."

"Yes."

"With Dobbin of all people. I've never seen Dobbin so energetic, rather like a *young* goat. I hope Jack doesn't mind."

"He doesn't appear to mind. He's not even looking at them. He's turned away from them, leaning on his elbow, looking in the opposite direction, it appears at Pamela. But don't you wonder about Pamela? That she might mind?"

"Pamela? What should she mind?"

"Dobbin prancing about with that girl."

"No one would ever mind Dobbin. He's so... he's so Dobbin."

"Anyway, they've stopped."

"They've flung themselves on the grass. And now the others are gathering up the picnic. It's over. They're going in." Sylvia turned and handed the glasses to Robb. "Now, I must go."

He put the glasses down on the window ledge and turned to her. "Stay awhile longer. I'll open some wine."

"I couldn't. Really, I can't." Sylvia broke away abruptly and went toward the door.

"Champagne. I have some on ice," said Robb running after.

"I must feed the chickens."

"Don't go."

"I must practice my music."

"Wait."

"I won't hear another word." Sylvia's voice was light, tremulous.

"All right, but you must promise to see me again. Tonight." Robb's voice was also light, and slightly theatrical, somewhat in the manner of a blithe spirit.

"I couldn't."

"You must."

"I can't."

"How can you say that? How can you ignore this thing that has happened between us? You can't stop something like this. This is bigger than both of us. You must see me tonight. Leave your door unlocked."

"What about Michael?"

"When he's out cavorting in the woods."

"How do you know he'll be out cavorting in the woods?"

"I don't. I just thought... it's the full moon isn't it? Isn't he a full moon nut?"

"No, that's me. You must not come to the house... the others..."

"Meet me, then. Later, after dinner. Pretend you're going to bed. No one will know."

"Oh, I don't know. I'm so confused."

"You owe it to yourself to explore this miracle. Otherwise, you'll wonder, we'll both wonder, for the rest of our lives, we'll wonder. You owe it to us. You'll never know..."

"Oh for heaven's sakes." Sylvia's voice lowered a couple of notches. "All right." She reached out a hand for the door.

"Promise?"

"Promise. As long as you promise to be good."

"I'm always good."

"You know what I mean. We'll meet to talk, talk only."

"Of course. What else?"

"And only for a few minutes."

"Only a few minutes."

"Where then?"

"The glade."

"Glade?"

"You know it," said Rob. "You told me about it, about finding it, in the spring."

"Oh yes, I know the one you mean."

"Meet me there as soon as you can get away."

"I can't promise when."

"I'll wait."

"I'll try. But something might happen..."

"I'll be there waiting. All night if necessary."

"Good-bye."

"Au revoir."

Sylvia burst from Robb's back door, ran down the steps and along the path through the trees. It was only when she reached her own back door that she remembered her berry picking hat. Worse still, she'd completely forgotten the berries.

THE AFTERNOON NAP

ii

Upstairs in the Davenport Suite, as Sylvia had jokingly referred to the guest room which boasted Pamela and Dobbin as its first customers, a conversation was taking place.

"You're red as a lobster," Pamela was saying.

"Perhaps I did overdo it," Dobbin responded.

"You're going to peel."

"As usual." Dobbin was lying on the bed studying his chest. A pile of students' papers lay beside him. In his left hand he held one of the papers, in his right a red marking pen, which blended perfectly with his skin tone.

Pamela was sitting in a wing chair near the window filing her nails. She looked up across her poised hands at Dobbin, but instead of her customary annoyed look when he did something stupid, her regard was one of concern. Her typical comment on such occasions was something to the tune of, 'You'd think someone with a PhD in Hegelian ethics, a postdoc in Marxist theory, learned articles in all the current prestigious philosophy journals would have the sense he was born with and stay out of the sun when he has the famous Davenport delicate complexion.' What, in fact, came out of her mouth was, "Maybe there's some cream or lotion in the bathroom cabinet. I'll have a look."

She put down her nail file and, still in Sylvia's drapery that she had donned for the picnic, swished out of the room. After much rattling of bottles and jars from the bathroom across the hall, then the closing of a cupboard door, she appeared in the bedroom doorway. "I found some lotion," she said, crossing the room toward the bed, opening the jar top as she moved. "Lie on your stomach," she directed in a manner that was modified from the usual ninety per cent efficiency and ten per cent human kindness to the extent of emerging as a direct inverse of that manner.

Pamela perched herself on the edge of the bed and looked at the considerable area of burned skin that was Dobbin's back. She set to her task. In the past, when he went out in the sun without protection, she had felt only exasperation. Would he never learn? Did he expect that she would always be there to apply lotion? To complicate matters, she was slightly repulsed at having to touch other people's damaged or diseased skin. Her distaste for this sort of physical contact was one of the deciding factors in her decision to go into the administration area of health care. But today she slathered the cool cream on Dobbin's blistering skin with the tenderness and mercy of a saint tending a leper. She did not mind the most humble of tasks, the most menial of labours, for she was doing it with love in her heart. In soothing Dobbin's pain, in alleviating his distress, she was easing the pain and distress of mankind. Because of the love she felt for Jack, her heart opened to everything and everybody. All God's creatures, including Dobbin, deserved her consideration, her pity, her love. Poor Dobbin, she thought, he can't help it if he's a fool.

As for the fool, he was suspended in a haze of sensual pleasure. He considered the possibility of promoting the circling motion of his wife's cool fingertips on his back into something more, but he was not sure that he was up to it with inflamed skin covering half of his body. Better forget it for the moment. Focus on something else. The negative dialectic. That was what he was trying to work out this weekend. That, along with, of course, participating in his friends' celebration of their new house, was the purpose of this trip, to give him a change of scene, a change of pace, so that he could gather his thoughts, so that he could renew his mental stamina. He must have his thought on a subject clear before he could present it with clarity to an audience and expect them to understand. To start with he would present the bipolar position. Then he would demonstrate that such a position was simplistic. They would discuss Marx's dialectical materialism, history as a dialectic, action and reaction, reaction as a foregone conclusion. They would talk about the intervention of other factors so that, as it turned out, the reaction could not be predictable. He would promote a discussion that was meant to conclude that the starting position was faulty, that polarizing the working class and the bourgeoisie was too simple, that there were any number of exceptions, of crossovers, of things not being what they seemed. He might use the example of Iago's 'I am not what I am.' To help his students understand a concept, he often used examples from literature and film, especially film. Young people nowadays could relate to audio and visual much better than they could to written text. And yes, *Othello* was an excellent example. It presented so many metaphors of extreme opposites, black versus white, isolated port versus mainland. It illustrated the constant flux between appearance and reality.

And so Dobbin ran with his idea, feeling the joy and exhilaration he always felt when he caught one out of the air, like a football hero who runs with the ball tucked under his arm and never wants to stop, not even when he makes it to the goal post.

When was the joy of his idea replaced by a joy of a physical nature? When did thoughts of the young lady enter his mind? He could not have answered the question. All he knew was that at some point his mind got away on him. Perhaps it was the soft cloud of sensuality in which he was drifting, perhaps it was that thoughts of Iago had led to thoughts of Desdemona, but several minutes later he came to the realization that he had been thinking of dancing on the grass, more specifically he had been thinking of the young lady dancing on the grass. After they had freed the butterfly, she had thrown down the net. Swirling and soaring, she had seemed a fundamental expression of life and movement. She had grabbed his hand, he was hesitant at first, but then she took his other hand and they skipped and pranced to the same inner music, so that they were in tune, in rhythm, in perfect accord. He had felt lifted, lifted. He, Dobbin, had felt as if he were flying.

Hold on. Hold on, Dobbin caught himself. What are you thinking, foolish man? Harness your thought and rein it in. You were going to use the example of Othello. Iago as evil which appears good, Desdemona as good which appears evil to Othello – an example that was clear, that his students would relate to... but something else was nagging at his mind. It was as though something or someone was knocking on his brain, demanding entry. That young woman again. Well, all right, if you insist, Dobbin instructed himself. Think about her, think it through, then file it away and get on with Monday's lecture.

Dobbin knew that he had had a delightful time teaching the young lady to swim and showing her how to wield the butterfly net. When they had let the creature go, he was aware that they had shared an important moment. Together they had felt a particular thrill as the yellow wings spread and fluttered away into the bright day. Such was the life of a teacher. A good teacher shared many such moments with his students. A good teacher was pleased at the progress of a student, a good teacher took pleasure in the student's learning experience rather than in his own teaching experience. So if he felt satisfaction about the day, it was all right. It was the satisfaction of a teacher when his student has come to a new understanding. And yet... in the kitchen, standing next to her... he could still smell her vanilla smell, he could feel her small brown shoulder against his bare arm. The touch had caused something like an electric jolt to flash through his nervous system, something that was almost like a pain. He had moved his arm away, quickly. Still, he recalled her shoulder vividly.

Again, Dobbin arrested himself from his dreaming. The young lady had done very well today with the swimming. One more lesson and she would have it, at least a good bit of it. Perhaps they would have time tomorrow morning before breakfast, or even later today. The light lasted now until late evening. And it was certainly warm enough. Might he suggest such a tryst? He was momentarily alarmed that he had used such a word in his thinking. He told himself that he was being ironic. The word, in fact, simply meant an appointed meeting. Yes, he would suggest it. And with this decision, it seemed to Dobbin that a weight was lifted from him. He felt light, as light as when he had gambolled on the grass with the butterflies.

As Dobbin drifted in and out of his dreaming, Pamela, who was back in the wing chair applying fresh red polish to her toenails, became a dim outline. And when he let himself be carried heavenward with the butterflies, he lost sight of her completely.

Candy stretched her shapely bare legs from thigh bone to toe tip. It was blissful to stretch, to relax, to be by herself. She had had an exciting day, a busy day, with no time to think. Now she wanted to reflect on things. What had happened? Staring up at the flowered wallpaper on the slanted ceiling, she listened to the silence of the old house. Where was everyone? Were they all napping? No wonder, in this heat! She was saved only by that wonderful breeze coming through the window.

Candy felt good. She, with Dobbin's help, had freed the butterfly. In that act there was significance, as though by freeing the butterfly she had freed herself. But her preparation for freedom had started before that. It had started before she jumped up out of the circle on the grass and grabbed the spotlight, before she helped make lunch. When they were in the kitchen, the *thing* was already loosening, the thing that held her in its grip and would not allow her to be herself, the thing that pushed her into that terrible silence that was like invisibility. Her wariness of the others was already loosening because she had learned to swim today. Yes, the start of it was the swimming lesson. Without that, she would not have stepped into centre stage in the kitchen, she would not have danced with butterflies on the grass. The swimming lesson had instigated her wet struggle out of her cocoon, the unfolding of her damp wings, her free flight.

And when, after watching the butterfly flutter up and away into the trees, she had returned to the group, she had not returned to her silence. What had happened, starting in the lake and developing in the kitchen and during the picnic and being completed with her dance on the grass, was that she had lost her self-consciousness. And then she had become so excited about... not about chasing the butterfly, no, not that, but about the freedom of the activity itself, she had forgotten herself. And because she forgot herself, she gave no thought to what the others thought of her, whether it was her high-heel sling backs and short leather skirt or her midnight skinny-dipping in the lake with a married man. She was outside their opinions, humming happily on her own, lost in her joy of being alive, of being able to dance.

Thinking these thoughts and watching the curtain at the window balloon and deflate with every fresh gust of air, Candy's eyes glazed over and closed. Her long lashes nestled into the delicate hollows above her cheekbones. When they lifted again, suddenly, sharply, it was in response to a knock on her door.

At that moment, Jack was also flat on his back, on a lounge chair on the grass near to where the picnic had taken place. He had taken off his shirt to make the most of the sun's rays. On his chest, little flecks of copper glinted amidst black swirls of hair. An open magazine was propped over his face. He appeared to be asleep, ankles relaxed, toes pointed outward. But even though his eyes were closed his mind was alert. He was thinking about Candy or, more rightly, he was thinking about Pamela. Strange how things happened. He'd never really seen Pamela before. It had taken Candy's tackiness to make him appreciate Pamela's classiness. This afternoon, he had turned from the flawed Candy and seen the flawless Pamela. He had turned away from the dancing and Candy making a spectacle of herself. The fact that Dobbin was encouraging her did not alleviate the situation. Dobbin would encourage anybody. That was why he was so good at his job. It was Candy who should show some restraint in the company of his friends. Why he had brought the girl – she could almost be his daughter – here in the first place was an enigma to him. But he had not seen her before, really seen her. He had not seen that she had no class, that she was not his style. He liked smart, slick, sophisticated lookers, bright but not intelligent, whose conversations were lively with the latest jargon and buzz phrases. His type was definitely not this fluffy-haired child who said gee and gosh, who in her wake left a swath of untidy debris – handbags, hair clips, sunglasses, chewing gum wrappers, earrings, as well as something that was difficult to pin down, something like a scent. But it was not perfume or lotions. What she conveyed wherever she passed and left behind had something to do with the very molecules of her being.

For a moment, Jack let himself drift in the uncertain territory of Candy's molecules. Then he shook himself back to the here and now. Whatever it was that she projected, he had not known about it when he had invited her to spend the weekend with him. He had been an idiot over her shapely ass and her long dancer's legs.

As for Pamela, she had been there all this time, in front of his eyes, and he had failed to see her because they were such old friends. Perhaps, he had deliberately not seen her because she was Dobbin's wife. He had strict rules about other men's wives. But now, for some strange reason, he did not care about that. It was as though he was in a dream or under a spell. Turning away from Candy, turning toward Pamela and looking at her as though for the first time, his eyes had been opened. He could not believe, Jack simply *could not* believe, lying here now on a lounge chair in the sun, that he had never before noticed Pamela's black hair and classical features, her wide mouth, her lively eyes. And her body – tall, slim, she could wear clothes like a model. Yes, there was no doubt about it. He had the hots for his old bud Pamela.

But what about Candy? What to do with her for the next twenty-four hours? Perhaps Michael would come to his rescue. Jack had noticed Michael's lascivious glances in Candy's direction when they had arrived yesterday. He had thought little of it at the time. It was Michael's way to go on the alert whenever any female who was not an absolute dog crossed his path. And, if Jack did not approve of Michael's methods since he was a married man, well, could he help it if things simply turned out that way? Who was he to tell people, Michael in particular, how to run their lives?

Yes, if Michael took Candy off his hands, thank you Michael.
Jack did not consider the possibility of Dobbin taking Candy
off his hands. He did not suspect for a moment that Dobbin might
be involved in anything further than swimming lessons. That Candy
could be interested in Dobbin was beyond consideration. That
Dobbin might be interested in anyone or anything other than the
negative dialectic or his wine formulae would have been
astonishing.

"What are you doing?"
"What are *you* doing?"
"Nothing."
"Are you going to lie down?"
"Yes... no. In a minute. I was wondering if I have enough
lettuce for the salad. Maybe I should go out and pick more lettuce."
"There's a huge bag of lettuce in the fridge."
"Is there? Oh, I must have picked it yesterday."
"Don't you remember whether or not you picked lettuce?"
"No, yes, of course I remember. It's just... did I pick enough?"
"You've got enough in the fridge to feed a warren of rabbits.
Why don't you lie down?" Michael patted the bedspread beside
him. In an effort to encourage Sylvia into thoughts of napping
so that he could tiptoe out to organize his scenario for the
midnight hour, he had stripped down to shorts and sandals. These
he had retained for quick and easy escape.
"Hmmm?"
"Lie down."
"I can't." Sylvia was rummaging in the night table drawer
for pen and paper. For nearly half an hour she had been opening
and closing drawers, rearranging items on shelves, pacing and
talking to herself. "I have so much to do," she carried on. "Why
don't you start your nap without me?"
What Sylvia wanted was a comatose Michael. She must
tell Robb that she could not meet him tonight. She must have
been insane to agree to a rendezvous. She was a married woman!
If Michael would go to sleep, she could quietly slip out and over

to Robb's.

"Now what are you doing? You sound like a gerbil."

Sylvia had found a piece of paper but she was still looking for a pen. "I have to make a list."

"Why are you so wound up?"

"What do you mean?" Sylvia brought her head up sharply. She looked directly at Michael, her eyes uncharacteristically challenging. "Don't lie on top of the bedspread."

Michael stood up from the bed. He took one long stride half way across the room and plunked himself onto a hard wooden chair.

"Oh yes. Be a martyr."

"I can't sit on the bed. I can't sit on the chair. Where shall I sit?"

"I didn't say don't sit on the bed."

"My ears must be deceiving me."

"I did not say that you can't sit on the bed. What I said was, pull back the spread. You know how that bedspread wrinkles."

Michael stood up abruptly and grabbed his blue plaid shirt from off a chair. He started putting it on.

"What are you doing now?"

"I'm going out."

"Why are you going out? Where are you going?"

"Some place where I can sit on the bedspread."

"Don't be silly. Come back here this minute and lie down and have a nap."

Michael turned at the door. This little quarrel was shaping things nicely into his hands. He had to get away from Sylvia's company. He had to get Pamela alone and suggest a rendezvous in the glade. Then he had to get Dobbin alone and suggest... something, he hadn't quite decided what, yet. All he had to do now was say something nasty and leave in a huff. But, no. That wouldn't do either. A distraught Sylvia would pace, would look out windows. An alert Sylvia knew everything that went on in her house. She kept track of activities, even of other people's thoughts, the same way she kept track of fridge contents. He must have her asleep, at least resting, with her antenna out of commission. "You need some time to yourself," he said.

"You don't know what I need," Sylvia accused. "You don't know anything about me." She slammed shut a drawer.

Michael was beginning to think that she was right. Either that, or Mars had just entered her sign – wasn't Mars the aggressive planet? However, he continued in the lower register, "I know how you get if you don't have time to yourself." Suddenly inspired, he continued. "Why don't you practice your music? You've been with other people all day."

"What is that crack supposed to mean?"

"It wasn't a crack. What's wrong with you?"

"Nothing's wrong with me. Why would anything be wrong with me?"

"I haven't the faintest notion. You seem upset, that's all."

"Are you accusing me of something?"

"Of course not. Although, come to think of it..."

"Talk about the pot calling the kettle black."

"This conversation is insane."

"Oh yes, when I say something it's insane. Yet you can say anything..."

"I haven't said anything."

"You know very well you made a snide remark about me being with Robb all day and neglecting my guests."

"I haven't even mentioned Robb."

"You don't have to. I know what you're thinking."

"I'm not thinking anything. Why would I be thinking something? What *have* you been up to?"

"There. You see."

"See what?"

"I won't stand for these accusations."

"What are we talking about?" Michael looked at his wife with dismay. Was she suffering from heat stroke? Sylvia never acted this way. Twisting the defensive into the offensive was his tactical manoeuvre.

"You have never acknowledged my existence," Sylvia raged

on.

"I married you, didn't I?"

"Oh, yes, big sacrifice. Thank you very much. That doesn't give you the right to tell me what to do. *You* say I'm tired. *You* say I need to lie down."

"I'm leaving." Michael turned the knob.

"And you didn't marry me. I married you! You didn't really want to marry me. You wanted me to move in with you. I was the one who insisted on getting married."

"This is irrelevant."

"So now our marriage is irrelevant."

"What I mean is... it's a done deal."

"It can be undone."

There was a long moment during which neither said a word. They were looking at each other with startled eyes. Sylvia was thinking, what have I said? With a few thoughtless words, she had disrupted the universe. How fragile was everything after all. How utterly fragile were the tenuous threads which held human lives together.

Michael was the first to move. He opened the door. "I'm going for a walk," he said. His voice was unusually quiet. "Down to the beach. I need to... think about a script I was reading." He grabbed up his hat and went out and closed the door softly behind him.

Sylvia waited only a few moments. She must go after him. She must take back her words. She ran to the door. She turned the knob and pushed. But what was this! Michael's blue plaid shirt dimly visible at the end of the shadowed hall, Michael's old slouchy khaki hat, his arm and loose fist raised to Candy's door.

In an instant, Sylvia's regret switched to anger, red and hot. She stormed out of the room, slamming the door behind her. She turned toward the opposite end of the hall and marched down the stairs.

PART FIVE

DANCING UNDER A BLUE MOON

i

Sylvia burst through the screen door letting it bang behind her. Her intention was to boldly, in full view of the world, march straight over to Robb Goodfellow's and fling herself with complete abandon into his arms right then and there. She crossed the porch, took the steps in deliberate sequence, and was advancing across the grass between the two houses when Jack caught her. He was in a lawn chair with a magazine over his face. He seemed to be asleep. But, as she passed, he reached out his hand and caught hers and pulled her down to his side. With his other hand, he removed the magazine, revealing an enraptured countenance that Sylvia even in her consternation could not help but note. "Have you ever noticed Pamela's toes?" he asked.

"Toes?"

"Pamela has perfect toes." With the hand that was not holding hers Jack stroked his chin and gazed up at the sky. His voice was full of wonder.

"I suppose she has," said Sylvia, trying to recall what Pamela's toes looked like.

"Like peas in a pod. So even. And perfectly shaped."

"I've never really noticed."

"How could you not notice something like that?" said Jack in disbelief. "They're a work of art."

"Pamela *is* looking rather well these days," ventured Sylvia.

"Well!" scoffed Jack. "I suppose you could put it that way, if you want to describe absolute perfection as 'looking well'."

Sylvia wondered how to excuse herself and continue on her

way.

"Isn't it funny," Jack went on in rhapsodic tones, "how someone can be there all your life and you don't see them, then one day you do. You see someone's feet for the first time. You see toes, perfect toenails, like a line of red jelly beans. You want to nibble those toes."

Sylvia heard the part about nibbling toes and was startled. What in the world was Jack going on about? And why that strange look on his face? And that tone of voice? That was not Jack's voice. His was always so terse, almost sharp, even when he was saying something as ordinary as 'good morning.' She jumped up, upsetting him and the lawn chair onto the grass. "I have to go," she said, looking down at the sprawled Jack who was starting to lift himself up.

Just then the lady herself came into view with freshly red finger and toe tips. Barefooted Pamela, in Sylvia's silk the colour of spring leaves, swished down the back steps. Jack set the chair to rights and grinned at her. Standing, he flexed his biceps and tensed his abs in the attitude of a precocious Adonis who knows that he is handsome and adored. "I think I'll move my nap into the study," he said, his tone broadly suggestive, his look level and smouldering. He turned and strode up the steps and into the house. Pamela, staring fondly after his departing figure, said to Sylvia in a voice resonant with admiration. "Have you ever noticed Jack's arm?"

To one side of Pamela, through the trees, Sylvia saw a movement. It was Robb's car moving towards the road.

Michael, after he left Sylvia, went down to the beach. He knew that he should be using this time to set up the midnight glade scene, but he was too disturbed. He had to admit to himself that he was thoroughly unsettled by Sylvia's remark. He sat himself down on a piece of driftwood and thought about things. There was Dob and Pam – he still wanted to save their marriage. That still was important. But even more important to him was his marriage. 'It can be undone.' Those words chilled him to the marrow. Sylvia had never spoken to him that way before, never used that cold tone of voice before. She could not have meant those words. How could she? She was Sylvia, his Sylvia. She loved him. Just about everyone he knew was separated or divorced from their first partners. But he and Sylvia were different. There was something special between them, he did not know what it was, he could not name it exactly, but something which, he realized for the first time, could not, should not, be undone.

How might he mend things with Sylvia? He supposed he *could* stop fooling around. It had occurred to him once or twice that he *was* despicable, balling his best friend's wife who was also his wife's best friend.

Michael had always resisted denying his urges because he did not want to jeopardize his artistic integrity. He had to experience all of life, the highs, the depths. What kind of actor would he be if he limited himself? Sylvia understood this. Perhaps because of her music, she understood the need to be free to be a creative person. They had talked about this before marriage, in the small untidy coffee houses they had frequented when they had first met. They had talked about middle class values. They had agreed about the falseness of the morality of the middle class. They had said things like, 'an artist who is not free is not an artist,' 'a person who is not free can not be creative.' He still believed that. While he subscribed to the theory that art happened not in freedom but in the space between freedom and discipline, he construed as part of the postulation that first you had to know and feel the freedom to which to apply discipline. The problem with marriage, then, it seemed to him, was how to be free within the confines of a relationship.

He had always thought that a loose arrangement would best ensure the freedom of the individuals involved. He had always thought that not sharing yourself, that is, your innermost self, with the other person would keep the self intact. Two individuals living amicably together, yet going their own ways, pursuing their own interests, their own talents, that was his idea of a successful relationship. But now he had to consider that there might be another way. Was it conceivable that if two people were very very close, *that* might also be a sort of freedom? If two people were so close that they shared their innermost thoughts, anxieties, passions, in short, if they shared *themselves,* would not such a sharing allow as much, or more, freedom as being niggardly with oneself? For could not two be greater, larger, than one? two embodiments, two human beings bringing with them into a relationship all the complexities of their human hearts? As far as creativity was concerned, since two personal freedoms were involved, would there not then be two springs, two reservoirs from which to draw? Might not a person have a broader base of integrity, and thus greater strength of character, in the long run?

Michael had to catch his breath. Monogamy as a possible solution came to him as a staggering thought. He supposed it was worth a try. But could he do it? Well, first things first. He must explain things to Pam. She was a sensible, rational woman. And she loved Sylvia. She would agree with him.

Dinner was again set on the terrace. The standards, however, had slipped since the previous evening. Plates were not lined up precisely. Cutlery was flung rather than laid. The cloth was askew. Candy did her best, since no one else appeared to be going to do it, but, with an absent organizer, the event and, consequently, the enterprise lacked a guiding hand. She found scissors and cut fresh flowers that were in plentiful supply in the garden, but she could not find a vase and so stuck them into a glass jar. She could not find new candles so used stubs that she found in the kitchen. Sylvia seemed both distracted and agitated and so was not much help. Candy could see that her hostess was different than she had been the previous evening. She was distant, not as friendly. She seemed sad. But, then, maybe the previous evening had been the exception. This afternoon, when Dobbin was at her door, they had heard another door slam behind them. They had seen Sylvia's back marching along the hall and disappearing down the stairs in what appeared to be abrupt angry movements. Yesterday and this morning, she had seemed so mild and gentle. Well, you never knew, and Candy, in particular, admitted that she did not know. She was the stranger here. Whatever the case, Sylvia's general inertia was interrupted by periodic episodes of activity that reminded her of a wound-up whizzy toy released from its spring. Her head would twist suddenly upwards, suddenly sideways. Her eyes would dart. When Candy looked in the direction of Sylvia's flung glances, there was nothing there except the neighbour's cedar cabin through the trees.

Dobbin found Candy when she was cutting the flowers. "Those are the loveliest ones," he said. "Those blue ones." He interrupted her when she was carrying plates to the table. "Can I carry those for you?" he asked. She perceived that he liked being near her. She thought it rather sweet and his wife didn't seem to mind. In fact, Pamela seemed to be hypnotized by Jack. She hung on his every word, which as far as Candy could hear was weirdo stuff. And Jack was paying far too much attention to his friend's wife. On the other hand, Dobbin didn't seem to notice. He was too busy taking care of her needs – did she want another glass of wine? a cheese biscuit? He made pleasant, if not entirely understandable, conversation. She found comfort in him. He was the only one in this crazy assembly who did comfort her. He was so thoughtful. How considerate of him to knock on her door this afternoon and propose a swimming lesson for later. He was, no, not like a dad or a teacher, but more like a protective older brother.

On the deck, Michael was barbecuing. He didn't really know what he was doing, but Sylvia, who normally took care of the task, had wordlessly handed him a package of meat and wandered off. Jack had instructed him in starting the barbecue but neither he nor Pamela, who were standing nearby, noticed the clouds of smoke arising from under the hood. As for Michael, he kept forgetting the task at hand, concerned instead with his wife's words of the afternoon. And not the least of his problems was the conundrum of how to get his friends to the glade at midnight. He must think up a plausible story but he could not think.

Finally, when the smoke became alarming, he whisked several charred bits off the grill and onto a platter. This he plunked down at the centre of the table. He called the company to come. Somehow, other food items made an appearance. Bowls and platters and bottles of wine exchanged hands. The behaviour of the assembly, Michael was quick to observe, was as odd as the table setting. Jack would not shut up. All through dinner, mister competent, efficient, ever-so-cool medical man in charge of every situation chattered like an out-of-control schoolboy. While his topics ranged far and wide, his major concern seemed to be toes. "Toes are like teeth," he announced. "Don't tell me none of you has ever noticed? It's so obvious." He cast a scathing eye on the company, as though to say, how can people be so obtuse? "Like teeth in a neat row," he went on, "two large incisors, then tapering either side." His eyes implored, begging for understanding and agreement. And Pam, instead of attempting to monopolize the conversation in a loud voice, beamed at Jack when he raved about toes, at Dob when he said pass the buns, at him when he said nothing. When she did speak, her voice was modulated, almost soft.

What's up? wondered Michael. Pam's moony and Jack's looney. Could there be something to this full moon business after all?

And Sylvia seemed disturbed to the point of lassitude. Michael knew that her behaviour was a result of this afternoon's quarrel. They never quarrelled. That was the great thing about their relationship. More correctly, Sylvia never quarrelled. Even when he tried to start something, she would answer quietly and keep her voice pleasant. But, he realized, people who never quarrel find quarrelling intensely disturbing. The result of her disturbance was that she had lost interest in both the dinner and her guests. She did not join in or even pretend to follow the conversation. She would turn her head quickly to the side, then stare in that direction for minutes at a time. During one such quick movement, with an involuntary twitch of her wrist, she spilled a glass of wine. She did not jump up to clean up the mess. She only righted her glass, saying, "never mind, it's an old cloth."

Michael gasped. This was a Sylvia he did not know. Perhaps

this stranger *would* leave him.

And what had got into Dob? Throughout dinner, he sat with a silly satisfied smile on his face. He did not join the general talk. Normally, he loved conversation, taking delight in keeping it up in the air. Since he had read everything and, what was more amazing, remembered what he read, he was a gold mine of information. Now this highly intelligent, knowledgeable individual was reduced to a grinning idiot. Michael had never seen his friend like this. "What's your opinion, Dob?" he asked. Dobbin gave a little start, a little shrug, a sweet little smile of apology, and immediately went back into his reverie. Michael regarded him with dismay. His vision of what was to happen at midnight in the glade depended upon Dobbin and Pamela having an epiphany of their first romantic moments and then doing what came naturally, but if this spell which had been cast on Dobbin did not lift, doing what came naturally would lack a certain thrust.

Candy was the only one at the table, besides himself of course, who seemed to be on solid ground. She was more sure of herself than she had been the evening before. Her appearance, too, was modified. She had given up on the gel and was letting her hair do its own thing, which gave to her a charming gamin-like quality. She ignored Jack's talk about toes, returned Dobbin's silly smile, and jumped to help Sylvia with the spilled wine.

When they got up from the table, arms laden with empty bowls and platters, smeared china and cutlery, stained goblets and depleted wine bottles, Michael cornered Dobbin beneath the elm. "What's up?" he asked.

Dobbin, holding forth a wobbly stack of plates, looked at him with an ambiguous smile.

"Hey, Dob, this is Michael, hello there, anybody home?" Michael, also carrying plates, swayed toward Dobbin and looked him in the eye.

"To be sure," Dobbin shifted his weight onto his other foot, still smiling benignly, like a father indulging a pesky child.

"To be sure what?" queried a confused Michael.

Dobbin's eyes showed some puzzlement. "Someone's home?"

he responded as if testing an answer to an exam question.

"Who's home?" returned Michael, who had lost track of his original question.

Dobbin's pale eyes now revealed a sort of wariness, as though he was not sure but that he might be in the company of a sharpie.

Michael, in exasperation, was about to throw in the towel and march into the house when he was struck by the light of inspiration. "We're getting up a little entertainment for tonight," he said instead. "In the glade. Midnight." He tried to remember Sylvia's prattling about the position of the stars and planets. "Full moon, that sort of thing." Then he had another brilliant idea. "Everybody's doing something."

"Doing something?" queried Dobbin.

"Performing. Amateur theatrics, entertainment." Michael warmed to his subject. "Amateur entertainment night."

"Did you say everybody?" queried Dobbin.

"Everybody." Michael's voice was firm.

"Jack's young lady? Candy?" For the first time, Dobbin said the name, and in naming her he felt a new intimacy with her as if she had become a part of his life.

"Of course," said Michael, without attaching any importance to the fib or, in truth, giving it any thought at all. Indeed, he was too caught up in his third brilliancy. "I was wondering if you'd do a piece from Cyrano."

"Cyrano?"

"de Bergerac. You know, *Cyrano de Bergerac*, one of the world's greatest lovers."

"Oh him."

"I have the book in my study. I'll find you some appropriate lines."

Sylvia's blue moon, a perfectly spherical globe, hung against a backdrop of velvet indigo sky. Beneath it, through an opening in the trees, the glade in the moonlight was ready to receive the players. Alder, birch and willow provided a suitable backdrop. In the foreground were tall ferns and grasses. Near the pond, watercress and wild strawberries fused in lush abundance and patches of Queen Anne's lace mixed with bluish purple thistle blossoms. Wild flowers – daisies, buttercups, bluebells, brown-eyed Susans, forget-me-nots – waited like an expectant audience, their faces upturned in the pure clean light of the moon. Fallen logs circled the edges of the space. Sweet white and purple clover dotted the cool damp grass. Hydrangea, tall on the bank of the trickling brook, nodded its heavy blooms. All nature was inspired and incited by this night. Birds chirped, squirrels chattered, cicadas whirred, frogs strummed, owls hooted. It seemed that every creature of the woods was moonstruck and did not want to sleep.

But where were the actors?

In her room, Sylvia, putting on makeup, looked at the face in the dressing table mirror and was startled. Who was this stranger staring at her with large unfamiliar eyes? She closed one eye, the left one. Parallel to the delicate curve of her eyelid was a wobbly black line. Her hand had been trembling so, the eyeliner pencil had involuntarily skipped a little jagged dance. She opened her eye and observed through half-closed lids. The eye shadow was too bright a green. The mascara was too thick – her lashes were matted together. Her eyebrows were too dark – they no longer matched her hair. As for her hair, its natural curl had become more intense in the heat and humidity of the day. Strands of tangled golden threads stood out around her head like a sprung brillo pad. Her lipliner was crooked – one side of her mouth was fuller than the other. Her lips were filled in with bright crimson. Her cheeks were almost as bright as her lips. What am I doing here? she wondered. What am I doing sitting in this stuffy room, trying to be somebody I'm not? Why am I neglecting my guests?

I look like I'm made up for a performance, she decided. But isn't this what one did if one was meeting one in the moonlight? Not that she intended having an assignation in the true sense of the word. The only reason she was meeting Robb Goodfellow in the glade was to tell him that she could not meet him. She had been trying to tell him that since late afternoon. Although her first impulse after seeing Michael at Candy's door had been to march over to Robb's and fling herself at him, she had come to her senses and then wanted to completely reverse her position. She had decided that, while Michael may be a despicable form of lowlife, she didn't have to lower herself to his standards. She had watched throughout the evening for the return of Robb's car, for a light in his window. Where in the world had he gone? He had begged her to meet him. How could the evening progress without him? If he did not act his part, how could she act hers? Did he not intend to keep their date? Sylvia felt a fresh wave of gloom. True, she had been going to tell him that she would not meet him, but that didn't mean she did not want him to want to meet her.

Robb, at the time that Sylvia was putting on her makeup and thinking these things, was in the Blue Banana Bar and Grill in Wildwood well into his third martini. Robb loved martinis but he seldom drank them because he found it difficult to stop at one. They were so short, one gulp and he had downed an ounce and a half of gin. It was too easy to drink too many and get too drunk. Because of his writing, Robb seldom allowed himself to get drunk. Tipsy, maybe, mellow, of course, but down and out drunk, no. He could not afford to lose a day at his word processor. Since he always woke up at five a.m. no matter what time he had gone to bed, getting drunk not only left him with a headache and a fuzzy brain, but exhausted. By the time he got himself sorted out again, one night of excess could cost him two or three days of production.

But today, after Sylvia had left and he had sat down at his computer, after what seemed an eternity, he had done something he did not allow himself to do when he was working. He glanced at his watch. One minute gone. He calculated. How many minutes until midnight? Nine times sixty, five hundred and forty. Should he stay here and glance at his watch five hundred and forty times? No. His nerves, his muscle, his bone, his blood would not take it. He jumped up. He would go into town, browse in some of the shops open for tourists in the summer evenings, have a bite to eat and thus pass the time until the witching hour.

Towards nine, he congratulated himself on the success of his plan and headed for the Banana. He had managed to put in several hours in a pleasant way. At The Pottery Den, he had got into an interesting discussion with the owner as to various methods of firing and glazing. He had spent at least an hour in the secondhand bookstore browsing through a stack of new old books. He had strolled over to World News and leafed through the 'Britain' rack.

It was after he had downed his first martini that he started to feel guilty about abandoning his characters for real life. This had to stop. He had a responsibility to the project. His characters needed him. They could not live without him. After his second martini, he thought he could hear them calling to him, 'save me, rescue me.'

Through the blinding clarity of a third martini, it hit him. His problem was that Sylvia had become a real person. She was no longer merely a myth. She was no longer Aphrodite rising from the waves, but a flesh and blood woman with a mind of her own. A real person demanded energy and attention. That was why he was losing his grip on his material. That was why his characters were acting up. Too much was happening outside the pages. Real life had become more real to him than his play. Real life was distracting him from his work. He was losing his characters because he was busy trying to keep track of real people. And people weren't doing what he expected them to do. Pamela was supposed to leave the berry patch first, not Jack. Michael was supposed to be chasing after Candy, not trying to save his friends' marriage or be deeply concerned about his own.

Robb had two choices, whether to join real life or go back to his play. He should not meet Sylvia tonight. He should excise her from his life, cut her as a thorn out of his flesh, cast her as a mote out of his eye. Damn, but those dudes in the old testament knew what they were talking about. Ah, but those were real men back then, men who had the courage of their convictions, men who stood up and were counted. But would that be fair? Casting her out. Would that be kind? No, definitely not. How could you have a beautiful woman waiting for you in the glade and not turn up? That would be like saying no to life. All right. He would give her his time and energy. To hell with the play. He would become involved in real life. He had already made a start by coming to town, already he felt himself to be in a different country, a country where real people walked real streets, real people sat in bars and ordered real drinks. He looked up and saw himself in the bar mirror. He would buy himself some new clothes, something trendy. He would get his hair styled. Yes! Get ready, Real Life, he declared to the mirror, here I come.

Meanwhile, back at the lake, Sylvia was contemplating wiping the whole mess from her face and going to bed. But she knew that she would not sleep. She would lie awake and stare at the ceiling and see Robb in the glade, see him alone in the moonlight, pacing, looking at his watch, hoping, hoping. "I'll wait all night if necessary," she heard his words of the afternoon. She could not bear to think that she was deliberately inflicting pain on another human being. She should not have said that she would meet him, but now that she had said it, she must do it. Besides, she had to get out of this room. She must do something to relieve her hurt and betrayed feelings at seeing her husband so openly and blatantly cheating on her. She must do something to alleviate her dismay and confusion at seeing Michael's true nature. This weekend, she had seen the truth of two men – her husband and Robb. Robb was a man with feelings, not like Michael who was an incredibly superficial person. Robb was a man who thought of others, not like Michael who only ever thought about himself. Robb was a man who had sworn his love for her, not like Michael who was in danger of suffering whiplash every time a female crossed his path.

While Sylvia was thus contemplating and Robb was ordering a fourth martini, Michael was dashing about from kitchen to living room to deck to kitchen, then back to living room, a blur against the backdrop of amber evening light. Time was winging and he was not organized, which was to say that he did not have everyone else organized. The details of the enterprise before him were leading him to a state of hypertension. At one point, it occurred to him that perhaps he should forget the matter. Let Pam and Dob find their own way, let them break up, what did he care?

But he did care.

The situation was rife with last minute problems. Where was Dob? He must speak to Dob. He must be sure that Dob knew how to get to the glade. And Pam. He must meet with Pam before Dob arrived in the glade. He must extricate himself from this situation with her. That had become of prime importance. His own marriage was in jeopardy. But he had not yet convinced her of the necessity of a meeting.

Accordingly, when Pamela was alone on the deck after dinner, he followed her.

"Look at the moon rising through the trees," she said, turning to him.

He kept his voice low. "We have to talk. Meet me in the glade at midnight. No. Eleven-thirty."

She turned more fully to him and said in a sweet voice so unPam-like he could scarcely recognize it as hers, "It's all right, Michael, really it is, everything is fine, everything is wonderful."

Recovering from her saccharine tones, he blurted, "That's just it. Things aren't wonderful. I have to speak to you. We have to talk."

"Dear boy, there's nothing to talk about."

"Yes, there is. We have to get things straightened out."

"But darling, things are straightened out." She put both her hands on his shoulders. Michael could not help but notice how enormously attractive she was this evening. She was wearing a long flowing robe of deep blue which he recognized as belonging to Sylvia. Her dark hair hung loose, her striking features were becalmed and glowing with a luminosity which seemed to come from inside her smooth creamy skin. He felt the full power of her tremendous energy, her irresistible force. "Michael," she said, "I love you."

Michael was shocked. "Shhh, you mustn't say that. Jesus,

what if Dob should come out here? What if he's standing inside
that back door right now? Jesus, Pam, have a little discretion."
    "No, Michael, I really mean it. I truly love you. Oh,
everything has become so clear. Don't you see?
    "No, I don't see and frankly I'm shocked. We have to discuss
things. You must meet me..." The door slammed behind them
and Jack was upon them spouting a mile a minute his inane
nonsense about toes.

    Dobbin was nothing if not conscientious about his
responsibilities toward a group project. For the remainder of the
evening, he occupied himself in glancing at a slip of paper and
muttering to himself. A worried look had replaced the former
vacuous smile. He had never had a theatrical assignment before
and, frankly, he felt a little nervous about it. He was having trouble
remembering the lines. Prose was one thing but poetry was an
entirely different matter. One thought did not follow logically
upon another. In short, it didn't make sense. Also, his spirit had
taken a bit of a plunge. The truth was, he was disappointed about
the cancellation of the swimming lesson. Since late afternoon
when he had knocked on Candy's door, he had been looking forward
to that event. Throughout dinner, he had occupied his mind with
various scenarios, various possibilities of instructional methods.
Would it be helpful for the young lady if he was to place his hands
beneath her torso while she tried out her arm and leg movements?
    Dobbin was not the only one having trouble with his lines.
Michael still had to persuade Pamela to meet him in the glade. He
had bungled his chance in the few minutes they had been alone on
the deck after dinner. His timing had been off. He had not been
quick enough. For, after Jack arrived on the scene, the others
soon followed, settling in for the remainder of the evening, only
occasionally going into the house to replenish refreshments or to
use the facilities. Michael knew that this business must be handled
secretively and cleverly. He must speak into Pamela's ear and his
words must be brilliant. They must grab her attention immediately.
He had tried to sit beside her but she had risen and glided off. He

had tried to meet her eye but she had refused contact. What could he say to convince her that a meeting was necessary? Then Sylvia, surprisingly, yawned hugely and said that she couldn't keep her eyes open. Candy had already gone into the house on some pretext or other, Jack had dashed inside to get Pamela another drink, and Dobbin was focussed on rehearsing his lines. Michael looked grimly toward where Pamela reclined limply on a chaise lounge.

While Sylvia was putting on her makeup and Michael was scheming and Jack was getting Pamela another drink and Dobbin couldn't remember his lines, Candy was trying to get together her bathing attire. She excused herself from the gathering on the deck and went into the house. She knew about a communal hamper in the hall cupboard where Dobbin had earlier found her a suit. The fact that she cared about what she would wear made her realize that the situation was becoming more complicated. Earlier in the day, she had given no thought to her costume. Kneeling at the open door of the cupboard, she dug into the hamper. She held up a scrap of material that had once been the top of an old bikini. But where was the bottom? She reached into the box and stirred things around. She pulled out a black saggy bag no better than the morning's costume. And here was something else. Straightening, she held a piece of yellow fabric in front of her body. This suit had more shape than the black but it was far too large. She sighed and sat back on her ankles and played with the idea of wearing nothing at all. This thought caused her to feel suddenly shy, a feeling which she did not immediately understand since she and Dobbin had totally disrobed the evening before. But, she decided, last night, carried away by the night and the moon, she had acted impulsively. And, if she was being totally honest with herself, in this situation she could no longer view her body objectively, as an instrument. She acknowledged that she was personally and emotionally involved.

All through dinner, Candy had been pleasantly elevated into a buoyant effervescence. She was looking forward to the evening's event. And the person who had so affected her was none other than a middle-aged professor, soft around the middle and starting to lose his hair. It was all quite weird. What had started as an appreciation of the man's thoughtfulness and consideration was turning into something deeper. Candy was not overly analytical about such things. She knew only that there was something about the way he looked at her across the dinner table, as if he was really seeing her, and the way in the afternoon he had tentatively knocked at her door, the way he had stood there clumsily, his face creased into a boyish conspiratorial grin, the way he had almost shyly suggested the swimming lesson, which had moved her to tenderness.

When Jack was returning to the deck from the kitchen, Pamela's drink in hand, he passed by the hall cupboard. Candy was upturned, head in the clothes bin, tossing articles across her shoulder. She had dressed for dinner in the black leather skirt which stopped near the top of her lovely thighs. What Jack was faced with, unexpectedly, before he had time to look away, were two perfectly symmetrical waxing moons showing beneath the upturned hem. Before he could control himself, the feeling assailed him, the same one as on the beach when he had looked through the trees and seen her, pitiful and shivering, flailing about awkwardly.

Candy, hearing someone behind her, looked around. Caught in the closet light, her face had the clear innocent look of a cherub. The down of her hair made a halo around her head. One cheek was smudged with dust from the cupboard. Quickly, Jack looked away. Again, as earlier, he felt that he had seen something of another person that was too personal. He set his mouth in a decisive, grim line and stepped quickly past.

Candy blinked in the light. She was holding up a particularly peculiar looking garment, constructed of spandex and what appeared to be black fishnetting. It looked like something she might have worn at Roxy's for her exotic dancing. For a moment, her heart went out to it, it was so absolutely perfectly weird. Then she gave it a look of disgust and threw it violently to one side. The porch screen slammed shut. She sat staring for a moment at the rejected small heap of netting on the floor. It was so pitiful, it needed her. With a passionate gesture, she grabbed it up and hugged it to her breast.

ii

The night continued warm and still. The glorious moon rose higher. Around it, stars flitted. Jupiter retrograde in lighthearted Gemini stood in splendid assertion to serious Saturn. Venus ascending in the west, effected a passionate aspect to Mars. The moon was full in the wise and spiritual sign of Pisces, bringing clarity and a release of secrets. The time was expedient for the comedy to begin. All nature contrived in its production. The glade was the perfect setting.

"Pam, there's something I have to tell you."

"Dear Michael. You don't have to tell me anything. I understand everything."

"Pam, you are the most unundestanding person I've ever met."

"I know, but I've changed."

"Since when?"

"Since the miracle happened."

"Miracle?"

"I don't want to go into the details. It's all too new. All too precious, too... miraculous." Pamela took a step, reached the edge of the glade, then turned so that Sylvia's blue robe billowed around her. She made one of those theatrical gestures which had become part of her new image. Since when? Michael asked himself. At lunch, during the picnic, when she had put on those improbable silk pyjama things, he answered himself. Pamela always wore aerobic tights and T-shirts or tailored slacks or, for formal occasions, sheaths and tunics. And now she was wearing a garment with yards of material and swishing around like Katherine Hepburn. He had to admit the act *was* attractive. But it was not his old Pam.

"Whatever in the world are you talking about?" Michael was sitting on a log near the brook, arms braced on his knees, hands clasped firmly in front of him, observing Pamela's performance with a studying, somewhat critical, eye. He'd changed directly after dinner into jeans, which he always wore to rehearsals. If Pamela had not been so involved in her epiphany, she might have noticed that Michael also was acting differently, as if he, too, had undergone an experience of immense proportions. She might have noticed a more serious Michael, one who realized that there were consequences to actions.

"Something. Nothing," Pamela exclaimed as she postured and turned. "Suffice to say, my eyes have been opened. I now see the world in a different way. And this new vision allows me to understand everything."

Michael could only stare. Was she drunk? He didn't think so. But she had stopped speaking. It was his turn to say something. He tried to take a cue from her last words. He could not remember what they were. He shook his head to clear it. He must say his little speech, the one he had come here to give, the one he had dragged Pam here to hear. By eleven o'clock, he had known that he had to take drastic measures. Dobbin had descended to the grass where he had added pacing to his muttering. Sylvia had gone to bed. Candy had disappeared. Jack had bent close to Pamela's ear and whispered something, then headed inside. Michael had run dry of ideas for conveying a subtle message to Pamela, so he grabbed her hand, firmly, pulled her up from the lounge and said, "Come on, let's go for a walk."

"But...," Pamela had gestured toward the departing Jack.

"What?"

"Jack wanted me to go for a walk with *him*."

"How about Candy?" Michael had inquired, for while he could not help but be aware that there had been a breakdown in communications between Jack and his girlfriend over the space of the day, he was not aware that the situation had fractured completely.

"Michael," Pamela had looked at him with fond exasperation, "believe me, a meeting between us is not necessary."

"Believe me, Pam," Michael had made his voice grave, his face stern. "It *is* necessary." He had kept the firm hold on her hand and began to tug.

She had given in, but not without the last word. "Well, if it will make you feel better but I assure you there's no need for it."

As they had made their way to the glade, Pamela still reluctant, Michael still insistent, he had rehearsed what he was going to say. Now, he must do it. He must do it before Dob's scheduled arrival.

"Pamela," Michael started. His voice was serious.

"Look at the stars," Pamela gestured to the heavens. "I've never seen the stars like this..."

"Pamela," Michael interrupted rather sharply. "Listen. Just listen for a moment." His voice lowered. "Hear me out." He paused, a bit dramatically. "I don't think we should see each other again. I mean, in that way."

"You mean you're breaking up with me?" Pamela swished to a stop, legs apart, feet braced.

Michael looked at the flowing drapery which was taking a stance before him. "If you want to put it in high-school terminology, yes."

"But dear boy, you can't break up with me."

"Why not?"

"Because I've already broken up with you."

"You have?"

"I thought you knew. I thought it was obvious."

Michael was suddenly affronted. "You can't toss me out like an old shoe," he spluttered.

"Why not? You were about to toss me."

"That's different."

"I don't see how."

"I'm not rejecting *you*. I'm doing the noble thing. For Sylvia. For Dob."

"Since when have you ever done the noble thing?"

"That's a terrible thing to say!"

"You're right. It is. I take it back. Even if it is true. Oh Michael," Pamela said in a soft voice, the very nicest voice Michael had ever heard issue forth from those resolute lips. "I love you," she went on. "Come here." She pulled him to his feet. A long silence followed, then nonsensical cooing, then satisfied sighs. "I'll always love you. You know that."

"Yes, I suppose I do. I love you, too."

Another silence ensued, this one longer than the last. It was finally broken by Pamela. "Hold on," she said, "or we'll be back in the soup."

"Yes, you're right. We do get on, don't we? We've had a lot of fun together, a lot of laughs. I do hate to give it, us, up. It's rather sad."

"Oh Michael, don't you see? True love is a higher thing, a greater thing. Jack has taught me that."

Jack?" questioned an incredulous Michael.

"Yes, believe it or not. Jack. I now know that love is more than two little people with our petty concerns. Love is larger than all of us. Love is a force. Out there." She flung up her arm.

Michael looked wildly across his shoulder. "Where?"

"There," and with a meticulously manicured finger she pointed to a caragana bush. At that precise instant, as though on cue, Dobbin walked out of it and into the glade.

Sylvia plunged through the trees. She scarcely felt the lash of branches against her face. Their slap was not nearly as painful as the slap in the face she had just experienced by her very own husband and her very best friend. A thorn bush caught the edge of her cotton skirt. She yanked viciously at the material to free herself and kept on. She stubbed her toe on something sharp. Around her, everything was illuminated by moonlight. Trees and bushes seemed animated with excitement. Sounds were magnified by the clarity of the night. Close by a brook danced and trilled its way into the lake. Somewhere an owl hooted. Crickets snapped,

frogs hiccupped and burbled. Nature was content, even happy.
But Sylvia felt none of the joy that was loose in the night. Her
makeup had come undone. Rivulets had cut gullies in it from her
swollen eyes to her chin. Streaks smeared her cheeks where she
had wiped away tears with the back of her hand. A sort of
slobbering spittle had blurred her lipstick. Scratches covered her
hands. In her fleeing she had stumbled over a root and fallen
headlong along the path. Small bits of twigs and stones were
embedded in her palms and forearms.

Adrenalin spent, she slowed her random flight. Still she could
hear the voices in the glade, murmuring voices, terrible voices,
terrible words. She would not let herself think about the specific
words, but the tone, the intimate tone of the voices, filled her
head. How could they? she cried inside herself. How could
they betray her so? How could Michael do that? and with Pamela?
How could Pamela do that? and with Michael? Michael and
Pamela, of all people. Oh, she knew that Michael was not reliable
in this regard. But Pamela!

By chance rather than design Sylvia found herself back on
the path. Getting her bearings, she trudged dejectedly in the
direction of the house. Lost in her misery, she walked right into
what she at first fancied was a bear, but no bear had ever smelled
that strongly of gin.

Robb happened to look up at the large brightly lit clock in
the Blue Banana. He was able to make out that the small hand
was near eleven. He stared at the clock and thought, I have to do
something. What? Then he remembered in a rush. "Gotta go,"
he said as he slid off the barstool.

"Are you sure y'wanta drive in that condition?" Nick
Capelli, who both owned and operated the establishment, had lived
in the area all his life. His folks had immigrated from Italy and
started a grape orchard and now owned a winery. He looked
after his customers, so when Robb mashed out an "ish awright,
I'm okay," Nick knew better than to argue with him. Instead,
when Robb went out the door, he picked up the phone.

When Robb climbed into his vehicle parked in front of the bar and grill, his blood-alcohol content was well over the legal limit. However, the least of his concerns was his physical condition of which, in any case, he was ignorant. All he knew was that he had to keep his date with Sylvia. Once behind the wheel, he realized that he had drunk a little bit too much, so he was careful to drive slowly and obey all the rules. What he was not fully cognizant of was the fact that he was driving very slowly indeed, about ten miles an hour. However, his speed made it easier for Harvey Purcell, the local RCMP constable, to catch up with him, pass him, slow down in front of him and stop, forcing Robb to also stop. Harvey then drove him the rest of the way home in the police vehicle, at what seemed to Robb an excruciatingly slow pace. "I don't suppose you could speed things up?" he tried.

"Nope," said Harvey.

Harvey guided Robb to his door, steered him to his bed, and took off his shoes. With the idea of immobilizing the young man further, he then removed his pants and shirt and hid them in the bottom of a closet. With the advice to sleep it off, he turned and left. As soon as Harvey was out the door, Robb sat up. He tried to find his clothes but came up, instead, with brown velour pyjamas his aunt had given him one Christmas and which he had never worn. Gotta get to the glade, gotta get to the glade, his mind kept repeating as he thrashed his way through bush. He knew where the glade was. Of course, he knew. He knew the whole territory like the back of his hand. It was just that, at the moment, he could not have found the back of his hand. He knew that he was supposed to meet Sylvia, but that was only part of his distress. Through the thinning fog of alcohol that surrounded his head, he also knew that he must find out what everyone had been doing while he had been getting bombed in the local bar and forgetting all about them. As the last of the Goodfellows in the area, it was his job to watch things at the lake and he had abdicated his duty. Where was everyone this minute? He had no idea. Deeply engrossed in such concerns, he was startled when a body walked into him, pushed itself off his chest and cried out a miserable, "Ohhhhhhhh."

"Sylvia?" questioned Robb. Was this really Sylvia, this caricature with strangely curved eyebrows and garish lips, with wanton hair and black squiggles dribbling down her cheeks? Where was his wood nymph, his earth mother, his goddess?

Sylvia had forgotten about Robb. The last thing she wanted at this point in her life was a rendezvous. But here it was, smack dab in her path, uncertain on its feet and grinning foolishly. As Robb swayed, he wove himself into a shaft of moonlight. In the spotlight, once more he took on the guise of hero. Once more, she had been disappointed by one man only to have another appear before her. It seemed that whenever she needed a hero, Robb was there. If anyone could rescue her from Michael, if anyone could make her feel wanted and needed and attractive, it was Robb. He was in charge. He was a playwright while Michael was only an actor. Robb knew how to write a romantic tryst into the plot, so let the play begin. She would play her role. She had not come here with the purpose of having a tryst, but by god she would have one. She would pay Michael back. What was good for the goose was good for the gander. Oh how thankful she was that she had not managed to catch Robb earlier and change the plan.

Sylvia advanced upon Robb. Suddenly, Robb felt alarm. He took a step backwards. Sylvia advanced another step. "Hey," said Robb. He put up his hands, palms outward. He saw a face in the moonlight, unnaturally white, unnaturally ravaged by tears, lips swollen large, hair Medusa-wild. "Hey," he said again, "Are you okay?"

"Yes," Sylvia said, advancing further. "I am finally okay." Neither the voice nor the words seemed to belong to his sweet flower.

"Are you sure? You have a strange expression on your face. Your eyes are glittering." Robb stepped another step backward.

Sylvia threw her arms around his neck. He felt the physical presence of this person, now a stranger, knocking him sideways into a bramble bush. He put a hand down to brace himself and felt it land on a bed of prickles.

"What're you doing?"

"Make love to me," gasped Sylvia, flinging herself on top of him.

"Whaaat? Now?" Robb was suddenly cold sober.

"Yes, this very moment." Sylvia started kissing him madly on the face, on the mouth.

"Hey, stop it," cried out Robb.

For answer, Sylvia grabbed at the cord that held up his pyjama bottom. In trying to undo it, she pulled it tighter. Robb arched his body up, which rolled them both over against a tree trunk. Robb raised an arm to save himself from smashing into the sturdy wood and caught the blow with his elbow. His arm tingled and went numb at the same time. "Owww, Oh, Oh!" he howled.

Undeterred, Sylvia thrashed around on top of him, attempting to pull down his pants and pull up her skirt at the same time. Legs and arms seemed to be everywhere. Robb was not sure which were his and which were Sylvia's. Then Sylvia sat up and tore off her blouse, throwing it aside. Robb averted his eyes. This was not the way he wanted it to happen. This was not his idea of a dignified seduction.

Robb took the opportunity to gasp, "Sylvia, stop! This isn't like you."

"Yes, it is," she panted.

"You're not yourself."

"I was never more myself in my life."

Robb tried to get himself out from under. He struggled to sit up, to kneel, but he was finding out that Sylvia was quite heavy. Also, he was in a weakened state. He could not seem to gather his muscular frame together to raise himself up off the ground.

"You can't stop now," cried Sylvia.

"What do you mean? I haven't even started!"

"Make love to me." Sylvia had extricated herself from her outer garments and once more flung herself on top of Robb.

"Sylvia, this is not a good time."

"Oh, I know I've been difficult," Sylvia said between kisses. "I've been cutesy. I've been coy. But I'll make it up to you."

"Stop! Sylvia, I've had a very rough night. Stop! Sto...op!"

194   *Cecelia Frey*

Down on the beach, Candy, a light jacket thrown over the black spandex and fishnet swim suit, sat shivering on a log. She thought it must be past midnight. She had left the house at eleven. For a while she had walked up and down the beach, admiring the moon and the stars, looking out over the water glittering with reflections of both heaven and earth, cabin lights around the lake as well as stars. But for the last half hour or so, she had done nothing but wait.

She had been certain that Dobbin would come. He was not the sort of person who would not come. And, after all, this was his suggestion. She had not knocked on *his* door. He had helped her with the flowers and with the table. At dinner, when she looked across the table from time to time, she found him looking at her. Was it possible that, after dinner, he had changed his mind? But why? Had he had a change of heart? Of conscience. But they were doing nothing wrong. What was a swimming lesson, after all? Still, perhaps to a man like Dobbin, it *was* something. He was such a weird old fuddy, so serious, so sweetly naive, rather like a boy, really, not like Smiling Jack.

She shivered again, not because of the night, which was warm, but because she was feeling uneasy. Everything here was so strange, so different from what she was used to in Vancouver. I'm on a beach at midnight waiting for a man to teach me to swim, she thought. That she would have to enter black cold water in the darkness had not registered in her brain when she had agreed to the meeting. Last night they had only played near the edge, but tonight she would be expected to walk into that waiting blackness until it was up to her waist. She would be expected to stretch herself out on top of it, to give herself to it. She dug her bare toes into the sand that still held the warmth of the day's sun.

She began to wonder if she had the right time and place. What, exactly, had he said? "Meet me down at the beach about eleven." Unless he meant eleven tomorrow morning. 'Down at the beach' could mean anywhere along the shoreline but, practically speaking, this stretch where she was sitting, where the Wilde property fronted the lake, was what the people at the house referred to as the beach.

Could he have come and gone before she arrived? She had been here well ahead of time, but maybe he had been even more ahead of time. When she had returned to the porch after changing into her swimsuit everyone, including Dobbin, had disappeared, even though all the lights were on and the unwashed dinner dishes were still piled in the sink. But she had come directly down the path. Surely, she would have met him. Unless he had taken another route and was on his way up when she was on her way down.

Sitting in the darkness, Candy began to feel spooked. The moon and the stars were all very well, the beach was wide and white in the moonlight, the lake was lovely, the sound of water slapping gently against a wharf was kind of soothing. But how about those crazy shadows? Shadows in the city were one thing. She knew what to expect in the city. But here, she could not be sure. She had heard of monsters living in these lakes. And what of bears and cougars? Or snakes and squirmy things? She drew up her feet and held them above the sand.

With a shock of alarm, she saw a dark figure standing near the edge of the water. She knew right away that it was not Dobbin. This figure was shorter, more compact, than Dobbin. As she continued to stare at the shape, it seemed alien and threatening. Her heart started to beat violently. Her eyes were paralyzed in their focus. Then the figure moved and she recognized Jack.

Jack was thoroughly disgruntled. Things were not going well. When he had set down his empty brandy snifter and whispered into Pamela's ear to meet him on the beach, he had expected that she would. She had not, of course, been able to give him an answer. Michael had been sitting close by with Dobbin not far distant. But now he had been here, he glanced at his watch, half an hour and no Pamela. Jack was restless. He recognized the feeling. He definitely needed an outlet for his energies.

Looking out over the water, not really seeing it or the reflected moon or the stars, he tried to figure things out. He could have sworn that Pamela was as smitten with him as he was with her. Throughout the afternoon and evening, she had sought him out. She had stayed close to him on the deck before and after dinner. She had laughed at his jokes. A woman did not laugh at a man's jokes for nothing. Yet, at the same time, she had eluded him. All afternoon and evening he had been pursuing her toes, the very idea of the nibbling of which elevated him to orgasmic heights, but he was no closer to catching them now than he had been at the start. He was certain that Pamela felt the same raptures as he. That was the puzzling thing. He went over it all again in his head. He had been peering through the trees and she had been standing over him and he had suddenly turned and seen her bright toes all in a row. Then he had raised his head and seen, he was sure of it, that she was staring at his body in wonder and delight, a stare for which there could be only one explanation. His first response had been surprise – Pamela, of all people. He had not considered Pamela in that way. She was an old buddy, she was Dobbin's wife. But her chemistry could not be denied. From that moment, he knew that sooner or later he and Pamela would get together. If years of womanizing bachelorhood had taught him anything at all, it was when a woman was ripe for the picking.

What had gone wrong? During lunch, things had seemed to progress as he might have predicted. Pamela had contrived to sit near him on the grass. Several times, he had caught her looking at him. Then there was the way she had laughed and swung her hair. There was about her an aura of deferred delights. When everyone else disappeared for afternoon naps, he had spread himself in full view on a lawn chair, visible and approachable. He was certain that she would find him. And she did. But then Sylvia was there. That was his fault. He should not have stopped Sylvia. But he had not been able to help it, he had had to talk to someone about Pamela. He supposed it was like the criminal who gets caught because he has to tell someone about his crime. Still, he had rallied. He had got up and gone into the house. He had brushed Pamela as he passed, giving her a message with his eyes, with his tone of voice. He had lain down on his bed in the study, but Pamela had not made an appearance. After a while he had got up, dressed, and gone into the kitchen, looking for someone, anyone. He had felt the need for a drink and he made it a rule never to drink alone.

Finished analyzing the afternoon's farce, Jack was about to start on the evening's, when from behind him he heard a definite gasp. He turned quickly. Could it possibly be? but, no, it was only *that* person.

"What the hell are you doing here?" he demanded.

Candy could see in the moonlight that his face was angry.

"I don't know," she stuttered, unprepared for the shock of being alone with Jack, the situation which she had been avoiding most of the day.

"You must know. Try not to be stupid." Jack felt terrible as soon as the words were out of his mouth. Try not to be an asshole, he told himself. But he felt so upset seeing her sitting there on the log shivering and quivering, her knees pressed together, her long thin legs splayed out from the knees in an awkward, heart-wrenching manner, like a newborn fawn raising itself for the first time, that he had to do something to quell the feeling that threatened him.

When Jack was six years old, his mother took him to see *Bambi*. It was a hot summer afternoon. The theatre was cool. His mother bundled him into a seat and they sat together holding hands. It was one of the finest memories of Jack's young life, up to that point. Then the dreadful thing happened. He was not prepared for it, the hunters, Bambi's mother dead. He had sobbed and sobbed. His mother finally had to take him out of the theatre. They sat on a bench in the lobby and she stroked his hair and erased his tears with her thumb and assured him that it was only a movie. But with that movie something unsettling had entered Jack's life. Before that, the concept of death had not occurred to him. He was a city child. He had never had pets. Death in books was confined to dragons and other outlandish creatures. Jack was a happy child until that moment when death entered his life, when he knew that mothers could die, that people you loved could be taken away. He became a happy child again. He became a normal boy. Except that he never could join in with playmates who fried ants with magnifying glasses or caught bees in jars. He was astute enough to know that perhaps that was why he had gone into medicine, so that he could have some control over death. But, of course, he could not control it. No one could. And perhaps, again, that was why he had switched to dentistry.

All Candy knew was that throughout the afternoon and evening Jack had not paid her the slightest attention. He had scarcely spoken to her but had directed most of his remarks to Dobbin's wife, Pamela. Of course, they were old friends. She knew that. But he was not, as she had thought earlier, like some dates who invited you and then casually ignored you. Rather, there seemed to be an intent to Jack's avoidance. Since this morning he had seemed to despise her. She couldn't think what had happened. Was it because she was not sporty or outdoorsy? But she had never pretended that she was. And that didn't make her a bad person, did it? No, it was more like she had something really nasty like gum disease. Even though Candy was not exactly enamoured with Jack any more, she felt her nerves strain under the tension. She felt uncomfortable in the position of being at the receiving end of another's anger and hostility. She wanted to get up and leave but she could not move. She started to cry, silently.

Jack saw her face in the moonlight. He had no desire to see a face that was soft and sad and now glistening with tears. He had no desire to see another person's pain. "Oh, bloody hell," he muttered and stomped off.

After he left, Candy thought of many things she might have said. 'I can be here if I want, you don't own the beach, it's a public beach,' and so on. Why can't I ever think of anything to say at the time? she wondered. No wonder he thinks I'm stupid. 'I don't usually say stupid things,' she might have said, 'only when I'm dealing with a jerk like you.'

Candy sighed. Her one bright hope of the weekend was Dobbin and he had stood her up. She may as well face the fact.

He was not going to come, that was all there was to it. It must be past midnight by now. Anyway, it was not a real date, it was only a swimming lesson. It was just that he had seemed so absolutely trustworthy, so absolutely straight. If he was not going to come, he was the type to let her know. She was sure of it. Maybe something came up at the last minute. Maybe something to do with his wife. Well, she could not fault that. Husbands and wives should be together. It was just that she had been looking forward so much to the swimming lesson. She *did* feel the tiniest bit betrayed. If he had changed his mind, if he had something else to do, he might have told her. Or maybe he had simply forgotten about it. Maybe it had entirely gone out of his mind.

Feeling alone and dejected, her pretty mouth in a downturn like a child's trying not to cry, Candy was struck again by the lights dancing on the surface of the lake and how they reminded her of Roxy's. The lake was like a big stage. What fun it would be to be part of that silvery glitter. If she could swim among the lights, it would be like dancing among the stars. Inspiration struck. There was no reason why she could not have a swimming lesson by herself. How surprised Dobbin would be when she told him that she had gone into the lake on her own.

But *could* she do it? Could she enter that cold water alone? without her teacher, without her friend? Yes, she could! She stood up from the log and marched to the edge of the lake, tossing her jacket on the beach as she went. The next step must be very firm, she told herself. She must not hesitate. She must not think. She must simply take the necessary step, like when she stepped from the wings out onto the stage.

She raised her right foot. She placed the whole of it into the water and positioned it firmly on the rocky bottom. A sensation of cold shot up her leg. Still, she raised her left foot and did the same. Right, left, right, left, she told herself. Goose bumps sprang up on her skin. She winced as the water reached her crotch, but she kept going until it circled her waist. Now she was on sand. Don't think, she told herself again. Here goes, and she pushed her feet off from the bottom and extended her arms before her head.

The sudden cold around her heart made her gasp. She could not breathe. She was clawing air into her lungs and not releasing it so there was no space for fresh air. She was suffocating. She started to panic. She lowered her feet. She could not find the bottom. Her head went under. Kicking, splashing, gasping, she righted herself. She stood panting and choking but still she could not get air into her lungs. Then she remembered Dobbin's words, "concentrate on breathing out, in, out, in, regularly, no matter how cold it is, no matter what else distracts you, you can do nothing else if you don't breathe." She expelled her breath as much as was possible and then took in air, not a satisfactory amount, but some. Again, she breathed out, all of her air, everything, she let it go. Finally, with the next breath in, her lungs filled. Her first instinct then was to say forget it and to head back for shore. But, no, she would try again, just once more. If it did not work the next time, she would admit defeat. She counted her breaths, long, slow breaths. You are relaxed, she repeated over and over to herself. How silly you are, she admonished herself. The water isn't deep. You can always simply stand up, she assured herself.

Again, she pushed off from the bottom. As she did so, she remembered to let out her air so that when she pulled her arms back and under her chest and took a breath in, there was room in her lungs for the new air. At the same time, she worked her legs automatically. As Dobbin had earlier noted, her strong dancer's legs were an asset. They kept going even when she did not direct them to do so. It was not until several turns later that she felt relaxed enough about her upper body movement to concentrate on her kick. Glide, kick, glide, she told herself. Knees together, quick snap to the sides, ankles smartly retracted, legs straight for the glide.

And suddenly it all came together, arm and leg movement and breathing. No longer did she have to stop after a few strokes to cough and splutter. No longer was she exhausted after a few strokes. Suddenly, she felt that she could go on forever. She could see now so clearly that it was simply a matter of coordinating physical movements and breathing, just like dancing. What had got in the way was the water. But if she worked with the water instead of against it, if she became part of the water, it seemed perfectly natural.

After some minutes of swimming back and forth, Candy stood up. The fishnet swimsuit was restricting. It caught her in the crotch and the netting was scratchy. This is a ridiculous swimsuit, she told herself. This swimsuit is not me. She had a habit of wearing garments that were not her. She would throw on whatever was lying around the flat, a boyfriend's old sweater, a roommate's boots. For stage roles and dancing, she put on the costumes that other people gave her. As a receptionist, she donned the white jacket that was part of her job. Why am I always wearing somebody else's clothes? Candy asked herself. She peeled down the fishnetting and stepped out of it. She threw it onto the surface of the water and watched it float away. She felt the water directly on her skin, without the barrier of fabric. Now she knew who she was. She was a swimmer.

She swam some minutes more before she detected a figure coming toward her through the water. She stood up. Almost immediately, she recognized Dobbin's large shape and deliberate movement. Naked as a newborn babe, he was approaching her with arm outstretched. She took his hand. They swam together, back and forth, back and forth beneath the moon, Candy lost in the miracle of her own movements, of the night, of this precious moment in time.

When Jack arrived back at the house, still disturbed at the sight of Candy in tears, still frustrated by Pamela's elusiveness, Sylvia, without a stitch on, was vigorously scrubbing a pot that was in the sink. Her buttocks were bouncing, as were her breasts which he could see reflected in the window. Not bad, he appraised. A little on the fleshy side but well-proportioned, with great pecs. He hadn't given it much thought before – what his friend's wife might look like beneath her voluminous garments.

Sylvia heard the door close and turned from the waist. "Oh, it's you," she said and turned back to her pot.

"What are you doing?" he asked, somewhat astounded.

"What does it look like I'm doing?" It seemed that she was trying to be snappish but her voice came out, instead, dispirited and sad.

"Where is everybody?" he tried.

For answer, Sylvia clanged the pot onto the drying rack, grabbed another and attacked it in the same manner. Jack did the only thing he could think to do under the circumstances. He took up a tea towel and started drying.

After a few moments, he tried again. "Is something wrong?"

"I don't want to talk. I've had a rotten day."

After a few more moments, Jack understood why Sylvia had disrobed. The heat of the day had settled into the narrow rooms of the old poorly ventilated house. In spite of the open window and the screen at the back door, the kitchen was stifling. "Would you mind if I took off my clothes?" he asked.

"Be my guest," she said without so much as favouring him with a glance. She drew her forearm up across her cheek as if brushing away something.

"I'll leave my shorts on." He put down the tea towel and started unbuttoning his shirt.

"Don't on my account. I couldn't care less. I'm not at all impressed with naked men."

"Really?"

"Really."

People are full of surprises, Jack decided. Still, he hesitated to disrobe entirely. There seemed something indecent about being naked with his friend's wife in his friend's kitchen. But it must feel good to be naked, he thought. Of course he was often naked. In his apartment, in his bed, in the shower, in the gym, with women, but this would be different. There was something absolutely freeing in the thought of being naked with a woman after whom he did not lust, doing something so ordinary as drying dishes. He slipped off his *Jockey* briefs and threw them onto a chair with his *Nautica* shirt and his *Calvin Klein* pants. He picked up the tea towel again.

After a few moments, he said, "Say, this feels wonderful."

For answer, she made the swiping motion again with her arm across her cheek. Jack saw reflected in the window something glistening there and realized it was tears. "Do you want to talk about anything?" he tried.

"I've been thinking," she managed, sounding only a bit weepy, "I wear entirely too many clothes, all those big skirts and layers of tops."

Jack didn't know what to say so he said nothing.

"People are more themselves without clothes on, don't you agree? I mean, there's nothing to hide."

"Yes, I believe you're right. This does feel very honest."

"We should all take off our clothes," said Sylvia. "And makeup. I just took a shower and removed my makeup. It feels so good to be nakedly myself. Maybe that's why I like swimming."

At that moment, the screen door slammed and Pamela burst into the room. Jack was both pleasantly surprised and dismayed. What would his amour think, finding him without clothes and with another woman? Thank Christ he had a body that could pass the nude test. He struck a bodybuilder pose, but Pamela's eyes were rivetted on his arm. She raised her head and beamed at him. "What are you two doing?" she asked in a syrupy tone.

Sylvia had clamped her lips the moment Pamela had appeared and she kept them clamped.

"Dishes," said Jack.

"Let me help. Do you have another tea towel?" asked Pamela. After a few minutes of silence in which Sylvia stayed clamped and Jack started to think that maybe the night would not be a total waste after all, she spoke again. "Whew, I can see why you took off your clothes. I'm going to take off mine."

"Mine," said Sylvia, but without force.

"I found this lovely gown in the spare room closet," said Pamela. "I didn't think you'd mind."

For answer, Sylvia scrubbed more vigorously yet another offending pot.

Sylvia's gown and Pamela's undergarments were tossed in a heap on top of Jack's clothes on the chair. Pamela resumed drying a dish. Jack drew in his breath. Here, indeed, was physical perfection. He tried not to tarnish the moment by having an erection. He forced himself to give his full attention to a particular spot on the pot in his hand.

Again, the door slammed. This time it was Michael. He looked accusingly at Pamela. "You pushed me."

"Dear boy," replied Pamela, "you're dreaming."

"I am not. I have the dislocated shoulder to prove it. And look at these scratches." He held out his arm, but no one looked.

"Well, I didn't mean you to fall down," said Pamela, picking up another item from the drying rack. "I simply could not stay there and see Dobbin making a fool of himself."

Michael suddenly realized that everyone was in the buff. Since he'd been in that condition with each of the three at one time or another, he didn't have any particular thoughts on the matter. "What's up?" he asked.

"Join us," said Jack. "You'll be more comfortable."

Michael, as it turned out, was surprisingly reluctant to take off his rehearsal clothes before the group. He said it would be like the worst nightmare of every actor, where he finds himself suddenly naked and exposed on the stage before an audience. Finally, however, he was convinced that he should by Jack and Pamela who took matters into their own hands and, with a great deal of fiendish glee, assisted him. Sylvia stayed out of it, she seemed to be deliberately ignoring him.

Later, no one remembered who first suggested going outside. Sylvia had to be coaxed. 'Come on.' 'Come.' 'It's so hot in here.' 'The grass will be cool.' 'Hurry.' 'Don't be slow.' They called to each other and escaped through the screen door. They ran down the porch steps and onto the grass where the magic of the moon released them from their foibles and lapses. At first, Sylvia refused to cheer up, but under the influence of the night sky she forgot Robb and what she had seen in the glade, forgot for the moment to be heartbroken or otherwise play the role of a tragic heroine. Jack looked up and saw the moon and the stars. He forgot his primal physical urges. It occurred to him that a physical relationship with Pamela was entirely too trivial, too mundane, for what was going on between him and her, or more precisely, between him and her toes. Pamela let herself be carried aloft by the perfection of Jack's arm. Michael forgot that his project had flopped. Pamela and Michael regained the innocence they had lost together. They all held hands and danced in a circle. Hearing the music that was inside them, they frolicked unsupervised and unobserved by Robb Goodfellow who was already snoring in his brown velour pyjamas on top of the bedclothes, his binoculars abandoned on the window ledge.

iii

Next morning, the sun came up as usual, without concern for the nonsense in which human beings had involved themselves the night before. The moon had passed the precise point of its fullness and was a pale sphere in the lightening sky. Both Mercury and Jupiter had resumed motion. The forecast was for moderating temperatures. And Robb Goodfellow was not at his computer. Although it was well after five, he had not even made it yet to his *Mr. Coffee*. When the CD player clicked on with Vivaldi's *Four Seasons*, he groaned and groggily assessed the damage. He ached all over. One arm was raw and inflamed. Both hands were seeded with thistle tips that he had not been able to remove the night before due to a failure of vision. He had an excruciatingly painful headache. He got out of bed, slowly, and stumbled to the bathroom where he ingested three painkillers. He stumbled back to bed and pulled the covers over his head. Let his characters take care of themselves.

On the grass beside the Wilde house, a robin ran, stopping every few steps to cock up its head and listen for worms. Suddenly, its bright yellow beak darted down. Bracing firmly on two matchstick legs, expanding a full fat bright copper breast, it lifted and tugged, stretching back its head at the same time as stretching its hapless victim between earth and beak. Above this scene of raptorial carnage, butterflies flitted. On the deck, a black squirrel appeared, thumping down amongst the brooms and watering cans, leaping to railing, springing to elm, its claws open and clutching the trunk bark, where it set up a curious quacking sound, much like a loud duck. Vivaldi's *Summer* could be heard faintly, drifting from Robb Goodfellow's window. As if to lend Vivaldi support, a robin, high in the leaves of the elm, burst into full-throated song, loudly declaring its territory. Another robin took up the challenge and answered in a clear trill. A third joined in. As the chorus persevered in raising a joyful sound, each member, it seemed, took its cue from the one before, not only continuing the melody but raising it another decibel in its progress.

With a sudden violence, the screen door burst open. Jack, clad only in boxer shorts decorated with red hearts, shot forth like a cannon ball. "Fuck off!" he bellowed, shaking his fist at the birds.

Candy in her unsullied bed, clad in nothing, sleepily opened her eyes. What's he carrying on about now? she wondered. She, too, had found the birds a bit much, especially when they had started at exactly 4:38 according to the bedside clock. But to act like a spoiled brat! Why didn't he grow up? She turned over, winding the sheet around her with her movement and immediately fell back into a deep sleep.

Unable to control the robins, Jack slammed back into the house and into his chaste bed. Jack was back to Jack, and he could not exactly remember or recall the feeling of last night when he had traded his physical nature for a brief foray into a higher realm. In fact, he was not in the best of tempers. Since he had not yet got laid, the purpose of the weekend had been sabotaged.

Upstairs, too, sleep was not doing its job of knitting up the ravelled sleeve of care. Directly above Jack, Sylvia was staring at the ceiling. She had been awake for some time, even though she had not gone to bed until after two. Normally, she was not a person to lie in bed once her eyes were open. Normally, she would be out for her morning swim. But Sylvia was deep in thought. She, too, had heard the robins and, for a moment, had been happy waking to another beautiful summer morning at the lake. For a brief moment, she recalled dancing on the grass and how joyful and carefree and uninhibited they had all been, but almost immediately, she remembered the scene with Robb. She squirmed

with embarrassment. She was thoroughly ashamed of herself.
Thank heavens he had had too much to drink. Otherwise, she
would be even sorrier than she was. How could she have acted
that way with Robb? Michael and Pamela, came the answer.
Again, she heard their voices in the glade. Again, she heard their
words. Again, she saw them kiss. Again, she was plunged into
gloom. But Michael and Pamela were no excuse for her losing
her principles. In the clear light of reality, she questioned her own
motives for going to the glade. Last night, she had told herself
that she was meeting Robb only to tell him that this nonsense
between them must stop. But then why had she painted herself up
and put on one of her best skirts? Oh, she was no better than
Michael and Pamela. "I have a confession to make," she said out
loud.

Michael was breathing deeply and evenly. Sylvia looked at
him. He was turned toward her, on his side, hairy and bare-chested
beneath a light sheet, both hands under his head. With his hair
curling on his forehead and his face petulant in repose, with his
full red lips and his beard, he looked like a god, one of the naughty
ones, say, Bacchus. I could forgive an affair, thought Sylvia. It's
the deception. She recalled Michael and Pamela in the kitchen
acting as though nothing had happened. How could he sleep so
soundly, so thoughtlessly, when he was a liar and a cheat? How
could he sleep when she was so upset? "I have a confession to
make," she said more loudly and jostled his shoulder.

"Hmmm?"

"Are you awake?"

"Ummm."

"I have to tell you something."

After a sudden snort and intake of breath, during which
Michael flopped onto his back, again there was silence. Michael,
however, had been disturbed. Like his neighbour, Robb
Goodfellow, he was feeling some physical discomfort from the
night before. As he turned over, he noted that his shoulder was
sore and the elbow on that side was definitely bruised. He was
now in the upper layer of consciousness where dreams are

remembered. He was having a dream about being in the glade with Pam, about Dob suddenly appearing, striking a pose and spouting poetry, getting it all wrong. In the dream, he tried to coach Dob, which only led to more confusion. Then, Pam left and Michael ran after her, trying to convince her to stay. She jerked her arm away from his hand, which sudden movement caused him to fall backward onto the ground. Michael saw himself crawling over to a log while Dob, lost in his own performance, continued to intone ridiculous dialogue, quite unconscious of the fact that he was mangling the words of one of the greatest lovers in history.

As Michael surfaced through the upper layer into the light, he had a clear picture of himself sitting on the log with his head in his hands. He felt the same acute sense of despair that he had felt then as he lamented the failure of his carefully contrived plan.

Across the hall, Pamela was coming to consciousness with the unsettling feeling that the sleeve of care was unravelling even before she set foot on the floor. Last night had given her pause for thought. Seeing Dobbin as a foolish lover had had a profoundly disturbing effect on her. One of the things that she had always admired about Dobbin was that he was not a fool. Hearing Dobbin reciting Cyrano's lines, getting them all mixed up because they were so foreign to him, seeing Michael correcting him, coaching him, urging him on and Dobbin looking at Michael with bewildered appeal, it had all been too much for her. She was used to a Dobbin who begged nothing of anyone. He did not have to because he was in charge of himself. She was used to a Dobbin who bore his humanity with dignity. An incompetent Dobbin made her feel uncomfortable. It had occurred to her last night – she could pinpoint the exact moment, a moment in the dancing, holding hands with Jack and Sylvia – that there was something wonderful about Dobbin. I'm so darn mean to him, she thought. Why? I'm mean to him because he's such an obtuse know-it-all, because he's so stodgy and pedantic. But he is a good, fine person, loyal and kind. As well as a good sport. He does his best. He would do anything for me. Where else would I find anyone like him? No place, that's where. Last night she had drunk of the nectar of truth. This morning she could taste the history of her own nastiness in her mouth.

Dobbin awoke with his joy intact. Having slept the sleep of the unaware, he lay awake beside his wife with his eyes shut. A lovely young woman is a good thing, he decided. Her presence, her effect on the world, is a truly marvellous phenomenon. He was happy and he was confused about his happiness and, because he did not like any kind of confusion, he tried to straighten out the situation in his mind. Why am I happy? he asked himself. What happened yesterday? Yesterday, he had danced with that young woman. He had taught her, or just about taught her, to swim. And then, at the end of a magical day, they had finished it off by swimming together in the light of the moon, a blue moon as he understood it. Fortunate that he had gone down to the lake after the entertainment in the glade, after Pamela had dashed off, and then Michael, leaving him alone and bewildered at the turn of events. What a mix-up. Michael didn't have the thing very well organized. Half the people knew about it and half had not heard of it. Candy, for instance. He still had trouble saying the name, even to himself. Perhaps part of the trouble was that it did not seem to be a real name. Would he have less trouble if it were Mary or Catherine? Her full name was Candice, she had confided that to him. He would call her Candice. She was not a frivolous Candy but a sensible courageous Candice. Yes, courageous. Think of how she had essentially taught herself to swim, how she had gone into the water on her own, in the darkness. What determination she must have had!

He thought of the way he had arrived on the beach, not really expecting to find her, thinking that even if she had kept their appointment, she would have gone back to the house by then. He had stood at the edge of the water and looked out and seen something. He remembered the little thrill he had experienced when he realized that it was, indeed, her. He thought of the way he had, without thought, taken off his clothes and walked out to her, the way she had taken his hand, the way they had swum naked in the moonlight. He thought of Pamela. He searched his conscience. The swimming had been such a pure act, such a pure joyous act. Perhaps earlier yesterday he had let himself be a little silly over a lovely young woman, but that had been, after all, foolishness. In the light of a new morning, he felt himself land on his feet. He excused himself – surely, a middle-aged man is allowed an occasional fantasy. Likely, it was healthy to let go now and then, as in the swimming. What a wonderful freeing feeling that had been.

Acting, too, was a freeing endeavour. He had felt free in his performance, as though the weight of his personality had been lifted from his shoulders. The weight of reality, he supposed. He wondered if he might try amateur theatrics in the fall. It might help him to be less stiff and formal, to be more fun. Pamela would like that. She'd like him to be a bit more like Michael. She was always telling him to loosen up. He supposed he might achieve something of the same feeling of freedom with Pamela as he had with that young lady... Candice. He knew that, with practice, he could become quite skilled at memorizing lines. It was simply a matter of getting used to fiction rather than fact. He was sure that there were all sorts of companies around. He would have to find out the details from Michael.

Brunch was set on the deck. The meal might have been an uncomfortable occasion if any of the company had been sufficiently tuned outside themselves to notice that the conversation had a halting quality and, in any case, was sporadic. However, all minds were distracted by their own concerns, which resulted in a consensual silence around the table.

Their hostess was in low spirits. Her party had been a failure. Her husband was having an affair with her best friend. Last night had been a disaster. But it had started Friday evening when her eyes had been opened and she'd been attracted to her neighbour and, at the same time, seen the truth of her husband, a transparent Don Juan. First Candy, then Pamela. And how about Dobbin? His betrayal? Hadn't Pamela said something in the kitchen last night about Dobbin, something about him making a fool of himself in the glade? Had Dobbin, too, come upon them? Sylvia looked at poor Dobbin with a great deal of sympathy. How did he feel about being deceived? But Dobbin didn't seem downcast or dejected. On the contrary, he seemed to be his expansive benign Dobbish self.

But, oh, what were they all to do now? How could she go on with Michael? How could she and Pamela remain friends? How could Dobbin and Pamela go on? The magic circle was broken. Sylvia tried to wring her hands which were in her lap, but they were still sore from the stones and twigs. She was back to wearing gauzy material. However, whether it was the weather or a vague recollection of her revelation of the night before, she was down to one layer.

She had abandoned her grand plan for brunch. Waffles and muffins did not appear. She could not even get up the spirit necessary to ladle out pancake batter. Candy, who now had the self-confidence to tackle any endeavour, did it for her. Pamela set out fruits and the remainder of the cheeses that she had brought. Michael, again, had to take charge of the barbecue. Uncharacteristically, he turned his back to the audience, the blue plaid of his shirt presenting a formidable barrier to the rest of the world as, tongs in hand, he flipped sausages and thought how no one appreciated him. All he had got for his trouble was a bruised shoulder and aching ribs. No one cared that he had put in all that effort trying to get his friends back together. No one appreciated his concern for his friends. He had gained nothing in doing the noble thing and breaking up with Pam, only lost a great bed partner in the bargain. As for his wife, she was angry with him, and he would never be able to tell her the truth – that he had chosen her over his old friend Pam.

Pamela had returned from la la land. Yesterday was like a dream from which she had awakened. Yesterday, she had let herself be swept away by nonsense. Still, it had been fun. She had felt herself plugged into the old fun-loving Pamela. Perhaps she would not let go of yesterday entirely. But you cannot live in a dream, she told herself, peeling a kiwi onto her plate. She was back into joggers and T-shirt. My heart has been opened to accommodate a transcendence of all that is mean and unworthy, she decided, a little grandly. My own petty concerns are not what give life meaning. Life's meaning is found in something outside myself. And although she knew that she would inevitably forget that piece of wisdom from time to time, perhaps she would remember it often enough. She felt so good about breaking things off with Michael, so self-righteous about taking the high road, she passed a slice of kiwi to Dobbin. She thought about the circle of friendship around the table, how it remained intact in spite of blunders – although, there *was* something wrong with Sylvia. Sylvia was not acting her normal good-natured self. Jack, too, seemed subtly altered. She could not put her finger on it, but he was too serious for Jack. And Michael wasn't performing. And Dobbin – what had got into Dobbin? He had poured her coffee, bending over her, putting his hand on her shoulder, all of which must mean that he was thinking about her, that she had a place in his mind.

Candy would have been feeling great except that she was fretting to herself about the drive back with Jack. Her victory over her fear of the water and her triumph of the swimming challenge and her enthusiasm for the day were dampened by the thought of having to spend several hours in the company of an unpleasant person who would corrode her happiness. She supposed she could ask Dobbin and Pamela for a lift, but she felt awkward about the complexities of the triangle. She was uncertain of Pamela's thoughts on the skinny-dipping, and she did not want to spend five hours in the confines of a car with an irate wife.

Meanwhile, Dobbin, already in his driving costume of yet another fresh blue plaid shirt, slouchy hat at the ready, lifted to the company a serene face. Unaware of the emotional states of the others around the table, he was at peace. Before him was a platter of fruit and cheeses. He lifted it to pass it around the table. On his right was that charming young lady Candice, on the other side was his good wife Pamela. The platter wavered in his hands a moment. He did not think. Rather, it was his heart that moved his arms toward the left.

Jack was vacillating between defence and offence. He had an overall sense that he had acted badly this weekend. Yet, how might he have played things differently? Was it his fault that he didn't realize until he got here that this person was entirely unsuitable and out of her league? That an act of kindness on his part had backfired? Of course, he had considered having sex with her, he wouldn't be human if he hadn't, but by and large, he had thought to do the kid a favour, she of the rundown heels and the firetrap walk-up. Bring her here for the weekend, let her have a lake experience, enjoy his friends' hospitality. And then to have her turn out to be so, Jack searched for the appropriate word, so feeble. And could he help it if his eyes had been opened to the charms of Pamela? He might have, perhaps should have, foreseen an unfortunate experience with Candy, but the thing with Pamela had been out of his control. Turning suddenly, seeing those toes and then Pamela in a new way, in a revelatory way, that had been one of those rare events that happened once in a blue moon. But he was over that. He didn't know why. Except that, last night, dancing under the stars, he had transcended the physical to soar in the upper air, and perhaps the residue of that experience was still with him. Whatever, as he comprehended it, having gone to bed drunk on the nectar of Pamela's toes, he had awakened cold sober, viewing yesterday as a dream. Too much sun in the berry patch, was his diagnosis. This morning, Pamela's toes were only vaguely recalled and, since they were enclosed in joggers, he could not stimulate his memory by gazing at the real thing. He smiled ruefully to himself. Yesterday was one of those crazy things that he would laugh about in the future, that he could laugh about now for that matter. Life must, and would, go on. Strange thing, life, how it was absolutely continuous, unless of course it stopped. But generally speaking, one thing ended and another began. Like eating, he thought, watching the platter of pancakes being passed up and down the table. One meal ends, another begins. He saw the platter held aloft in Michael's hand, like the communion wafer by a priest. And it was then, at that very moment, as he always thought of it after, looking up, looking across the platter of pancakes, he saw Candy's laughing face. Someone had just complimented her on her cooking, she was pleased that her pancakes had been a success. Quickly, as before, he averted his eyes. Then just as quickly, he caught himself. What are you afraid of? he asked himself. You have climbed mountains and jumped out of airplanes. You have held the scalpel in your hand over countless mouths. You have made the incisions necessary to reconstruct jaws. You have never been a coward. You're not going to start now. He turned his head back and looked squarely across the table.

Candy was without makeup. She had given up on her hair. She thought she might go for one last swim after brunch. She was looking down at her plate, unconscious of the others and of herself. Her mind seemed to be contriving fantasies like a child at play.

The uncomfortable feeling that was like a pain started again in Jack. Still, he did not let himself turn away. He knew what to do with pain. He was a dentist wasn't he? He knew that you have to go with the pain, feel it, accept it, endure it. Pain is, after all, only pain. He knew people who had made friends with pain, who actually missed pain when it was gone. If you cannot avoid pain, then you have to incorporate it into your life. He knew people who, by acknowledging it, turned it into something greater. Jack let himself go with the feeling. He let the pain enter him, become part of him. He wondered if he would be able to make friends with it. At this point, he was not sure. And what he felt on the other side of the pain was a great surge of feeling that was not pain, although he was not sure what it was. But it released him from confusion. He now knew what he had to do. He now knew his duty. His duty was to alleviate pain. Was not that why he had gone into medicine? Had he not had some exalted idea of relieving pain and suffering in the world? But alleviating pain was only part of it. He should also try to not cause pain. He should try to be more considerate of this person he had brought here for the weekend. He must look at her. He must *see* her.

Jack suddenly realized that he was staring at Candy with a manic intensity. As if she felt his scrutiny, she looked up and across the table at him. He did not look away.

Robb spent the better part of the morning with his eyes closed and a cold cloth on his forehead. He thought briefly about his neighbours – let them take care of themselves. When he could stand up without becoming dizzy, he rummaged in the bathroom cabinet until he found some ointment for his bruised muscles and tweezers to pluck thistles from his hand. By late morning, he was, once again, at his station with his glasses. What happened? he asked himself with alarm. He should not have gone to town. Yesterday, in the berry patch, things seemed to be under control. Jack had been smiling lasciviously, Michael had been preening, Pamela had been scowling and Sylvia, ah Sylvia had been sweetly maidish. True, during the picnic on the grass, he had noted a slight change in Michael. Jack and Pamela, too, had not been quite themselves. And Dobbin dancing on the grass had certainly been different. But modest Sylvia had still been her gentle self. What had happened to change her into less than his goddess?

Robb admitted that seduction had been his plan. But it was to be a contrived stylized seduction, not two animals engaged in shrieking sex. He had planned to proceed with soft words and kisses, slow caresses, a breathing in of essences. The culmination of the act he had not foreseen. It existed in a mist somewhere at the end of hours of sweet sensuality. What he wanted was an angelic muse suitably responding to his overtures. He definitely did not want a lewd, lustful, sex-crazed earthling pursuing him madly through the trees, a primitive creature jumping on top of a man, her skirts raised and pulling at his trousers. And the fact that nothing had actually happened because he had been unable to perform due to several too many martinis did not elevate the situation one iota. Conversely, it shattered the courtly romance aspect of the story and placed it firmly in the area of farce. No. Things had not turned out the way he had wanted them to. He felt a profound disappointment, even a deep sense of loss. Yesterday, he had thought himself different from his neighbours, wiser and more intelligent, experienced in life at the lake and in these woods.

He had prided himself that he stood outside their silly, petty nonsense. And now he found himself part of it, every bit as muddled as they. He did not know how to proceed. He had lost the thread. In the light of morning Robb knew only one thing with absolute certainty. Sex and Sylvia did not go together.

Jack and Candy were standing at opposite sides of the red convertible under a noon sun positioned in the emotional sign of Cancer. Candy had decided to bite the bullet and go back to the city the same way that she had come. It seemed cowardly not to. If she could face that cold dark water, if she could teach herself to swim, well, then, surely, she was up to the challenge of Jack. Also, something had happened with Jack at the table. He had looked at her for the first time since Friday evening. And it had not been a casual glance. Rather, he seemed to be really seeing her, a little the way Dobbin had during last night's dinner, except Dobbin's consideration had been more like that of a fond teacher. Jack's look had something more in it, something she found totally intriguing. She decided to try and find out what that look meant. Just to be on the safe side, though, she had stuffed into her bag a paperback murder mystery that she had borrowed from Sylvia.

Jack watched Candy bend to the door handle. Since brunch he had been thinking about pain. He had decided that emotions cause pain and that all human beings who feel emotions feel pain. Then he thought about pain as it pertained to him. How exactly did it feel? Like something was being torn from him, he came up with, say his thigh bone out of his hip socket, although, in this case, it was a feeling being torn out of him. As Jack figured it, referring to several psychology courses he had taken during his training, when, as a child, he had first found out about death and that death had been connected to his mother, the force of his emotion had been so overwhelming, he could not deal with it. He had never dealt with it. But this weekend these hidden emotions had been pulled out of him by Candy. He had responded by pushing them back down, but now he must have the courage to let them surface.

The pain had already become part of him. He could feel it inside, unyielding, uncomfortable. Face it, he said to himself, with her you will never stop feeling this pain because you feel the vulnerability of her flesh and blood. Would it be worth it? He did not know. No one knew things like that. But, in any case, the question was irrelevant. Now that his eyes had been opened, he could not pretend that he had not seen. Even if he never met her again, he would still have the pain. And, he surmised, if he kept looking at her, kept seeing her, he might learn how to become a better person because of it. On impulse, Jack went around to the other side of the car and opened the door for her.

Candy glanced at Jack. He was looking at her with a scrunched up, desperate expression on his face. Her nature responded. No matter that last night she had hated him, that this morning she couldn't stand him, that overall she thought him a terrible, horrible, rude, thoughtless, inconsiderate person, now that she perceived in him a need and that need was directed at her, she could not help her impulse to put her hands on that face and smooth out the scrunches. Quickly, before her hands got away on her, she stepped into the car.

Jack, in cap and *Armani* sunglasses, rounded to the driver's side. Tossing his *Vestementa* jacket into the back seat, he hopped in. He put on his driving gloves. "All set?" He turned toward Candy who, clad again in the toreador pants and tube top, had kicked off her heels. She had abandoned the hair gel for the fluffy look and had not got around to doing her makeup. With a quick movement, Jack removed his hands from the wheel, stripped off the gloves, threw them into the back with the *Vestementa* and started the motor.

With cheerful waves they drove off. At the end of the lane, as Jack turned the wheel at a sharp right angle onto the main road, he wondered if he might entrust the story of *Bambi* to this woman at his side. He had never told another living soul. Of course his mother knew. He might even introduce Candy to his mother. That would be another first. As for Candy, she thought she might tell Jack about her career as an exotic dancer. But she didn't think that she would ever tell him about her magical midnight swim. That would forever remain between her and Dobbin. Even if Dobbin never gave it another thought, which she thought likely, she would hold it precious and private in her heart, a special happening. And, she vowed, if she continued to be a receptionist in Jack's office, she would refuse to wear that white jacket.

Following close on the wheels of the Mercedes was the yellow Dodge, its chrome-tipped fins reflecting the sun, shooting spears of light so that it looked like a fire-trailing comet. It was not until they were on the road that Pamela remembered that she had been going to tell Dobbin that she was leaving him. Oh well, she could always do it another time. And maybe she would never do it. Could he help it if he was a stodgy unromantic know-it-all? She looked across the wide seat toward him. With his light wispy hair, the settled creases in his skin, the chin already doubling, he was very much her plodding Dobbin. Had she ever looked at him through rose-coloured glasses? She didn't think so. They had not had that kind of relationship. But maybe it was time they had. Put on the glasses, she told herself. Apply magic. Be generous. See your husband as your hero. She kept her eyes steady on Dobbin's profile. Could she do it? Could she effect the transformation? This would be a test. She settled down into it. She loved tests.

As for Dobbin, he was still working on his lines. It was simply not in him to give up until he had mastered the thing that was in his mind, which at the moment was the immortal speech of Cyrano.

"Did you have a good time?" Pamela's voice intruded.

"Great. How about you?"

"Yes. I think we accomplished our mission. Gave Sylvia and Michael's little place at the lake a good christening. Except for last night. What a mishmash."

"I did wonder what happened to the others. I understood it was to be a grand gathering of entertainment."

"Really? That's the first I heard of it."

"Michael didn't tell you? We were all supposed to meet in

the glade."

"That's Michael for you. He always gets these ill-considered ideas that never quite turn out."

"Michael is a great actor," said Dobbin. "But he lacks organizational skills."

"Those lines from Cyrano," said Pamela quickly, wishing to avoid any discussion of Michael. "Last night. They're so lovely." She bit her tongue on adding, 'even if you did get them wrong.' "You know," she said, "I had the idea that you were saying them right at me."

"I was," said Dobbin. What he meant was that since she was the only member of the audience, of course he was saying them for her.

And Pamela passed the test, for she chose the merciful interpretation of his words. She slid across the smooth upholstery and put her hand on his knee.

For once, Dobbin's lack of communication skills stood him in good stead. He did not reveal, nor did it become an issue in his mind that such a revelation was necessary, that he had naturally thought that Candy, along with the whole company, would be in the glade, and that it was her face that had inspired him, her face that had kept popping into his mind as he had done his darnedest to memorize and deliver those lines.

Dobbin kept his eyes on the road but he felt the pressure on his knee, a pressure which moved up to his inner thigh, and which erased thoughts of anyone else in his mind but his own good wife. "'Ah, in your presence, such confusion grips/My heart that it grows as wordless as a kiss,/If kisses could but wing in winged words,/Then you could read my letter with your lips.' Aha!" shouted Dobbin, raising his right hand from the wheel in his excitement. "I think I've got it!"

Pamela was astounded to realize that he must have been practicing those words in his mind all morning. Who but a latent romantic would do that? And so she convinced herself that she finally understood her husband and what he was talking about. And away they sailed down the silver highway in their winged chariot, allowed to believe for a little while longer that they were immortal.

    Michael and Sylvia stood at the end of their driveway and watched the cars until they turned the corner and disappeared into the trees. As he waved his friends into the distance, Michael thought how life is, after all, a series of performances. You went out on the stage, you did your best, but there were always accidents, errors, miscalculations. Even after weeks of rehearsal, nothing was ever entirely predictable. The challenge of live theatre, as he perceived it, was in resolving the imperfections on the stage during the performance. That was what he was addicted to. Not perfection but imperfection. Each night, rising to that challenge. And every once in a while it all came together. You pulled it off. Afterwards, you tried to analyze what you had done. But you never could, not entirely. In the end, it was simply a case of sometimes the magic working, sometimes not. Like last night, somehow out of that mess in the glade, success had been achieved. Or it appeared so. At least, the people who had come together left together.

    Michael was feeling much better than he had at brunch. Close observation of his friends during the meal and after had told him that Pam and Dob were back together. He did not know how it had happened but, as he breezily put it, his not to reason why. Perhaps Pam had, after all, been in love with him, Michael. Perhaps that *was* why she had got the bright idea of leaving Dob. Just because she had denied it, just because she had countered his news of breaking up with her with her news of breaking up with him, didn't mean a thing. That was Pam for you. She had to be the winner. Ah well, let her win. He, too, had won, or at least he had not lost. He had not lost his old friends. This morning, Pam had once again been his pal. Nothing was said, but he could tell from the atmosphere between them, one of easy camaraderie. Yes, Michael felt good about himself. He did not know how he had done it, but he had accomplished what he had set out to do.

    Then, just when Michael was savouring his victory, like a dash of cold water, came Sylvia's voice, "I know about you and

Pamela."

Sylvia, while Michael was silently philosophizing about the theatre, had been standing paralyzed in a state of shock. When Michael and Dobbin embraced, two blue plaid shirts melded, two slouchy khaki hats coincided. Her world shifted dramatically beneath her feet. She could no longer believe her senses. She no longer knew what she had seen down the long shadowy hall. And if she had been mistaken, if she had seen, not Michael, but Dobbin, then might she be mistaken about the other? No, she told herself, sternly. I *did* see Michael and Pamela in the glade. I heard their voices. For if she had not seen and heard such, the scene with Robb was even more humiliating. She was even more at fault for her actions of yesterday. She must speak up. She must have her belief validated. "I know about you and Pamela," she said.

Michael was careful to keep his face turned toward the road and not to change the expression on it. His spirit, however, spiralled downward.

"What are you talking about?" he countered.

"You and Pamela are having an affair. I saw you in the glade last night. I heard you."

Michael tried to think. What had been said? He must stall for time. "Heard what?"

"You and Pamela swearing undying love for each other."

Remember the old rule, Michael swiftly thought. Admit nothing and put her on the defensive. "You mean to say you were hiding in the bushes!" he exclaimed. "When we desperately needed some members in the audience for our little entertainment! Why didn't you come forward? Why didn't you bring a flute and play some music? You might have even brought your cello, although, admittedly, it is rather large for hauling through the trees."

"How was I to know that you had planned an entertainment?"

"I told you."

Sylvia thought a moment. He *could* have told her. She had been so distracted last evening, she hadn't heard anything anyone said. But she must not give in. "You certainly did not," she replied.

"Yes I did."

"No, you didn't. I would have remembered something like that."

"I know I told you."

"I don't remember..." Sylvia caught herself. She had just about fallen once again for Michael's weaseling tricks. "Don't change the subject on me. I heard you in the glade."

"Then you must have heard Dob."

"Dob?"

"Dob was there, too. Look, I don't know what you saw and heard. Perhaps it was our rehearsal. Pam and I were rehearsing our parts from Cyrano. Don't tell me you missed Dob's performance! The performance of a lifetime!"

"I..."

"And Dob was so proud of himself, too. You might have had the courtesy to stay and watch."

"I..."

"What did you have to do that was more important than our friend's first acting gig?"

"What do you mean?" Sylvia's voice was high. "What are you accusing me of?"

"I'm not accusing you of anything." Michael's voice was calm. "It's your business if you have no interest in our friends."

"No one, *no one,* could be more supportive of our friends than me." Sylvia's voice trembled at Michael's injustice.

Michael suddenly remembered his ace. "Then where were you during yesterday's lunch?"

Sylvia just about capitulated. She just about flung herself on the ground and clasped Michael's knees and wailed, I'm sorry, I did neglect everyone terribly for my own selfish pleasure. Forgive me, forgive me. She just about decided that she had been wrong about everything. But, then, her head cleared and she came to her senses. Michael had once again turned the issues back on her.

"To get back to my original question," she said firmly, if no longer confidently, "I heard you and Pamela in the glade. I saw you kissing."

"And I'm telling you," answered Michael. "We were

rehearsing. And for that matter, of course we love each other. We've known each other for so long. We're like brother and sister. Maybe we did get carried away with the wine and the night," he went on. "As we all did when dancing on the grass. But that's all it was, that is, if it was anything at all. Which I can't rightly remember. I think we all drank copious amounts of wine at dinner. But," Michael took a deep breath, "believe me, Pam and I are not having an affair."

"Are you sure?"

"Of course I'm sure. How could a person not be sure about a thing like that?"

Sylvia realized that she was never going to know with certainty what had happened this weekend. She could not be positive about what she had seen or that Michael would tell her the truth. She thought of the law. If an eyewitness might be wrong, if there was any possibility of doubt, then there could not be a conviction. Still, she wanted something more. She needed more from Michael. Some assurance, some definite assurance. "Swear?" she said. She tried to make her voice strong.

Michael looked at Sylvia. How easy it would be to return a victorious blow. He could act outraged at her harbouring even the possibility of him and Pam having an affair... how could she think such thoughts about her best friend, let alone her husband, etc. But in seeing her so easily manipulated, so trusting, he found that he could no longer torment her in this manner. He realized that the thing that was special between them, the thing that he had not been able to name yesterday when he was sitting on a log at the beach analyzing the situation, was love. For the first time, he admitted the fact to himself. He loved his wife, not with a superficial romantic love but with a deeper love. And the realization came to him that he had been at fault in his marriage, that he had not seen Sylvia as an individual apart from him, an individual with likes, dislikes, personality quirks, desires, that were distinctly hers. He must try and do better in that regard. He must learn to see her as a person, a person whom he loved. He vowed to make it up to her, all his past indiscretions. But how could he make it up to her if she gave him the boot? There must be a way around this. He thought about the vow he had made to himself to stop fooling around with other women. He had made that vow yesterday, at approximately five p.m. Anything that had happened before that had happened in another existence and was water under the bridge. If Sylvia knew, it would only upset her. It would accomplish nothing. "I swear to you," he held up his hand, "I am not having an affair with Pam."

Sylvia looked at Michael. Friday evening her eyes had been opened and she had seen her husband as the fop and fool that he was. Now she had to make a decision. To accept him the way he was, or... what were the other options? To try and change him? But then he wouldn't be Michael. Anyway, she was not sure that she could change him. He was pretty solidly Michael. To leave him? She thought about life with Michael and a possible life without him. Life without him would be dull, she decided. He makes me laugh, she concluded. The options then are, she instructed herself, accept him the way he is and be happy most of the time or don't accept him and be miserable most of the time. Happiness versus misery, take your pick. Misery seemed pointless. Happiness would depend upon whether or not she could let him be who he was. She knew that he would never be a good husband. He was not husband material. But, she reminded herself, it was not because of her virtue that she had not had an affair, or, at least a one-night stand. Sylvia decided, in light of the situation, the better part of prudence was to question Michael no further, the better part of mercy not to strain it.

Instead, she put her face up to the sun. She closed her eyes. She had so wanted everything to be nice this weekend. She was a person who wanted life, itself, to be nice. But life seemed to take on a life of its own. How had things got so out of hand? Well, it was over. Now she must tidy up the house, feed the goat and chickens, weed her garden. But first her music. She had not practiced for three days. The callouses on her fingertips were softening. She turned toward the house, thinking that she missed her friends already but she would see them soon. Meanwhile, she had some wonderful memories, the berry picking, that had been fun. She recalled the sound of berries plopping into the pail, the berries, their colour, their bruised colour.

And suddenly she remembered. Her eyes flew open. She blinked her lashes. "The saskatoons! They're still at Robb's."

"Forget the saskatoons," said Michael, taking her hand. "They'll be mush."

I could make jam, Sylvia just about said. "Let them stay mush," she said instead. And hand in hand they ran up the porch steps, Sylvia with the knowledge that practicing her cello would be the second thing she'd do. Just before she went into the house, she looked across her shoulder. She thought of Robb's binoculars on the ledge and wondered if he were, right this minute, looking through them. Just in case, she gave a broad wink before the screen slammed shut behind her.

Robb at his window adjusted his binoculars and brought the figures of Michael and Sylvia close. But something was wrong. Was it the binoculars? Was it the focus? Where was his tall glorious goddess, his Aphrodite striding forth from the waves? When had she been replaced by this rather shortish, rather dumpish, almost plumpish, you might say stumpish, perfectly ordinary human being. Why had he once desired to press his thin lips against her full luscious red ones?

Robb felt sad the way he always felt sad when a play was over, when the last words had been said, the last songs sung, the curtain calls ended, when there was nothing else to do but leave the theatre and enter real life. For even though Sylvia and Michael would be staying on for the summer, even though there would be other summers, the enchantment would be replaced by the reality of being friendly neighbours. He would keep a watch on the place when they were in the city during the winter, he would gather any stray mail, watch for nesting raccoons. He'd probably take on her goat and chickens, for Christ's sake. He could envision it all. He and Sylvia would one day create a myth over the scenes in the berry patch and the midnight wood. They would acknowledge the effects of the droning summer heat, the unusual alignment of the planets, the blue moon. Remember that summer weekend, they would say to each other, the time we were fools. It would always be their little secret from Michael. As for Michael, he, too, would have his little secret, and Robb, of course, would never let on that he knew.

Robb lowered his glasses. He felt lonely. The weekend had coincided with his finishing a draft of his play, and he would feel this way until a new enthusiasm, a new play, demanded a new set of characters.

Things would settle back to normal. But not quite. For with every project as with every experience, a subtle shifting of perspective of both reality and fantasy took place, so that things were never the same again. Perhaps because of the blue moon, perhaps because Sylvia had been a very special muse, the jolt to Robb's world seemed more pronounced this time. This time, thought Robb, the shift will be sharper than ever before.

Robb had lived his entire life in a transient tourist place where weekends and summers could not last forever. He knew from experience what he had to do. Today, he would work on his manuscript. There were always more edits. Tomorrow, he would drive to Vancouver and give the play to his producer. Then he would come home and start something new. He'd had enough of real life to last him a good while. Real life always let you down. He'd find another play to write. He always had. He always would. Meanwhile, the cat was making sounds around his ankles, demanding to be fed.

ABOUT THE AUTHOR

Cecelia Frey was born in northern Alberta, grew up in Edmonton and now lives in Calgary. She received a B.A. in Philosophy from the University of Alberta and, after raising a family, returned to the University of Calgary where she completed an M.A. in English. Her thesis, *Organizing Unorganized Space: Prairie Aesthetic in the Poetry of Eli Mandel*, is concerned with the impact of undefined space on the creative consciousness. She has worked as an editor, teacher and freelance writer and has for many years been involved in the Calgary literary community. Her short stories and poetry have been published in dozens of literary journals and anthologies as well as being broadcast on CBC radio and performed on the Women's Television Network. Numerous reviews, essays and articles have appeared in a wide range of publications including newspapers such as *The Calgary Herald* and *The Globe and Mail* and journals as varied as *Westworld* and *Canadian Literature*. Three times a recipient of the Writer's Guild of Alberta Short Fiction Award, she has also won awards for playwriting.